Tag was watching her

And Dusty was beginning to feel clumsy. She began to climb down off the rickety old stepladder. In three strides, Tag was across the room and lifting her effortlessly off the last step. Unfortunately, her shirt snagged on the nail she used to hold her paint bucket and ripped right up the back as Tag placed her on the ground.

Dusty tried to ignore the fact that her shirt was no longer in one piece, just as she tried to ignore the fact that Tag hadn't removed his hands from her hips. What she couldn't ignore was the way his eyes were burning into hers.

"Dusty," he whispered huskily, letting his hand slide up her bare back. Then his lips fastened on hers, warm and hard, in a kiss that seared her soul....

ABOUT THE AUTHOR

"I was forty-three when I finally found out that I wanted to be a writer when I grew up," says Anne Laurence. "But only a writer of romance novels. They're my favorite kind of books. I wouldn't want to write anything else." A widow, Anne makes her home in St. Louis, Missouri. She has three children.

Always Say Yes

ANNE LAURENCE

Harlequin Books

TORONTO • NEW YORK • LONDON
AMSTERDAM • PARIS • SYDNEY • HAMBURG
STOCKHOLM • ATHENS • TOKYO • MILAN

Published March 1990

First printing January 1990

ISBN 0-373-70394-5

Printed in U.S.A.

To Larry

PROLOGUE

IT WAS FUNNY how the rain could alter a person's perception of the world—even of such a familiar world as Dusty's own city neighborhood. Getting off the bus after eleven o'clock, she was struck by the stench of exhaust held suspended in the damp air of the late spring night. Even the noise of the bus's engine seemed muffled, as it pulled off leaving her in the quiet of her residential street.

Dusty had reservations about her old slicker and rain hat. Water sluiced down a crease in the rubbery hat and continued its course inside her collar and down between her shoulder blades. Her shoes and panty hose were soaked clear through. Oh, well, at least this was the last night she'd be coming home late. She'd just taken the final exam for an interesting psychology course and was looking forward to her summer holiday. As much as she loved teaching kindergarten and as much as she needed night school to hone her skills, doing both was a challenge even for someone with her energy.

As she walked, with her bright yellow rain hat continually slipping forward to half cover her face, Dusty barely noticed the march of streetlamps and regular pattern of look-alike houses. She'd been raised on this block, and knew nearly every home and inhabitant. It was a stable neighborhood. Had been for the entire twenty-four years of Dusty's life. And that had been good for someone like her, for someone with a less than stable family situation.

Well, it was stable enough now, she supposed—now that there was only her and her father. There were no more arguments to come home to, but, on the other hand, as everyone knew, Ox Landry was rarely at home and never on time. He put his dedication to police work well above family and home—and always had.

Pushing her hat back off her face once again, Dusty became aware of a parked car, with someone sitting inside behind the wheel. She didn't recognize the car and thought it was strange that the occupant was just sitting there.

Her first thoughts were for her own safety. She even considered then rejected the possibility that her dad might observe his eleven o'clock quitting time and arrive home at any minute. Fortunately she knew she could dash into almost any house along the way, and that gave her courage to carefully note the name and make of the car, the license number and the color, though the latter was hard to define in the half-light.

She decided she wouldn't look at the man in the car when she walked by him, but her glance as she strode past was automatic. And just as she looked at him and he looked at her, a cigarette lighter flashed in front of his face.

She almost laughed with relief. He was hardly going to pounce on her if he was lighting a cigarette. Then, just before her rain hat fell into her face yet again, just before the smoke screened his features, their eyes met and held. He was clearly distinguishable for that instant—photographically so.

Her next cause for curiosity was the whine of wheels she heard coming from behind her. Turning to look, she saw a police car. Her dad was home on time, after all. Pausing, for she had almost reached their house, and squinting up her eyes against the sheeting rain, she waved to him.

He merely pulled over to the curb, his windshield wipers in steady motion. Before she could take it in, he was out of his car, down on one knee, pointing his revolver at something behind her.

His shout of "Run, Dusty!" startled her. The stranger's car was racing past her, swerving around her dad's car. The deafening roar of gunfire exploded in Dusty's ears. Then the assailant's vehicle skidded down the quiet block, shuddered around the corner and was gone.

Dropping her books and running toward her father was automatic. But her raincoat became a horrible, rubbery weight, slowing her down. At last she reached her father where he had fallen half beneath his open car door. An urgent need to do something gripped her. But he ordered her to let him be. As concisely as ever, he asked her to call headquarters on his police radio—which she did. After reciting the information she'd memorized concerning the assailant's car, she returned to her father. Sitting down on the wet pavement, she took his much larger hand in hers and forced herself to look at him. She'd been afraid of what she might see, but his very masculine face remained unmarred.

Their neighbors began to emerge from their houses and gathered around the spot where she clung to Ox Landry's large hand. It was obvious to Dusty that everyone knew there was nothing to be done, and she turned from their sober, lamp-lit expressions to the broad features of her father's face.

"Dusty," he said, his voice still firm but more earnest than she could recall ever hearing it before. "I'm sorry, you know. I mean, I realize I've been less than a perfect father, and—"

"Please, Dad," she interjected. "Just rest until the ambulance gets here."

"It's no good, girl, so let me try to tell you what I should've said a long time ago. I cared...about you and Leslie and your mom. I really did. I just didn't know how to...to..."

Tears joined the rain that coursed down Dusty's face. "I understand. I think all of us did."

The deep love that Dusty had secretly harbored for Ox Landry rose to the surface of her small being. Such a wash of love flooded into her heart that she sensed he felt it, too.

"If you'll forgive me, maybe I can think that your mom and Les would as well."

"I forgive you," she said simply.

The years when she had doubted this man's love, had longed for his love, had felt deprived of his love, were all purged in a few minutes that she would count as the most healing minutes of her life.

Once her father disappeared into the ambulance, Juan Alvarez, his partner on the force—a man who was his best friend and one of hers—arrived on the rain-drenched scene and took her into a fierce embrace.

Struggling with his own shock, his horrible anger, Alvarez spoke roughly into her ear, "Oh, God, Dusty. Who did this?"

A picture flashed into her mind, perfectly in focus and illuminated by the warm glow of a cigarette lighter. But although she envisioned the killer clearly, she couldn't say who he was. She only knew that one day soon she'd look into his face again. If he didn't see to that, she would.

CHAPTER ONE

"OH, GOODNESS," Dusty sighed, unconsciously smoothing the taut tug of her jeans across her lap. "I don't know what to say. I mean, it's not that I don't want the chance to help. I've told you since day one that I'd do whatever I could to find that...that creep who murdered my father. It's just that I don't think I can stand the confinement anymore. This has been..." She gave up. After six months of protective custody, there just weren't enough words to describe her frustration.

Captain Alvarez lounged next to Dusty on the serviceable couch, his sympathetic gaze following hers over the hotel sitting room. It wasn't that the place was a dump, but after six months any place could become a prison.

The third figure in the room remained motionless, staring out at the brightly lit view that Dusty had come to know by heart. The stiffness between the younger male's broad shoulders indicated that Detective John Taggert wanted little part in this morning's discussion. He'd made that clear since coming through the door.

Not for the first time, Dusty found herself wondering what John Taggert's problem was. She'd met him briefly once before and, while she couldn't recall him precisely, she'd been left with a good impression. Oh, it was obvious that he was angry, but there was something else expressed in that aloof stance of his. There was reluctance, and weariness, and a...a reflection of her own worry.

Putting aside both her anxiety and the ever-present threat of depression, Dusty forced her gaze back to the familiar features of Captain Alvarez. She knew this was already hard for him, and she wasn't making it any easier.

She felt bad about that. Juan Alvarez meant a lot to her. He wasn't merely her father's partner on the Organized Crime Task Force that had been her father's life for so many years. He was like an uncle. "Maybe if I could have a couple of weeks at home...some time to pull myself together," she suggested at last.

"Dusty," Alvarez said, leaning toward her, his flat, round face close to hers, "this *creep*, as you call him, knows where you live and work. And probably anything else he needs to locate you at any time. He saw you when he—"

"You can say it. When he killed my dad. I told you—I'm doing fine. I can talk about that just fine. Ask the therapist. It's just this being cooped up that's driving me crazy. And now, to think of going into another 'safe' situation...of being caged in again after six months of this place...well, it's hard."

"Being on surveillance won't be as bad as this," Alvarez said.

At that point, John Taggert shifted his weight, wordlessly giving his opinion of the setup Alvarez was suggesting. Taggert was in charge of the surveillance operation, and he didn't want the additional responsibility of having Dusty along.

"Of course," Dusty said, feeling the smart of his unspoken rejection, "the fact that I might be able to identify the murderer is the most important consideration. It's just that I've been hoping—I've been assuming—that any photos, any revealing information gathered from the surveillance, could just be brought for me to look at so that I can get back to my life."

"And normally that's the way it would be. Usually, once six months is up, the Witness Protection Program ends. The funds aren't there to protect people for a longer time period. But just because your six months is up doesn't mean you're safe."

Getting up from her place on the couch, Dusty paced away. "Oh, I know, I know. And I appreciate your concern. You understand that."

As if he didn't, Alvarez went on to firm up his position. "I feel responsible for you, Dusty. I've always felt that way about you and Leslie."

"And both my sister and I realize that, too. You and Aunt Marge have always been there for us. Don't think we don't remember that."

"And now," Alvarez said, undeterred, "what with no one being at home with you, we're even more concerned about you. It's not as if you have anybody anymore. Not with Leslie married and in New York, and your dad . . . gone."

Dusty pasted on what she hoped was a convincing smile. "You forget that I have my neighbors and friends. Anyone I'd ask would be glad to come over and spend a night. Or—"

"That's not the point," Alvarez said, finally getting to his feet. "We're talking about a very dangerous man. This guy's not to be taken lightly, to be handled by amateurs."

When her back stiffened, Alvarez knew to regroup. Dusty Landry could be as stubborn as a Missouri mule. It was easier to reach her through her big heart. "Look, Dusty. Save me some sleepless nights, will ya? Otherwise Marge'll be on your doorstep at all hours."

Dusty knew she was being finagled. She also realized that Alvarez was genuinely concerned. In any case, Detective Taggert was shifting his weight again, and she wasn't about to wrangle in front of him. She half thought it was a good idea for her to be involved in the surveillance, anyway. It would give her a real sense that she was doing something...that she was involved in finding that creep she'd seen only once. The one whose picture was still crystal clear in her mind.

Suddenly Dusty was caught up short. She hadn't noticed it before, but the morning light was coming in the large plate glass window at just the right angle to make it a reflective surface. She could still see the all-too-familiar view of downtown St. Louis framed by the giant steel band of the Gateway Arch. But it was the figures reflected in the window that she noticed now—hers and Detective Taggert's. His was impressive-looking. At over six feet tall, with midnight black hair and the right bulk to dress his large frame, he was the kind of man who dominated any scene. But it was the piercing quality of his pale blue eyes that arrested her. He had been watching her all this time. Still, he didn't glance away. It was she who did that.

Beside a man like Taggert, Dusty knew that she looked like a kid. Even at twenty-four. She was short—"petite" her sister had always been dear enough to say. For her size, she had a perfect figure, but in a world where leggy, thin-as-a-reed women were the fashion, she had no illusions. Her rust-colored hair and equally rust-brown eyes and eyelashes weren't fashionable, either. Nor were the freckles dusted across her nose—the ones that had earned her her nickname. Somehow, in Taggert's ice-blue stare, she saw herself clearly for what she was. Gamin and cute? Maybe. She'd certainly heard that. But attractive to a man like Detective Taggert? Hardly.

Turning toward Alvarez again, Dusty endeavored to put her odd train of thoughts behind her. "You said that the surveillance would be better than this safe house situation, didn't you?"

Both she and Alvarez had gone back to sit on the couch, and he appeared relieved to hear the interest in her voice. "To most people involved in safe house setups, anything is better. But in this case...the one with Tag...it'll be different. The two of you'll be in an apartment in a residential neighborhood. A four-family flat, isn't it, Tag?"

At Taggert's brief nod, Alvarez went on. "There won't be a team of cops on rotating duty, only you and Tag on your own. You'll have to use your head, of course. I mean you'll have to remember not to blow your cover, but you'll have more freedom than you do here. If Tag agrees, I don't see any reason why you can't get out some, take care of the groceries—that sort of thing."

Hearing Taggert's indrawn breath, Alvarez's eyes switched to him. "Why don't you sit down, Tag? All that standing's got to be hard on your leg."

Dusty had noticed Taggert's limp when he'd first arrived. She saw it again as he reluctantly took his superior's advice and sank painfully into a plastic-covered armchair, holding his leg stiffly extended. Dusty also saw the automatic rub he administered to himself, but when he caught her eye, she was, once again, the one to look away and pick up the conversation.

"Won't we stick out?" Dusty asked. "I mean, you said that this surveillance would be out of a four-plex apartment building in a residential neighborhood."

"That's the point," Alvarez said. "That's why we need you. Normally we'd put a female partner in there with Tag. His partner, in fact, Ellen Daniels, went through a similar stakeout with him on his last case. Only in that instance it was really rough."

"Really rough?" echoed Dusty.

"Yeah, you know. They were in a crude neighborhood and a worse hotel. Still, the job itself was pretty much the same. Tag installs his listening equipment, bugs the rooms he's watching, sets up his camera and then collects the evidence."

"What do I do specifically?"

"Your most important job will be to watch for this guy you saw...the one who killed your father. But aside from that, you're supposed to make the surveillance look like a normal situation."

Dusty frowned. "How precisely do I make this look normal?"

"By acting the part of newlywed bride to Tag's newlywed groom. You live together in the apartment . . . I mean, separately in the apartment. But the minute there's any public contact, you act your role and he'll do the same." Alvarez's eyes ran quickly to Tag's, then just as quickly back to Dusty's riveted stare. "Nothing to it."

When no one in the room responded, or even moved, Alvarez went back to pleading his case to Dusty. "Look, we've got a really good lead here, and we're only talking two . . . three months for this surveillance. Each day brings us closer to the killer, and that's part of why I want you involved. Your father was on the verge of getting these guys, and so was the officer who followed him."

Dusty frowned. "Who followed Dad on this case?"

"Brinker."

"Brinker? You mean that Detective Taggert is new to it?"

"Just this week."

"But what happened to Brinker?"

Alvarez looked at Tag, but there was no help there. "They got him, too," he admitted softly.

"Oh, my God," Dusty gasped. This was shocking news. She would have thought she would have heard before now. But then again, maybe not. For all of their free talk concerning headquarters and the goings-on there, the cops who had been watching over her wouldn't have told her about Brinker. Not when she'd been recovering from her own bad experience.

The silence was thick in the room as Dusty scrambled to absorb this new fact. She had known Brinker. Sort of. He had come up through the ranks with her dad and Alvarez. She could see now that Alvarez was thinking along the same lines. He'd lost his best friend when her father died and another very good one with Brinker.

"Well," she said, on what she hoped wasn't too much of a weighted sigh. "Well, well, well," she added as a soft litany, then stood again. She simply had to go and look out the window for a minute. Standing there, gazing down as she had for—what was it, hundreds of times?—she didn't see a thing. *Brinker and her dad.* That creep and his cohorts had killed two good men, and that was a part of what this was all about. The law wanted these people very badly.

And so did she.

What did three more months of living in a prison mean in comparison? She knew she wouldn't be able to get on with her life until this thing was resolved.

"All right," she heard herself say.

Looking back, she saw Alvarez break into a smile. Taggert remained impassive.

"I knew I could count on you," the elder man said, rubbing his hands together. "Now, like I said, the surveillance is set up in a neighborhood just south of Forest Park."

Dusty was surprised. "I pass through some of that neighborhood on my way to Brockham Elementary."

"That's true," Alvarez agreed, "but it doesn't matter. You're to remain totally apart from your normal routine in life—just like you have for this situation. No contact with anyone. It shouldn't be hard. Everybody's used to your disappearance by now."

"I can call Leslie, can't I?"

"Before you get into the surveillance you can. But I don't want you making calls to anyone you know once you're in the apartment. You'll have to call your principal at Brockham Elementary again and extend your leave of absence. That shouldn't lose you your job if you tell him it's only for a few more months, should it?"

"I don't think so. He has a sub for me. I don't know what people are figuring I'm doing, but everybody who's been contacted has been pretty cooperative, even without knowing the specifics."

"People are more savvy about these things nowadays. The news media plastered the whole business of your dad's murder on everything that delivers. Anybody who cares knows you had to go into hiding."

Dusty sighed. This sudden turn of events wasn't as cut and dried for her as she was trying to make it appear. She disliked becoming involved in the work her father had done—the work that had tainted her childhood dreams, caused her to fear for him and, finally, taken his life. But under the circumstances, she didn't feel she had any choice.

"No, you're right," she said at last. "I haven't had any problems with people not understanding my going into this protection program."

"So," said Alvarez, his eyes switching to Taggert and back, "to get to the surveillance. Like I said, the apartment you'll share with Tag is located in a four-family flat. The ground-floor unit next door to yours is occupied by an old man by the name of Syd Desota. He's an uncle to the brothers who head the gang we're uncovering. Just what part the guy who murdered your father has in this group we haven't found out yet. He's still an unknown to us, and you're the only one who's seen him. It's our guess that he's been lying low since that night, just like you have."

Dusty forced a smile and, ignoring the way Taggert was quietly observing her, encouraged Alvarez with a nod.

"There won't be much activity, much coming and going, but this is a good link to the Desotas. They use the phone regularly when they're in town, and the old man relays messages when they aren't. The old man's apartment is a sort of clearinghouse. Not much happening on the surface, but it's our best bet and one that has to be watched constantly."

Once again Dusty didn't know what to do but nod her understanding, and Alvarez went on. "Tag's only been there a week. He's made sure the place has been bugged. He's got his equipment set up and ready to go. The electricity's on, the phone's installed and he's bought a couple of beds and card tables."

Dusty stared into the solid black of Captain Alvarez's eyes. She knew this man with his Mexican-American looks as well as any—had known him since she'd been a child. She realized that he cared for her, and she trusted him. Even in the face of what he was telling her, she trusted him and his wife, the woman she called "aunt" without being related to her.

"We're real close to winding this up, Dusty." Alvarez was at his most solemn now. "I don't need to tell you about the work, the lives, that have gone into this. You know that better than most of us."

Dusty's eyes flashed to Taggert. She was suddenly struck with the thought of how he must feel about being the next man up on a case that had killed two others. He had to love police work as much as her father had.

But peering into his cool blue eyes, studying the hard set of his handsome features, she couldn't read his feelings at all.

Getting stiffly to his feet, Taggert moved toward the door.

"What's wrong?" Alvarez asked, his eyes examining his companion's very pronounced limp. "Is your leg bothering you?"

There was no reply for a moment, and then the one that was mumbled was obviously false. "Yeah. It's my leg."

"I guess we'd better finish up," Alvarez said, his jet-black eyes again shining into Dusty's. He was looking very "uncle-like," and she knew she'd have to prepare herself for a little lecture. "Just remember that your most important job is to keep yourself safe," he began. "Use your head. Of course, it would be great if you could identify our man—should he visit Syd Desota. But our main goal is your security, and that has to be kept in mind no matter who comes to visit next door. Remember, too, that it's essential that you provide a good cover by acting the part of Tag's wife. You know, the young and devoted couple. That sort of thing. Finally, as soon as you move into the flat, it's you and Tag. He's in charge. No questions. You can trust him. He'll do what's best for you and you do the same."

Keeping her eyes away from the very masculine, very impatient figure hovering just inside the door, Dusty nodded. She found it odd that she could sense the friendship between the men, especially with the younger one acting the way he was. But once again she had to catch up to what Alvarez was saying.

"My assistant—you know him, Ted Jackson—he'll come by first thing in the morning and drive you and your clothes to the apartment. Don't worry about anything else. There'll be a little cash to make this look good."

Alvarez stood up, already softer and appearing more like the man she'd always been fond of. "Don't worry. You'll do fine. Tag's a good man. One of our best."

"I'm sure he is," said Dusty.

Suddenly it was she who became the comforter, and she patted her old friend's arm. "I'll be fine. You've done the best for me that anyone could and I know Dad would thank you, too."

Alvarez seemed almost unsure, but then recovered as he drew a deep breath. Putting an arm around her shoulders, he jostled her gently.

Dusty smiled. "I'll talk to Les tonight. I'll tell her you said hello, and you do the same with Aunt Marge."

"Yeah, yeah," he said gruffly. "Just remember. Two calls. Your principal and your sister. And you can't say where you are or where you're going. Only that it'll be a few more months."

Dusty smiled broadly. "Yes, sir."

"How's the food here?"

Since this sounded more like the man she knew, she chuckled. "It's pretty good for hotel food, if only room service would bring it up while it's hot. I think Charlotte's downstairs getting lunch."

Alvarez and Dusty were now moving in the direction of the door, where Taggert still stood, silently watching them.

"Anything we haven't thought of?" Alvarez asked him.

"No," the younger man replied, stiff to the end.

Looking down at Dusty and giving her a wink, her old friend tried to smooth things over. "It's just that he isn't used to the idea yet."

Dusty shot the other man a stiff little look of her own. "He doesn't need to worry about me. I can take care of myself."

Detective Taggert's reply was a disbelieving snort that raised her hackles. She knew she looked young, but she'd been through so much lately that she felt old beyond her years. Before she could say anything, the door was open and the three of them were making way for a female police officer carrying a large tray.

"Hey, everybody!" the casually dressed newcomer called out with a big grin. "I thought I'd bring our lunch and not only save room service the trouble, but have it nice 'n hot for a change."

Officer Charlotte Ross, third person down on the rotation of people who guarded Dusty, was country inside and out. She was big and friendly and had helped Dusty through many a restless night with her down-home logic.

While Charlotte went to set her tray on the small table in the window, Taggert escaped through the door without so much as a backward glance and Alvarez bid his final goodbye.

"We'll talk. Especially if you have questions. Maybe it would help if you called Marge tonight."

Dusty nodded and smiled and, with one more reassuring jostle, Alvarez was also gone. All the mental pictures that had kept her going over the past six months flashed through Dusty's mind—the cheery faces of children, their Crayola drawings pinned to the bulletin boards in her classroom . . . the other teachers at Brockham Elementary with whom she'd shared her tug-of-war days . . . All were now sadly beyond her reach.

Sensing Dusty's depression, Charlotte came over and put a reassuring arm around the smaller woman's shoulders. Dusty was used to people giving her hugs like this. She supposed it was encouraged by her height—or, rather, her lack of it—and she submitted as she always did.

"Come on, darlin'," Charlotte said in her deep country accent. "Let's have some of this delicious lunch I bought for us."

"Do you know what's going on?"

"Nothin' specific. None of us knows much about anythin' in particular."

Dusty sat down across from Charlotte and, after quibbling over who'd have the tuna salad and who the chicken, they began to eat. This was one of their running battles. Each always wanted the other to have her preferences. However, Dusty realized she must be looking as stunned as she was feeling, because Charlotte was doing her best to tease her out of her renewed sense of anxiety.

They both knew that Dusty had been counting the days since she'd been brought to this room, looking forward to being released. But now that wasn't going to happen and, somehow, Dusty felt crawly all over.

Especially when she considered who her lone companion would be for the next few weeks.

She wouldn't have Charlotte anymore...or even the two male police officers who'd been with her over the past six months. And while she hadn't got close to them, as she had to Charlotte, they had always been sympathetic—brought her ice cream, bucked her up when she got down.

"Charlotte, do you know anything about John Taggert?" Dusty asked abruptly.

The big female, with her teased hair and aquamarine eye shadow, stopped dead in her tracks and smiled a wide, knowing smile. "Why, darlin', don't tell me you got it, too."

"Got what?"

"Taggertitis," she drawled triumphantly. "The disease is real common among the women down at headquarters—especially among the single women. Of course, it only takes the minimum exposure for catchin' it, and I'd say you had yourself a big dose."

Dusty's reply was wry. "I'm not at all surprised that he's compared to a disease."

"We all figure it's not just the way he looks, which, in most cases would be enough, but the way he looks at you with those cool blue eyes."

"How long has he been on the force?"

"I don't know how long he's been a cop, but he's only been in St. Louis for six months. He's had a couple of undercover cases, and he got himself shot in the leg on the last one. Fresh out of the hospital before he came here. He's not supposed to be up yet, but he's a real workaholic. And very good. His partner's Ellen Daniels. Do you know Ellen?"

Dusty forced down her dry tuna salad with a gulp of diet cola. "No. I don't know her."

"She's real strikin'. Smart, too, and very precise in everythin' she does. Of course, nobody's sayin' anythin's going on between her and Tag, 'cause Ellen ain't the type. On the other hand, John Taggert's the kind that can make a gal change the very type of her blood."

Dusty had to smile. Charlotte was good for one's soul.

"Mind you," Charlotte continued, "there hasn't been any talk about John Taggert and anybody else, either. Nosiree, he plays his hand real close to the chest."

When Dusty started to chuckle, Charlotte looked pleased. "That's more like my darlin'. Got the roses back in your cheeks now. Tell ya what. Who's watchin' over you tonight?"

"Pulaski."

"Great! I'll come back, same time as always, and he can keep an eye out for us. A little skinny-dippin' up in that big blue pool on the top floor will do us both a world of good."

CHAPTER TWO

TAG SHIFTED HIS WEIGHT on the sun-heated seat of Alvarez's vintage Chevy.

"It's hot for late October," the older man said, looking over at him as his rattletrap coughed a reluctant response to his twist of its key. "Summers in St. Louis can be the pits, but I hope this is the last of the heat. Want some lunch? I missed breakfast."

"Lunch would be good. There's a bar near the apartment that serves great deep-fried chicken livers. How's that sound? You have to drop me off, anyway."

"Sounds great. Until later this afternoon, that is. Then it could get a little tricky for my stomach."

The two men fell silent as Alvarez concentrated on freeing them of downtown traffic. Tag liked Alvarez. He hadn't had much time for forming really close friendships since coming to St. Louis and felt fortunate that he had a superior with whom he could talk openly. As openly as he ever did, that is.

"So. How do you like Dusty?" Alvarez asked as they reached the busy double-decker stretches of Highway 40.

Tag couldn't help a little smile. "Don't push your luck."

"Look, I know you don't want her on your hands," Alvarez said, getting down to brass tacks.

"That's the understatement of the year."

"You have to admit she'll be safer with you than on her own in her dad's house."

Of course, Tag had to grant him that point. "It's not that I'm unwilling to help out. I know the trouble you've gone to to get her into this setup. It's just that..."

Alvarez gave Tag a quick glance. "It's just what? That you don't feel...what? Well enough?"

"No, I'm not worried about my leg. I know it'll come along with time."

"Hasn't your group therapy helped with—"

"Actually, I've met Dusty Landry before," Tag said, abruptly changing the subject.

"You have?"

"The night her dad was killed was my first day on the force here in St. Louis, and I ended up at the murder scene."

"Hell, that was a night. It's no wonder I don't remember your being there. What a zoo. All those neighbors. Sympathetic, of course, but still in the way. And, God, how I was feeling! To come up on that scene...Ox shot down right in front of his own house, Dusty sitting in the street, the rain pouring down on her, Ox...dying. She just sat there, holding his hand and talking to him very calmly as he faded away. I'll never forget it as long as I live."

"That's only natural. Ox Landry was your partner."

"Ox Landry was my best friend. Had been for many, many years."

"And that's why you're looking out for his daughter. It's a shame the way our Witness Protection Program switches off after six months. Whether or not the murderer's been caught, the witness is on her own."

Alvarez was quiet for a moment. "Actually, it goes deeper than my relationship with Ox. He was a big, beefy guy—a man's man—but he wasn't a very good father. Hell, let's face it, he was both a rotten father and husband. After Dusty's mother died, Marge and I sort of stepped in. To Ox's mind, all his girls needed was food on the table and a roof over their heads. I can say this now because I loved him like a brother. But that doesn't mean I didn't recognize his glaring faults."

Alvarez paused, as if reluctant to continue. "Hell, it's more than that, too," he admitted at last. "Dusty's so damn...I don't know...special. Well, you saw it that night at her house after Ox was taken off by the ambulance and we went inside. All that crowd of neighbors and friends—it went beyond the usual hubbub generated by a crime scene. It was genuine concern. And believe me, it wasn't for Ox. Dusty has a knack for winning over anybody she meets. Always has."

Tag could clearly remember that rain-soaked night and the crush of friends that Alvarez was talking about. The little house had been full to capacity. He could recall the newspeople commenting on the reaction of the Landrys' well-meaning friends as he pushed his way through the jam-packed rooms.

And then he'd seen Dusty. She'd been hunched over on the living room couch, her mop of red-brown curls a straggling mass, covering her bowed head. Someone had thrown an afghan over her shoulders, and she'd looked like a forlorn waif. Her expression was one he'd seen on so many others in similar circumstances—shock turning everything to a numb daze.

Even then he'd known she was, as Alvarez said . . . special. That, more than anything, scared the hell out of him. . . .

"Tag, did you hear what I said?"

"What?" he asked, snapping out of his reverie.

"I *said* that you'd better keep a close watch on her. Not that she'd do anything dumb. She's bright, you know. Very bright and energetic. It's just that she's sick to death of being hemmed in, and she's liable to . . . well, to push her limits. She's convinced, you know, that Ox's killer wouldn't recognize her."

"What do you mean?"

"Dusty claims that just as she looked at him and he looked at her, her hat fell over her face. She says the guy couldn't possibly have gotten a good look at her."

"That's nothing to count on."

"My feelings precisely. And thus my getting her to move in with you."

"Which I've agreed to," Tag said wearily.

A silence stretched between them. Tag broke it. "Didn't Ox suspect that they might be onto him?"

"Oh, yeah. We'd had word a few days previously that they knew he was hot on their trail."

"Why didn't he get pulled off the case if he'd been blown?"

"Huh," Alvarez muttered. "You didn't know Ox. He was like a bulldog. Once he got his teeth into something, he never let go."

"Not even with two daughters?"

"Like I said, you didn't know Ox."

"And now his dedication, or whatever you want to call it, has dumped his daughter in my lap."

Alvarez glanced away from the traffic to grin at Tag. "Now that's not so bad, is it? You've gotta watch her, though. I've had word that she's been sneaking up to the hotel pool at nights. She and Charlotte Ross have been skinny-dipping, for cripes sake." Alvarez chuckled like a proud but exasperated parent.

Tag couldn't join in. Dusty Landry might have the looks and winning ways of a girl, but he knew different. She was one-hundred-percent woman.

BY EIGHT O'CLOCK on the morning following her meeting with Juan Alvarez and John Taggert, Dusty was dressed and packed and sat waiting with Charlotte Ross for the captain's assistant to pick her up. She wore the sort of thing one would travel in: slacks, a shirt and a nice blazer in the autumn colors she loved. She called Leslie for a second time. She had promised her the night before that she would and, once they'd rehashed the whole situation again, there was nothing to do but wait. Wait and worry.

She dreaded the cool welcome she'd probably face at the apartment she was to share with John Taggert. It was funny how she remembered him so differently from the aloof male she had seen yesterday morning.

The night her father had been killed, she'd come down the stairs of her house and been told that Detective Taggert would drive her to a safe house. She'd been in shock, of course, but she remembered him as being totally helpful, completely sympathetic. He'd encouraged her to talk when she'd wanted to and fallen in with her silences when she was quiet, hadn't he?

Shaking herself free of what was obviously unexplainable, Dusty switched her attention back to her favorite watchdog, Charlotte Ross. She felt oddly nostalgic about leaving her, and it was evident that the large policewoman, with her teased hair and friendly smile, felt the same.

"Did you say Ted Jackson comin' for you?" Charlotte asked, catching Dusty's eye.

"That's what Captain Alvarez told me."

"And you're to act like...what?"

"Like I just flew in from New York."

Charlotte grinned. "And how do you act like you just flew in from New York?"

"I suppose I act tired."

"Well, darlin', you certainly look that. I shouldn't have taken you skinny-dippin' so late last night."

"It's not because of the skinny-dipping. I didn't sleep very well."

"You been dreamin' again?"

"It wasn't as bad this time. The dream stopped before it got going, and I felt good about that. In fact, I feel pretty good about this surveillance situation. I'm hoping I can really do something to help find the guy who murdered my dad. Then this whole nightmare will be over and I can get back to my life."

Charlotte put the last of the paperback romances she was collecting from around the room into the grocery bag she carried. "I think you're right. I think that havin' a direct part in solvin' the case will be like a key you can use fer lockin' the door on all the bad memories. Did you finish this one?'' she added, flashing a paperback under Dusty's nose.

"Yeah. And thanks for bringing your collection. You've made me a romance junkie.''

"That's good. You can't imagine how many of the gals pass 'em around at headquarters. I'll save 'em up again, and give 'em to you next time we see each other.''

"I'm glad you're planning on seeing me again.''

Charlotte looked slightly startled. "What do you mean, darlin'? You're not thinkin' you'll be killed on this surveillance?''

Dusty laughed. "No. That thought hadn't even entered my mind. I've been more worried about being closed in than being killed. I was just thinking we might not see each other again. It happens, you know. People who grow close drift apart when circumstances change.''

Dropping her sack of paperbacks, Charlotte put an arm around Dusty's shoulders. "You're not thinkin' with your heart, darlin'. There's nothin' in this world that'll keep us from visitin' once we have the chance.''

After a quick hug, the call came that Dusty's "cab" was downstairs. With one more hug, Dusty was on her way.

Since Charlotte had sneaked her out for little walks, the outside world didn't seem too strange. Still, it felt odd to be on her own again, though, of course, she wasn't really on her own. She was met by a friendly "cabbie," complete with uniform and a spiffy yellow Checker cab.

"Ma'am," Captain Alvarez's assistant said, acting his role and holding open the door.

Once they were inside, however, Dusty had to chuckle. "The next time you play the part of cab-driver, you'd better be more surly. No one'll believe a polite one."

Relaxing as best she could, she indulged Ted Jackson in his chatter about people they both knew. For all of her dad's neglect, Dusty had had regular word of the goings-on at headquarters from Juan Alvarez's wife, Marge. It had been Marge who'd taken over when Dusty's mother had died. It had been Marge who had seen to it that she and Leslie, then eleven and twelve, had been included in that part of a police department that serves as a family.

"You don't have to worry much today," her driver said.

"Oh?"

"Old man Desota, the guy in the apartment next to yours, is spending the day at a clinic downtown. He's not well, you know."

"No, I didn't know."

Jackson's comment put a damper on Dusty's recovering spirits. It was comforting, of course, to think that Syd Desota wouldn't be watching her arrival, but being reminded of Syd Desota was exactly the opposite of comforting.

At last Dusty's "cabbie" announced they were nearing her new "home." They were just a few blocks south of Forest Park, right in the middle of an area of apartments and two- and three-family flats. There was a main drag with the usual conveniences for the surrounding neighborhood: a Laundromat, a grocery store, a drugstore. There was even a hardware store, a hamburger joint and, best of all, a string of little secondhand shops that attracted people from more than just the local area.

Many of the streets were tree-lined, and all of them had sidewalks bordering little lawns of green grass that were now turning brown with the change of seasons. Her "cabbie" pointed out a small park the residents were restoring and patrolling. He said the neighborhood, in general, was being revitalized. It was easy to see which rental properties had been restored and those that hadn't. And when they pulled up in front of the one that was to be hers, she saw it was one of the "had nots." The little patch of lawn was choked with weeds and mud, and the shrubs were overgrown and unkempt.

Well what do you expect of crooks, Dusty? Good taste and civic responsibility?

She was still staring, trying to keep the unfamiliarity at bay, when John Taggert emerged from the downstairs door on the left. He was dressed casually in slacks and an open-necked shirt. But it was the body beneath the clothes that made Dusty's breath catch.

Dusty's attention was diverted for a moment when a young black woman with a boy who was probably her son followed Tag out onto the stoop, the battered screen door banging behind them. But then Dusty's eyes were drawn to Tag's handsome face. He was actually smiling, wasn't he? Or was it more like a gorgeous grin?

Before she knew what he was doing, he had the door of the cab open and was holding her in a hard embrace.

"Hello, babe," he said softly, lowering his mouth toward hers.

Dusty stared, wide-eyed, watching his lashes close on his pale blue gaze. When his lips finally made warm contact with hers, she stiffened. Then realizing she was supposed to be acting the part of bride to his groom, she did her best to accommodate her "husband." Lifting herself on tiptoe and lacing her arms around his neck, she pushed her soft curves into the hard wall of John Taggert's body.

He responded enthusiastically, like a newlywed husband should, holding her harder and closer. But when his tongue sought entrance to Dusty's mouth, she pulled away—not as far gone as she'd felt for a moment.

Tag had no choice but to release her, and Dusty made a show of playing the blushing bride—which wasn't difficult. She was blushing furiously.

Glancing past Tag to her new neighbor, she introduced herself. "Hello, I'm Dusty T-taggert," she said, offering her hand.

The lovely brown-skinned woman chuckled. "You almost used your maiden name. It's understandable, so don't blush. I'm your upstairs neighbor, Pam Peters, and this is my son, Brent—as your very smitten husband should have said. But his being a little tongue-tied is understandable, what with his having waited a week for you to get here."

"Oh . . . yes." Dusty knew she sounded inane. They should have discussed their circumstances so she would have known what to say. Should she have taken the name Taggert? Evidently so. Now that she was thinking better, though, she realized she could have simply said Dusty.

Only then did the complexity of what they were doing strike her, again leaving her a little befuddled. She felt as if she were on an emotional roller coaster. One minute she was confused and the next she was determined to do better.

"Tag says you've been married a month."

Pam Peters was speaking to her, while Tag turned back to pay the "cabbie" and get the luggage.

"Yes . . . a month."

"He really missed you. It's too bad you had to stay behind with your mother until she was feeling better. Is she okay now?"

"Oh . . . she's fine. Otherwise I wouldn't have left her."

"Even with a félla like Tag waiting? Honey, I find that hard to believe."

Dusty couldn't think of a comment, and simply smiled at Pam's friendly quip.

"I'll carry one of the suitcases," Brent offered.

Tag's reply sounded genuine. "Okay, bud."

In her confusion Dusty had forgotten Tag's limp, and she reached for the case in his hand. "Shouldn't I carry that, d-dear?" When he looked questioningly over his shoulder at her, she explained. "I mean . . . your leg."

"My leg's fine. It may not be good enough to get you over the threshold in any kind of style, but I can certainly manage my other husbandly duties."

Dusty again had no idea how to respond. Fortunately Pam Peters didn't seem at a loss for words and filled the awkward gap. "I just bet you can do your duty." Her light tease was accompanied by a joking leer for Tag.

Dusty could only follow the procession up the two flights of steps to the stoop with its wrought-iron railing.

"We share the same stoop," Pam explained. "Our door leads to the apartment above, and yours opens into the first-floor apartment."

While Tag disappeared into one of the four doors that were all in a row, Dusty nodded. Pam remained behind, talking through the screen door, as Dusty and Brent followed Tag into the front room of Dusty's new home.

"That's far enough, Brent," Pam called. "Put the suitcase down. If there's one thing you've got to learn, honey, it's when you're a fifth wheel."

"Are you sure you wouldn't like to come in for a minute?" Dusty asked, her voice betraying a plea.

"It's nice of you to ask, Dusty, but I'm sure the two of you need some time to say hello."

With a big grin, Pam left, and Dusty turned to look at the empty living room. Tag had gone into one of the back rooms with her luggage, and her heart sank as she looked around. Everything, from the hardwood flooring to the woodwork, walls and windows, was dingy and gritty. The only thing at all cheerful was the narrow stained glass window placed high in the wall.

The kitchen behind the living room was no cleaner than the front room and looked archaic. Even the back door looked worn and was loose on its hinges. Turning down the hallway, she saw that the decor didn't improve. On the contrary, the hallway was even darker and felt almost claustrophobic.

The first bedroom, the one overlooking the stoop, contained a cot, a card table displaying Tag's equipment and a couple of metal chairs. There was a lamp and an alarm clock on another chair by the cot, and a camera set up in the window, barely peeping through the dirty drapes. That was it.

The second bedroom had a brand-new double bed without a headboard. There was bedding, though, wrapped in plastic and piled on the fresh expanse of mattress. Once again there was a metal chair and a metal lamp. Dusty's luggage sat on the floor.

Her eyes switched to the bath but locked instead with the ice-blue stare of Detective John Taggert. He, too, was standing in the small hallway. She could tell the bathroom behind him was as dingy as all the rest, but she could also see he'd made an attempt at cleaning the old-fashioned sink and commode.

"Will you mind if I leave my shaving gear in there?" he asked.

His deep voice would have been pleasant if it hadn't been hard. Where was the man who'd grinned at her, the one who'd called her "babe" and kissed her with such devastating results? Again Dusty found herself having to change gears. *That was an act. Remember?*

"Your things won't bother me," she told him at last.

Limping past her, Taggert turned into his own room.

Dusty followed and stood in his doorway, nudging at his door until she could see him. "I was wondering if you should tell me what you've told the neighbors about us."

"There's not much to tell for the week I've been here. I thought my partner would be doing this and she knows how to roll with the situation." Taggert's announcement was terse. But getting no rise from Dusty, he went on. "Pam and Brent are the only ones to have shown any interest. I told them we've been married a month. I left you in New York to come ahead and find an apartment while you stayed behind with your mother who reacted badly to our marriage."

Tag casually opened a paperback, indicating he thought he'd given her enough of a rundown. Dusty tried again. "My driver said that Syd Desota is out. I suppose that means we don't have to be as careful today."

Muttering a noncommittal, "Um," Tag didn't even look up.

Dusty drew in a quick breath. She finally had to say what she had to say. "I don't want to be here any more than you want me here."

When Taggert ignored her, Dusty reminded herself that she was a primary school teacher and had to learn to hold her temper and practice patience. "I'd like for us to make the best of a bad situation."

Tag rounded on her. "Well, I'm not so nice. We're not talking about setting up an amicable, polite little household here while we wait to catch some crooks. This is a damn stakeout, lady. We're here to arrest a group of men who are nothing short of scum. They're dangerous. Damn dangerous. They've killed the two men before me. And here I sit with Miss Goody Two-Shoes who wants to be reasonable and make friends."

"I didn't say I wanted to be friends," Dusty blazed back, her good intentions flying out the window. "I simply wanted to do this the easy way instead of the hard way. But if you want it the hard way, you've got it!"

CHAPTER THREE

A REGAL EXIT wasn't easy when one was short, but Dusty tried. Marching out of Tag's room, she went to her own. How had she ever thought of John Taggert as sympathetic? She must have been more affected by her dad's murder that night than she'd thought.

Ripping her bed pad from its pristine wrapper she flung it onto the bed and went around shoving its corners over the mattress. She did the same with the plain white sheets and the fuzzy blankets and still hadn't calmed down. Stuffing the new pillows into the pillowcase, she finished her chore by putting on the chenille bedspread. After that she unpacked her clothes, and noted the filth of the closet, which added fuel to her fire. When she couldn't find so much as a broom or a pail, not even a cleanser, she knocked on Tag's door. When he didn't answer, she hollered through it, "I'm going to the store. I need some stuff!"

She heard him stir. In a moment he opened his door and handed her a few bills, evidently approving her plan. He exhibited no signs of his earlier anger. Hers was barely banked.

"Just some basic rules," he said. "You don't stick your nose out the door without talking to me first."

Dusty nodded brusquely.

"Use the rear door as much as you can, and when you use the front door, stop somewhere down the block and check the sidewalk, street and stoop before coming back in."

Dusty merely nodded again.

"The store is—"

"I saw the store on my way here," she cut in, glad to do so.

Stalking off gave her even more satisfaction.

"Pick up a bag of hamburgers and some coffee on your way back," he called, obviously unimpressed by her anger.

"Anything else you want lugged in for you?"

His jet-black eyebrow arched in masculine coyness. "Some cream?"

"Does that thing masquerading as a refrigerator work?"

"I don't know. Does it?"

Getting out into the brisk autumn air did Dusty a world of good. It was wonderful to simply be on her own again. Brent, who was as friendly as his mother, happened to be in the little side yard that ran along their building. He was glad to lend her the metal shopping cart that belonged to his mom, and trailed after Dusty through the grocery store, hardware store and the hamburger joint, where she stopped on the way back to the apartment.

It had always been easy for Dusty to talk to children, and nine-year-old Brent was no exception. Of course, he was the kind of child anyone could converse with, and Dusty enjoyed his company. He even accepted her admission of being a teacher with equanimity.

Retaining her restored sense of calm was Dusty's next goal. After the freedom of the bright weather outside, she found the apartment all the more oppressive. It was no wonder John Taggert was unsociable. Who wouldn't be after spending the hours he had in places like this?

It was almost heartbreaking, picturing the cot he slept on. He had to love his work as much as her father had.

On the other hand, that Taggert had bought her a bed—a double at that—displayed more plainly than anything the cosseting he thought she must be accustomed to. Of course, that had to be part of his resentment of her; he thought she was soft. Well, she'd show him. She could handle John Taggert, and she'd handle the depression of having to live in this grimy apartment, as well. Nothing would make her as sour as he was.

"Where do you want your hamburger?" she asked, giving Tag's door a sharp rap. Once again she heard him moving across the room to open his preferred barrier.

"I had them add mustard and pickles," she said as a first attempt at being civil.

"Fine," he muttered, not responding in kind, but his tone no longer cutting.

At least he didn't hold a grudge.

Oddly enough, Dusty found that heartening, even though he immediately turned away from her to eat in solitude. As he did so, she was again struck by a sense of sadness about the way he lived. Being alone most of the time, inhabiting seedy rooms and thinking seedy thoughts, couldn't be good for him, even for someone as obviously hardened and self-sufficient as John Taggert. Dusty had a soft spot, and somehow Taggert had reached it as easily as he had tapped her anger.

Since he kept his back to her, Dusty went to her own room to eat her hamburger. The middle of her bed was the only place she knew was clean, and she plunked down on it. Just that quickly her determination wavered. *Another strange and lonely room* was all she could think as her eyes moved over the dingy paint with its web of cracks. There were plenty of real webs, as well, draping the corners and clogging the creases where the ceiling met the walls.

The building was basically sound. It was just neglected and grimy. Some paint and a good scrubbing would make it a hundred percent better. The windows, unfortunately, were small and set high in the walls, and the drapes were ready to be trashed. But the bath and kitchen fixtures were serviceable and could be cute, in their own way, if placed against a better backdrop.

Why not fix the place up a bit? Painting wasn't beyond her abilities. Nor so expensive as to be unreasonable to request. Come to think of it, if she really were newly married to John Taggert, wouldn't she be fixing up this place? It would look strange if the pair of them only hid out, day in and day out, with nothing to account for their time.

Marching to Tag's door, Dusty applied her sharp rap.

"Yeah?"

Undaunted, she pushed the door open. "Is there any reason for keeping the doors closed before we're ready for bed? I mean, it's not like I don't know what you're doing in here.''

"That's not my reason for keeping it shut.'' His cocked brow told her she was the one he was hoping to close out.

Remembering her decision to react as positively as she could, Dusty stifled her automatic retort and went on. "What will people think we do here all day long?''

"What newlyweds do.''

"No. I mean, what have you told Pam and Brent you do for a living?''

"I'm a writer. You know, the destitute-artist-in-a-garret type who's going to make it big someday because he suffered the garret.''

"And me? What am I supposed to be doing in these small rooms twenty-four hours a day?''

"Suffering with me. When you aren't catering to my sexual excesses. All we artists have sexual excesses, you know.''

"No, I'm serious,'' Dusty insisted. "Most women my age do something.''

"A job is out.''

"I know that.''

"All right,'' he said, looking her straight in the eye, "what do you do?''

"I make a home for us. I cook and scrub and clean and paint—''

"Paint?'' he asked, cutting in.

"Can't you get a little extra money so I can buy some paint?''

Taggert sat peering at Dusty, something other than cynicism playing deeply in his eyes. It was as if he was looking at her, really looking at her, for the first time, and it made her heart race. What would it be like, she wondered, to have a man like John Taggert love you? This was such a stunning thought that it nearly unraveled both her and her determination to have this talk with Taggert. What was the matter with her?

The word *Taggertitis* echoed in her mind, and she saw a vision of Charlotte's grinning face.

"I can get some paint," Tag said.

"And furniture?" she queried. "Nothing fancy, just secondhand stuff."

"Okay. If it'll keep you out of my hair."

The cynicism was again entrenched in his deep voice and cool eyes. Knowing she'd been dismissed, Dusty didn't dare bother with him anymore. He might change his mind, and then where would she be?

She pulled his door shut behind her, then remembered he'd given her permission to leave it ajar. Turning, she pushed it carefully open again, her eyes sneaking to those of the man within. Although neither one of them said a word, both she and he recognized the meaning of her leaving it that way.

Still, Dusty continued to feel unsettled by the confrontation, especially by that close, heady examination he had made of her. Things were complicated enough between them without adding a sensual element to their relationship. Even to think of such a thing as her being attractive to Tag surprised and, at the same time, caused a ripple to run through her body. She was just as glad she was aware of the possibility, however. She could be on guard. It was unlikely he would approach her, but several weeks alone together was several weeks alone together. Who knew what could grow to seem natural under such circumstances?

To unscramble her thoughts, Dusty attacked the job of cleaning the bathroom with a vengeance. Then, after seeing that the refrigerator did work and unloading the groceries, she marched back to the bathroom and used all of her pent-up fears, questions and anger in cleaning the toilet, tile and porcelain. She spent the afternoon laying down a coat of bleaching cleanser, letting it sit awhile and then rinsing it and starting all over again. Happily the old fixtures responded.

The clean bathtub sparked thoughts of taking a bath, however, and that led to the question of towels, washcloths, soap...

Screwing up her courage, Dusty bearded the lion in his den yet another time. "Did you buy bath towels?"

"Sorry," he said, actually apologizing. Glancing up from the newspaper, he was slouched over, he added, "I carry my own and forgot to warn you."

"I'll have to—"

"I know."

By the time Dusty returned with the yellow bath towels that she thought would look cheery in the dingy bathroom, it was almost time for supper. She didn't dare approach "him" again, and so was relieved when "he" called out that "he" had ordered a pizza. She was even more amazed a few minutes later when she turned back from admiring her new towels and found him standing behind her just inside the bathroom door.

"You can use one of those for answering the door when the pizza comes."

Dusty thought she hadn't understood him right. "I beg your pardon?"

"You can wear a towel—and nothing else—when you pay for the pizza at the door."

"I will not."

"Yes, you will."

"And why will I?"

"Because I said so. Because a policewoman would do it. Because we're supposed to be newlyweds, and because the same guy who'll be delivering that pizza will be delivering pizza to any number of other places in the neighborhood. Not to mention the little tidbits he'll drop into the ears of the guys back at the pizza parlor to be passed along from there."

"You mean you want people to...?" Dusty began asking, dumbfounded.

"I mean, I want to build a solid, safe cover here. And that means we're to look like newlyweds. We all know newlyweds spend a lot of time in the sack. So that's what we have to look like we're doing."

"How eloquently stated."

Ignoring Dusty's comment, Tag went on doggedly. "Besides, we've been separated for a week and married only four. You've been out showing your sweet little buns all over the neighborhood today. A new wife who's been separated from her husband would hardly be haunting a hardware store, examining paint samples. We're going to show everybody that I have some pride, as well as a good bit of appetite. Nothing like a little blatant sex to keep a neighborhood astir. Now, either you put on that towel and muss up your hair, or I'll do it for you."

Dusty had been watching the long, masculine finger that had been jabbing the air for emphasis. "I'll do it."

"And one more thing, Dusty. Don't question me anymore. Give me some credit for my twelve years on the force. If I tell you to do something, you do it."

"All right, all right. I didn't know. I was thinking about—"

"We're married, remember? You've got no lily-white reputation to worry about."

"Okay, okay."

"Well, get going. The pizza's been ordered, and it won't be long before the delivery boy gets here. You think I haven't seen a nice little fanny like yours before?"

"No, but you haven't seen mine, and it's going to stay that way."

Tag snorted, and Dusty exploded inside.

"Out!" she declared, jabbing a finger into his hard chest. "We're only talking *appearances* here."

Two minutes later, when Dusty stepped into the hallway, naked except for the canary-yellow bath towel, her appearance seemed to absorb Tag's total interest.

"Will I do?" she asked as crisply as if she'd emerged for his inspection in dress blues.

"Turn around."

"Are you sure this is really—?"

His world-weary sigh had her doing as he asked, but she'd never before felt so small, so short, so inadequate. A flush rose to stain her cheeks. Damn her translucent skin. Damn John Taggert.

Finally her eyes lifted to his all-too-familiar blue stare. She noticed she came up to Tag's chin, and would have gladly given anything to be able to look him straight in the eye. "Well?"

Before she knew what he was doing, he had her hard against his larger body and was kissing her. She was torn between resisting, which would certainly allow the towel to slip, and standing stock-still in protest. She decided on the latter, but even that didn't make her point. Finally he finished and, as if that wasn't enough, he rubbed his day's growth of beard against her cheeks.

"Ow! Stop!"

Tag let go when it pleased him, then stepped back, his eyes shuttering over. "That's it. You look your part."

Not two minutes later Dusty found herself answering the rap at the front door. Indeed, the delivery boy looked both duly impressed and totally convinced when she exchanged her money for his box of pizza.

Slapping a couple of pieces on a paper plate, she retreated to her room. Certainly she'd completed her assignment as well as any policewoman would have. But she had a question that wouldn't go away. Did Ellen Daniels find her partner's methods and manners irritating? Did Ellen Daniels find his physical attentions unsettling? No. Surely that paragon was immune to Taggertitis.

Dusty felt more of her self-confidence return once she'd changed out of the towel and back into her clothes, but under her surface calm, she remained unsure of herself in this strange situation. She didn't usually depend on TV or radio or even on other people to fill her off hours, but, still, it was nice to have those sorts of distractions available. Here there was nothing at all. It seemed there was only silence. There wasn't even much light in the dirty, old apartment.

A metal swing lamp clamped to the back of her metal chair provided an adequate pool of light in her room. There was a pool of light in Tag's room. And there were other small pools from single bulbs here and there—one in the hall, one in the bath and, probably, one in the kitchen.

But Dusty couldn't keep her mind off the fact that one whole end of the apartment was dark and empty. It seemed foreign and eerily vacant. Thinking of it sent shivers down her back, and knowing that Syd Desota sat next door in a similar apartment, unknowingly awaiting "the inevitable day," added immeasurably to the creepiness of her situation.

Resisting the temptation to call her sister, Dusty took a long, hot bath. It seemed odd to put her toilet things next to Tag's in the now-clean pantry. She couldn't help her curiosity about his shaving cream and after-shave, either.

He was so quiet, so obviously content to be in that little room. And all for what? Did he have some deep allegiance to righting the wrongs of the world? She didn't think it had been that way with her father. But she didn't want to think about her father. Not tonight when she was already feeling off balance.

Oh, she was strong. But she had her weaknesses, her little chinks of vulnerability. She didn't, for example, like having John Taggert evaluate her so easily and then dismiss her as a nuisance.

She felt she deserved better than that. She had always gone to school and worked, as well, often holding down two jobs. She had made good grades and had put herself through university on scholarships. After that she'd continued to attend night school while teaching the morning and afternoon kindergarten classes at Brockham Elementary.

Of course, most people wouldn't understand why she kept educating herself. There was no corporate ladder to climb at Brockham Elementary. She simply wanted to be the best damn kindergarten teacher that any five-year-old could have. She, like so many in her position, believed that there was no more important year in a child's life than his first year at school, and she wanted to make each child feel successful and eager to move up to the next grades.

But Brockham Elementary seemed worlds away now. Snuggling down under her covers, she switched off the lamp and lay on her back.

An angular patch of bluish light from a streetlamp streaked her ceiling. Other than that, the room was darker and quieter than any room she'd ever slept in before. The occasional clank of her radiator was a new sound she'd have to get used to, just as was the pop of the water heater in a hall closet when it turned off and on.

This was the world of Ox Landry and John Taggert, a world that was oblivious to the warmer comforts of home and hearth. She'd have to live in it for many more days and nights.

She wouldn't cave in. She'd make the best of it and come out a stronger person. She'd also retain her positive outlook. She'd managed it throughout her stint in the safe house, and she could do the same here.

THE NEXT MORNING when Dusty awoke the apartment was silent and, looking out her door, she could see that the bathroom across the hall was unoccupied. Gathering her clothes—her jeans, shirt, sneakers—she got dressed. It was then that she realized Tag wasn't in his room. Nor was he in the kitchen or living room.

This was a startling discovery, and Dusty went back to his room just to be sure. No, he was gone. Except for the still-rumpled blankets on his cot, everything was straightened. Dusty's eyes ran to the stack of bestsellers, newspapers and magazines that kept him occupied when he wasn't at his card table. He was obviously a voracious reader and, just as obviously, hadn't moved out or been dragged off by Syd Desota.

Just thinking of that name turned Dusty's skin to gooseflesh, but fortunately she heard a key rattling in the back door. Walking to the kitchen, she met Tag just as he came in.

"I didn't know you'd gone," she said.

"I do get out once and a while. Otherwise I'd starve."

He indicated the bag he carried, and Dusty could smell the aroma of fresh coffee. Then, to her surprise, he limped by her toward his room. Only then did she realize that the little white bag was obviously too small to contain anything for her.

"I didn't know when you'd be up," he offered as an excuse, pulling out his coffee and Danish and setting them on the card table.

Dusty had never met anyone so inconsiderate, not even her father. That Tag had a good excuse for not having brought her anything held little weight when measured against the irritation she was feeling. Hadn't she brought him hamburgers yesterday? she wanted to ask tartly. Wouldn't he have brought something for Ellen Daniels? But she wasn't about to be the one to set this day off in the grooves of yesterday, so she gave an inch.

"I'll buy a coffeepot today."

Automatically reaching for his billfold in his back pocket, Tag handed her some money, once again without looking at her. Dusty turned and stalked into the kitchen. She'd write a grocery list that would knock his eye out, and then make him a lunch that would demonstrate how generous she was in comparison to his stingy hide.

By the time Dusty came in with his lunch, Tag was into his paperwork. He barely noticed when she set her offering beside his elbow on the table. Although he managed to eat it down to the last morsel, he didn't say thank you.

It was while she was taking his bowl away that he finally deigned to speak. "What was that?"

Positive. Be positive, she told herself as she forced a reasonable tone into her voice. "Lemon-egg soup. It's easy to fix and, since I picked up some second-hand dishes—a few pots and pans—I thought I'd try them out."

She could tell Tag had already lost interest. His eyes were switching back to his papers even as he sent her a brief nod.

Dusty spent her day cleaning the kitchen in the me-thodical way she had the bathroom. She felt she couldn't use it until she did. The refrigerator, stove and sink were equally old, but they responded. As she worked, she tried to accustom herself to the constant drip of the faucet, but by the time she'd cleaned her last cabinet, lining each one with fresh, sticky paper, she'd had all she could stand of the constant drip-ping. She made a close examination of the plumbing under the sink and found there was no shut-off valve. While that came as no surprise, it did make her task harder.

Getting yet another, even less patient okay from Tag, she beat her now-familiar path to the hardware store. Picking up a faucet, the sort that "just anyone can install," she sneaked back in as quietly as she could. She didn't dare arouse Tag again.

She'd installed a faucet before, only it had been on newer plumbing and with a handy shut-off valve un-der the sink. But she had a real penchant for tinker-ing and puttering and had done a lot at home. Without any hesitation she went to look for a shut-off in the basement, this time ignoring Tag altogether. She wasn't really leaving, after all.

Naturally it was very grungy in the cellar, but she was able to locate the four shut-offs for the individual apartments. They were in a neat row, one for each, just like the doors on the stoop. She puzzled for a long time, wondering which one she should turn off, her big brown eyes following the slender lines of pipe up the basement wall and through the joists. She finally de-cided there was only one possibility and gingerly at-tempted to turn that one off.

She had expected the handle would be difficult to move—its elegant fluting spoke of the age of the plumbing—and, sure enough, the tap was frozen in place. She was determined, however, and, rummaging around, she found an equally antique wrench. Applying it as carefully as she could, her small hands just barely got the grip she wanted. Still, it didn't budge. Not even when she put her full weight behind the wrench. Then, just for a moment, she thought she had it, only to be shocked into the reality of the handle spinning to the floor, completely broken off.

She automatically clapped her palm over the spewing water but saw that that was nearly useless. All she'd succeeded in doing was to change the course of the stream of water so that instead of splashing onto the old boiler, it gushed onto the floor. Fortunately the concrete floor had a decided slope, and the water formed into a neat stream running straight down into the drain.

"Thank goodness for that," she muttered, still trying to decide what to do. Just standing there was largely ineffectual, even if she was keeping the old boiler from drowning. Besides, the water was like ice and her hand was already numb. Her jeans and sweatshirt were soaked clear through along her front. Even her shirt, underpants and sneakers were wet.

She wondered if hollering would do any good or even if she should. After all, Syd Desota lived above the other end of the basement, hearing impaired or not.

Finally she had to do something, and so she hollered. Of course, the basement's concrete walls efficiently muffled the sound. Still, she figured Tag couldn't be too far. In fact, he was probably directly above her. It was just a question of contacting him.

Her eyes again ran along the peripheries of the dank basement. Someone was obviously a gardener. She had seen the small, immaculately kept plot in the side yard and, surely enough, this was where the blessed person kept his blessed tomato poles. Letting go of the spouting water, she dashed over and grabbed one. Then she ran back to replug the pipe with one hand, while with the other, she used the tomato pole to bang on the joists of the floor above her. Finally she switched to banging on the pipes themselves.

In a matter of minutes, while her one hand was frozen with cold, her other arm hurt from flailing the pipes with her stick, and she still wasn't getting any response.

She didn't know what else to do. Should she simply let the water spew out of the pipe and run upstairs to call a plumber? Wouldn't that be bad for the boiler? Should she continue to raise a racket? Perhaps enough of a racket to arouse even old Syd Desota? Still in a quandary and near to tears besides, Dusty couldn't believe it when Tag rushed down the basement stairs and stopped just inside the dim interior.

"What the hell . . . ?"

"Now don't get angry."

"Don't get angry? Have you no sense?"

Well knowing what he meant without him rolling his eyes in the direction of the other end of the basement, Dusty spoke brusquely. "Just call a plumber."

"What?" he bit out. "I should leave you here to get soaked and die of pneumonia?"

Tag's eyes perused the wall of pipes behind her, and Dusty was amazed when he pushed her aside to step into the spray. His strong hand reached for the major main and, with a truly blue curse, he managed to shut it off. The silence that resulted was deafening.

Dusty couldn't imagine why she hadn't thought to look for the main, and then didn't know what to say. "Thank you," she managed at last.

"Go upstairs and call headquarters. They'll send a plumber. And, for heaven's sake, get out of those clothes."

Dusty wasn't about to try to make a point, to apologize or even to explain. She was grateful for the excuse to get out while Tag cooled off.

An hour later she heard Tag come upstairs and go into his room. Straightening her shoulders, she also marched in, only to stop dead in her tracks. Tag stood inside, naked to the waist and unzipping his pants.

"If you'd either leave a closed door shut or knock before you barged in, you wouldn't end up being embarrassed," he snapped.

"I'm not embarrassed."

"Oh, really?" he asked skeptically.

As if to prove his point, he went on to push down his pants, his act revealing not only pale blue briefs but a beautifully formed masculine body. Beautiful, that is, except for his badly marred thigh.

Still, Dusty wasn't about to back off, not even when he eased onto his cot with a know-it-all glance to her and stripped off his socks.

"I feel that I should pay the bill for the mess I made."

Tag stood up, grumbling his reply without looking at her. "Forget it."

"I don't know about you, but I couldn't stand the drip."

"Even with Desota next door, you can't stand a drip?"

Dusty was reminding herself not to fire back when Tag sent her a pointed stare. "I'm going to change my briefs too, Dusty."

That decided it, of course, and Dusty backed out of the room. But she wasn't embarrassed. She was too busy thinking about the glimpse she'd had of Tag's leg.

To see such a perfectly formed, male column of leg so badly damaged was a shame. Her eyes had only flicked over it, but she had clearly seen the wide expanse of puckered flesh on his muscular thigh. Not only had John Taggert been wounded, but evidently he'd barely recovered from the operation it had taken to set him to rights. No wonder he limped. No wonder the pain often registered in the hard set of his features.

Once again Dusty sensed herself sympathizing with him in a way she would never have thought possible. He represented everything that had hurt her in her childhood. He, like her father, was a workaholic cop who cared for little else but his job. He put her off at every opportunity. He ignored her and didn't want her here. Still, she was drawn to him. Still, she felt an empathy for him. Perhaps because she had found out all too late that her father had regretted his similar life pattern.

When Dusty went into the kitchen to make supper, she found a new faucet installed on the sink. *How considerate,* she thought, her eyes welling foolishly with tears.

You'd better get off this emotional kick, she scolded herself, *or you aren't going to hack it.*

An hour later she went to Tag's room, pausing with scrupulous care to knock at his door.

"Come in," he called absentmindedly, again at work.

Moving to his card table, Dusty put down his plate, glass and cutlery.

"What's this?"

"It's called a home-cooked meal."

Thoughts of the shiny faucet that Tag had gone ahead and installed himself glowed inside of her. "Those are steamed carrots with unsaturated margarine. That's a broiled chop. And this is tapioca pudding. The glass has decaffeinated iced tea—of which there is plenty more—and there's a salad. What kind of dressing do you prefer?"

"You don't have to do this, you know. We have a budget."

"Oh, but I do have to do it. After six months in a hotel room, I have to do something with myself. I couldn't stand to live in this filthy place as it is, and I've always enjoyed homemaking."

Tag lifted a broad shoulder. "If you put it that way, who am I to complain?"

"About this afternoon—"

"Let's not go over that again."

"All right. I bought a little drip coffeepot today. If you want coffee after you eat, or any other time, just ask. However, I give you fair warning. The coffee will also be decaffeinated from now on. You drink too much coffee, and you have to admit it.''

Tag's mouth was full, but Dusty felt encouraged by his nod. Gesturing at his table and the machinery on it, she asked, ''Would you mind explaining what's going on here?''

While he continued to eat, Tag spoke more amicably than he ever had before. ''There's not much to tell. Syd Desota lives just on the other side of that wall.'' He indicated ''that wall'' with his full, lifted fork and, putting it in his mouth, went on. ''He's an old man and unwell besides. His nephews use the phone in his apartment on a regular basis, so I've bugged it. I've also drilled a tiny bug directly into the wall. I listen when there's anything to listen to, record the conversations I hear and make reports.''

Dusty's eyes ran automatically to the camera that was set up in the window that overlooked the stoop. She noticed how carefully it was placed so that it barely showed between the drawn drapes and the old venetian blinds.

After swallowing a bit more of the meal he obviously preferred to her, Tag responded to Dusty's pointed gaze. ''The camera's set up for photographing anyone who comes to the stoop. While the bugs are voice-activated, I have to be here to get pictures. Seeing as how Syd's visitors come by car, I listen for cars pulling up to the curb.''

''And you've been here a week? How much have you gotten?''

''Hardly anything. I've photographed a guy in a Cardinals' baseball cap and recorded an average of two phone calls a day. But don't worry. The guy in the Cardinal's cap isn't your dad's killer. He's a two-bit punk we're all familiar with.''

Dusty's unease at being exposed to the nitty-gritty of Tag's job must have shown in her eyes because Tag smiled a cryptic smile. ''Until my leg's healed, I'm on what's called 'light duty,' like this surveillance, for instance. The Desotas are in Miami getting together a drug deal, and most of the gang members are with them. There won't be much to do until it gets hot. Unfortunately that's the bad part. We can never be certain when it'll get hot. That's why I have to be here no matter how innocuous things look.''

''And that's also why you have time to baby-sit me.''

''Yeah, but don't for a minute forget why we're here. These men are dangerous—''

''I know. I've heard that one. These men are 'damn dangerous, Dusty.' ''

Her bit of teasing almost got her a smile from Tag. It didn't actually materialize, however, and, before she knew it, he was stern again.

''Just watch yourself, because, quite frankly, I don't have the patience or the inclination for it. I'm only doing this because Alvarez twisted my arm.''

''Yeah,'' Dusty said without rancor. ''I figured that.''

While Tag went on with his meal, Dusty leaned comfortably against the doorframe. ''By the way,'' she said, ''I went to the other two apartments to explain my plumbing mishap. Pam and Brent were gone, but I met the sweetest couple upstairs across from them. Their names are Jake and Bessie. He's a retired zookeeper. Since we live so close to the park, he used to walk to work every day. He kept the big snakes, and he has pictures of them in their living room. There's one photo of an enormous boa constrictor wound around him. He's a small man, too. Those photos gave me the shivers just to look at them, but he was so nice that it was hard for me to leave without letting him explain what he obviously thought was a great job. He says he kept mostly constrictors—anacondas, pythons . . .''

While she knew Tag had to take a professional interest in their neighbors, he'd obviously lost interest as she went on. When was she going to get the point that he didn't want to converse? *He doesn't need companionship,* she told herself, *even if you do.*

CHAPTER FOUR

ON HER SECOND MORNING in the old apartment, Dusty heard a knock at the front door that startled her. Walking into the dingy living room, she hesitated before answering. On the previous afternoon she'd seen Syd Desota returning from the clinic, and she couldn't get that picture out of her mind. Oh, he had looked like any other little old man, leaning on the arm of some scuzzy acquaintance who had helped him home. Still, his crabbed image flashed before her, keeping her where she was.

Fortunately Tag came in and, while he was scowling deeply, he signaled that she was to step aside so he could handle it. To watch him change gears the way he did, from frowning to smiling, was the next thing to surprise Dusty. The last was that their visitor was Pam Peters, their neighbor from the apartment upstairs.

"I know, I know," the young woman said with a big grin marking her smooth brown complexion. "I promised you some time alone before I came pounding on your door. I'm not much for keeping silly promises, however, and since I've got the afternoon off from that hellhole called a department store, I thought Dusty might like to come up for a visit."

While Dusty tried to appear as relaxed as Tag, she wasn't as practiced at playing the games he played.

Her eyes flashed to his, and Pam, being the savvy person she was, picked up on that, as well.

"Come on. Your bridegroom can do without you for long enough to take a break. Besides, I'm cutting my pumpkin today and I can use the help. I hate cleaning up yucky pumpkin seeds, and all that membraney stuff inside is even worse."

Dusty laughed and, catching Tag's almost imperceptible nod, said she'd love to come.

She did, in fact, want to and was glad to follow Pam into her cheaply decorated but cheerful apartment. "Wow," she said. "This is great."

"It's not so great, honey. It's only that anything would look great to somebody who lives where you do."

Dusty laughed. "Was your apartment as bad as mine when you moved in?"

"Not quite, but almost. I must admit I've had fun painting and fixing it up." Pam had walked to the stove and was offering a cup of tea with an eloquent move of a shoulder.

"Let's cut the pumpkins first," Dusty said. "Really, this looks like fun."

The three pumpkins on the spread of newspaper, the big and small knives and the waiting trash bag indicated that Pam had planned this little get-together.

"I haven't done this...well, since last year," Dusty said.

Even though kindergarten kids were really into Halloween and pumpkins, and Dusty was accustomed to enjoying the holiday, it felt as if it had been years since she'd enjoyed this kind of thing.

"Well, dig in," Pam announced, flourishing her knife.

"You mean I get a pumpkin of my own?"

"Sure. I don't make my guests clean up the yucky part without offering them a pumpkin. Anyway, I bought two extra for Brent and his friend and, since they aren't here, it's their tough luck."

"Oh, I don't know," Dusty said, hesitating. "I mean I understand how much kids like to do this."

Since Pam had plunged her wicked looking kitchen knife into the largest pumpkin with such relish, Dusty picked up the smallest knife and the smallest pumpkin and did the same.

"Actually, I love doing this," she admitted. "I don't even mind the icky insides."

"Good. Then you can scrape mine, too." Dusty was suddenly put on her guard by her hostess's next subject. "Brent says you're a teacher."

"Yes. Kindergarten."

"I take it you're looking for a job."

Now Dusty was thrown off balance. She could see that forming a friendship with Pam would involve not only watching what she said, but a certain amount of lying, and she didn't like that. "I . . . I've been looking, but . . . well, the school year just began and I haven't had any luck. There might be something after January . . . or so I've been told."

"I suppose somebody should be working," Pam said dryly, glancing up from her pumpkin.

Once again Dusty had to regroup. And lie. "Oh, you mean Tag's being a writer? Well, actually . . . he has a trust from his . . . maternal grandmother, and we're living off that. We decided to give his writing a

chance . . . while we're young and without responsibil-
ities.''

Pam looked entirely convinced as she murmured a
"You're lucky in that" and went back to frowning
down into the cavity of her pumpkin.

By the time Dusty and Pam had both their pumpkins cleaned and were ready to get into the creative
part, Dusty was feeling better. With the arrival of
Pam's son Brent, who was already well acquainted
with Dusty, things got even easier. He was accompanied by a smaller boy, one who was decidedly pale
and white when set against Brent's deep brown skin
and nicely built boy's body.

"Hey, Dusty," Brent said, his delight pleasing her.

"Hi, Brent. Have I taken your place?"

"Naw, I don't wanna do that. It's Mom who likes
that kinda junk." Peering at his smaller friend who
was hanging behind in the door, Brent proved that he
was being raised right. "Of course, I'd be glad to cut
pumpkins if Rog wants to."

"It's time you introduced Roger," Pam said.
"Dusty's never met him. Come on in here, Roger,
honey."

Dusty's eyes refocused on the smaller boy who was
making a try at fading into the woodwork. So he's shy,
she thought, her heart going immediately out to him.

"That's okay," she said, "I can say 'Hi' from over
here and Roger can say 'Hi' from over there."

Her turning back to the pumpkin obviously gave the
boy the mental and physical space he needed and,
while the others went on with their conversation, the
teacher in Dusty noticed that Roger continued to hover
in the background. She decided to ask him to help her.

She knew that would edge him into the group easily, but her plans proved unnecessary.

After a little more chatter, the boys left, and Pam looked across from where she'd started the third pumpkin. "Now that my son has publicly claimed he's not the one to like jack-o'-lanterns, I suppose I should consider myself uncovered."

"Yes, you should."

"I guess I'll have to stop buying them next year."

"Why's that?"

"I can hardly enjoy Halloween without Brent as an excuse."

"Heck, I wouldn't let that stop me. I don't need an excuse for enjoying pumpkin cutting."

"I'll say," Pam seconded on a wry smile. "The way you've slashed into that one makes me feel I've met my match."

"At least your match and maybe your better."

"And what does that mean?"

When Dusty turned her artfully grimacing pumpkin, the other woman let out a yowl of delight. "Now, honey, you've got to teach me to do that."

"I don't know if you've got the touch."

The two of them laughed comfortably, and Dusty realized what a release her little visit had become. "Thanks for asking me up here today, Pam. You don't know what this means to me."

"He's that bad, eh?"

Dusty didn't know what her new friend meant, and Pam laughed at the look of puzzlement on her face.

"Your husband. New husbands can be demanding. But I wouldn't have thought you'd complain. Not with the new husband you've got. The pair of you have the whole neighborhood talking, and its only been two days.''

Dusty was amazed. ''The whole neigh—''

''You can't expect to answer your door in a yellow towel and not have people talking. Not in a neighborhood like this one.''

''Oh, my Lord.''

''Not that any of us mind. I mean, it kinda gets the blood circulating.''

''But—''

''And certainly you don't mind. Not with a guy like Tag.''

''Oh ... I don't mind. I mean ... well ...''

Pam was laughing again, and her big smile set against her black skin, was her prettiest feature. ''Honey, I can imagine. I've had two husbands of my own.''

''Two?''

''Yeah, Brent's daddy and then Terance Peters. Of course, both of them are long gone and I'm the happier for it. But I do remember the early days, the ones you're experiencing now. And I say, enjoy it, because it can't last. Nothing that good can last forever.''

Once again the pair of them laughed, and Dusty realized how long it had been since she'd felt so good.

The eyes of the little boy she had met earlier surfaced in her thoughts, however, and she decided to approach Pam about her unease. ''Do you know Brent's friend, Roger?''

''Not as well as some of Brent's other buddies,'' Pam said, sobering, too. ''He's only lived in the neighborhood since this last summer. Brent met him in the park, and now they're in the same class at school. I know what you're saying, though. He's a forlorn little critter, isn't he?''

"It's funny, but that's exactly how I felt when I met him. He's not only shy but, like you say, forlorn."

"I hate to see it when a child's like that," said Pam.

"So do I. It's my guess that something very sad is going on in his life."

AFTER A WEEK Dusty's kitchen was well stocked and as clean as she could get it. The refrigerator was humming along, keeping things cold, making ice and sparkling inside and out.

She and Tag had settled into a sort of status quo, Tag sticking to his room and Dusty doing everything but. She cooked, she read, she planned, she escaped—when Tag let her—and she talked with the neighbors. All in all, she found she was sort of happy. The emotional roller coaster she'd been on during her first few days with Tag had settled into a much smoother track—as she had expected.

She'd spent a lot of time chipping and sanding paint until she was down to the sound stuff. Because she could stand only so much of that, she'd often stop, do something else, then go back to it. And, if anything, the place looked worse. Under the general dinge, she'd uncovered great patches of other colors from earlier coats of paint, but she continued undaunted. She enjoyed doing what she was doing and could picture what it would look like when she was finished. Unfortunately Tag couldn't.

"What *are* you up to?" he asked one afternoon when he limped into the kitchen for coffee.

"I'm preparing the walls before I paint. This is the hardest part and the most boring, but it's important."

Tag peered up at her where she was perched on top of an old stepladder. He took a sip of his coffee and crinkled his eye against the rising steam. "Where'd you get that ladder?" he asked. "It looks rickety."

"From Jake."

"Jake?"

"Our neighbor. The snakekeeper I told you about."

"Uh." Tag glanced around the room. "It looks like hell."

"I know," Dusty agreed cheerily. She found it was easier to roll with whatever Tag had to say and then go merrily about her business. Actually, she saw him so seldom she'd decided it wasn't worth getting upset over their brief exchanges.

"Where did you learn to do all this?" Tag asked.

"I started out helping my mother paint. My dad was never around, so she and I took care of the house together. I liked it, though, and once I was running the household on my own, I got into more complicated stuff."

"Like plumbing?" Tag asked innocently.

Hoping to forget the faucet incident, Dusty smiled and changed the subject. "What's Syd doing?"

"What Syd always does. His snoring puts me to sleep."

"Don't you need to go out once in a while?"

This was just one of the many things Dusty wondered about Tag. She thought about him all the time and had all kinds of questions she wanted to ask.

"It's one of the ironies of the game. Until the surveillance starts, you run yourself ragged. Then once it starts, you sit until it drives you nuts."

Dusty was surprised at Tag's bitter tone. She hadn't expected to hear him criticize what he obviously loved best. "If your partner was here with you, would you go out more often?" she asked.

"Yeah, I'd take a break now and again. Nothing elaborate. Just an hour here and there."

"Why don't you show me how to take over for short periods? You could teach me the basics. And you could wear a signal on your belt, couldn't you? Or what about some backup from headquarters?"

"I suppose," he mumbled, trying to leave the subject hanging.

"Would you look into it?"

Even when he walked off without answering, Dusty knew she had planted her little seed. Whether or not Tag would act on it, she didn't know. All she did know was that it would be good for him to get out and move around on his leg. And while she knew she could no more express her concern than fly, she remained worried.

Much to Dusty's amazement, her little seed planting bore fruit. Two days later, when she was again perched on her ladder with a special spackle for filling cracks in the plaster, Tag hobbled in.

"How'd you like to learn to take over for me this evening?"

Dusty endeavored not to sound too breathless over her minor triumph. "Fine."

Tag's eyes were moving from one snaking white patch to the next. "What's that?"

"I'm filling the cracks."

"Aren't you going to an awful lot of trouble for this place?"

"I want to be busy. Besides, if we were married, this is what I'd be doing. That's what you said you wanted, wasn't it? A good, solid cover?"

Tag's eyes were now passing over her anatomy, she noticed. Or, more likely, her appearance. She was wearing one of the two pairs of jeans she'd been living in for the past nine days, and her hair was tied up in a red bandanna. She also wore a favorite old shirt and sneakers. Suddenly conscious of the fine white dusting of the spackle on her face—the stuff had to be sanded down after it was dry—she decided she'd prefer to do without his continuing appraisal. "Is that all?" she asked at last.

"Am I being dismissed?"

"No. Of course not," she said more amicably, hoping he'd go away.

"I was mulling over your little picture."

"I don't know what you mean."

"You said this was what you'd be doing if we were married, and I was thinking about what else we'd be doing—once you came down off that rickety ladder."

"You've been cooped up for too long," she countered. "It'll do you good to get out for a while." Then another thought struck her. "Do...do you have a girl, Tag?"

Tag's smile was wry and only half genuine. "A girl? What a quaint, old-fashioned way of putting it. No, I have no girl. Not anymore," he muttered, walking out.

That evening Dusty showed up in Tag's room, still in jeans, but squeaky clean. She was glad to think he'd be getting out more. With her on his case, John Taggert just might end up with some healthy habits, Dusty thought. He was already getting three square meals a day from her kitchen and, although he never said so, he seemed to be enjoying it.

As she entered his room, however, Dusty felt uneasy. While she was always aware of their purpose in the apartment, she didn't allow herself to think about it too often. It was too scary.

Besides, Tag had never specifically told her what he did in his grungy room. Now he did, and Dusty found that his getting down to brass tacks made things easier.

She listened while he explained the basics of his equipment, following which he went through the procedure of contacting headquarters. Finally he described what she could expect. She could tell, just from listening to him, that he was good at what he did. She also thought he felt he could trust her.

This time spent with Tag made other impressions on Dusty, however. She was once again taken with the masculinity of him. She loved looking into his eyes when they were unguarded, as they were when he instructed her. She found him articulate and intelligent, while his hands were wonderfully expressive.

"Well, what do you think?" he asked, staring down at her where she sat at the card table.

"About what?" She could tell she had irritated him again. "I think I can do it. You say it's unlikely I'll hear anything, and I can certainly sit here and keep watch as well as you can. I do have ears, you know."

"Yeah, I know," he said, sweeping up his sheepskin coat. "Cute little ears that are just as sweetly dusted with freckles as the rest of your delicious hide."

He was gone before Dusty could turn around, and she would have given anything to have seen his face. Had he said that derisively? It hadn't sounded like it.

For one hour Dusty remained in Tag's room. Once she got used to the idea of Syd Desota being but a slim wall away, and once she got bored with hearing him moving about—making a can of something for his supper, she guessed, hearing a can opener—she started meandering around Tag's room. She looked through his newspaper and examined his books. She realized Tag had to have a real residence somewhere but couldn't begin to picture it. Was it just as empty of anything personal as this room? And what had his little comment about not having someone "anymore" meant?

When Dusty heard Tag's key in the door, her heart began to pound. Would he begin talking about himself again? She both feared and hoped he would. The moment she saw his face, however, she knew he wouldn't. He looked dark and unapproachable when he came through the door.

What could have happened to him in one hour? she asked herself, eying his tall frame.

She had her answer when he sat down. He was in pain. He hadn't been on his leg for any real amount of time since he'd been with her. This walk, out in the cold, dank night had taken its toll.

"Can I help you?" she asked, watching as he massaged his thigh.

"No."

"How about a hot tub?"

"No, I said."

Dusty knew to back off. "I'll go to bed, then. There's nothing to report," she added, still hesitating in the door. "Syd fixed a can of soup or something. Would you like—"

"I'd like you to stop your mothering," he said sharply.

DUSTY STARTED PAINTING the following morning. She'd decided to paint everything, including the woodwork, a pale but warm yellow. The place was simply too small to break it up with a mix of various colors in different rooms. She began in the bathroom. As she rolled the creamy paint onto the ceiling, she could feel a fine mist of paint falling onto her face.

"So, it's to be yellow," Tag commented from where he was standing just outside the door. He had given her a start and the ladder wobbled.

"It's definitely yellow," Dusty said, ignoring his disapproving glance at Jake's very old ladder. "You'd better like it, or at least grow to like it, because everything's going to be yellow."

Everything but his room, that is. She knew better than to tamper with his space.

"You've got tiny yellow freckles on top of your normal smattering."

Dusty never knew what to say when Tag made remarks like that. She couldn't tell whether he was being subtly derogatory or what. But it was more the light in his pale blue eyes that both confused her and set her heart racing. Finally she decided to meet his remark with her usual nonchalance. "I'm afraid I'm a mess in one way or another most of the time. It's part of doing this.'' When Tag didn't say anything, she asked, ''You aren't from St. Louis, are you?''

''No, Cincinnati.''

''Do you have family back there?''

''Yeah, a big one. My mom, my two brothers, their wives, four nephews and a niece.''

''That sounds great to me. How long have you been here?''

''A couple of cases.''

Dusty wondered briefly if Tag measured everything in terms of his work. Her father had. ''You were wounded on your last case, weren't you?''

Right away she knew she'd asked the wrong thing.

''Yeah,'' he murmured, dropping his eyes.

Just then they were interrupted by a knock at the door. ''I'll get it.'' Tag said, already halfway down the hall.

Not a minute later Pam Peters stuck her head around the bathroom door. Her large brown eyes moved over the small space and stopped on Dusty.

''So you decided on the yellow.''

''Yeah, it's yellow.''

''I've heard how you've become a permanent fixture at the hardware store, so you must know what you're doing.''

''You've been talking to Mr. Cooms. He's wonderful about explaining things and keeping me on the right track.'' Dusty placed her paint roller in its tray.

''Don't stop on my account. I'm on my way to the store and thought you might like a pumpkin or something.''

Dusty smiled. After cutting their pumpkins, she and Pam had spent Halloween evening sitting out on the stoop, welcoming their little trick-or-treaters.

Of course, Tag had been disapproving, but she'd ignored him. It had been an unusually warm night, and she and Pam had had a good time. But all the while he'd hovered behind his bedroom curtains, watching over her. Just as he now came to casually lean against the bathroom doorframe.

Turning to him, Pam grinned. "How's your book coming along? Now that Dusty's here, I imagine you've slowed to a snail's pace."

Tag matched her grin with a glorious one of his own. "As a matter of fact, I've hit a fertile spot. Dusty's my very own inspirational muse."

"I guess I don't know much about muses," Pam said as he gave them a nod, then walked toward his "study."

Pam turned back to Dusty. "I thought you'd like to go to the park with Brent and me sometime. We always go on the weekend to get out for a while."

"I've heard about the park. You mean the one the neighborhood's been restoring, right?"

"Right. It's nice now. And it's safe, which is even better. How about this weekend?"

Dusty nodded. "That would be fine."

"What time is good for you?"

"Any time. You say."

"Should you ask Tag?"

"Ask Tag what?" Tag asked, coming lazily into Dusty's view.

"About going to the park."

"Morning would probably be better," he replied, his eyes holding Dusty's briefly before sliding back to their visitor.

"Well," said Pam. "I have to get to the store. I'll see ya."

Tag watched Pam leave, not even turning to Dusty when he heard the door click shut.

"I don't think I've ever met anyone like her," Dusty said.

"What do you mean?"

"I haven't known her for very long. Yet I feel as if we've been friends forever."

"Um" was Tag's not uncommon reply. "I'm thinking," he added, "that this decorating bit is a good idea. Particularly with such an outgoing neighbor as Pam and especially in a gossipy neighborhood like this one. But you'd better get down off the ladder and come with me for a minute."

Dusty heard the seriousness in his voice and peered at him questioningly.

"Somebody just came to use the phone next door and I've got a Polaroid I want you to see."

"You mean while . . . ?"

"Yeah, while Pam was here. That'll show you how this thing can change from one minute to the next. It should also demonstrate how careful we have to be."

CHAPTER FIVE

TAG GAVE DUSTY a minute to clean up and was waiting in his little sanctum when she came in. Although the paint she was using was water-based and supposedly washed off, she was sticky with it, particularly the fine splattering across her face. Tag didn't seem to notice. He was all business. As Dusty took the chair at the card table, he dropped a fresh Polaroid picture into her hand.

The shake of her head was automatic, even as she stared down into the swarthy features of the man who had just been photographed coming up the front steps. "It's not him. I mean, the man who killed my father. It's not him."

She wondered why her heart was beating so fast. Nothing had come of this first little encounter with the reality of their circumstances, and yet it was horribly unsettling. Tag remained businesslike, however, turning to stuff the picture into a manila envelope. "I didn't think it was him."

"Why not?"

"The guy who killed your dad is a bigger fish. Oh, it's true that he's new to the Desota gang. He solidified his position with the Desotas by doing what he did to your dad, in fact. But this guy in the photo must be a tadpole by comparison."

"I still don't understand why you say that."

"Because of the way Syd talked to him. You have to remember that Syd is only tolerated because he's related. He was never worth much to the gang. He'd hardly be able to give this guy the gate without feeling he could. And give this guy the gate is what he did. The guy was hardly there and he was back out on the street. Pam almost bumped into him on the stoop."

Dusty couldn't help the release of her fearful sigh. "This is as much of a nightmare as all the rest."

Tag didn't reply. His mouth was again set in grim lines as he readied his manila envelope. "I've got someone coming for this. We'll have to identify this character no matter who he is, and headquarters will need the film."

"Syd didn't call him anything, then?"

No, he didn't. Say, do you want to hear the tape? I could play it back if you want."

Dusty shuddered. "No. No. I don't want to hear. How soon will this messenger come from headquarters?"

"Don't worry about it. I only have to meet him at the corner. You can go back to your painting."

Dusty wondered if she could. With little jolts of reality like this, the easy pattern of her days was revealed for what it was. An illusion. Oh, God. Could she return to that illusion again? She didn't think she could bear it if she couldn't.

Pausing in the door for a minute, Dusty looked back at Tag. He was shrugging his shoulders into his sheepskin coat. He looked wonderful, standing as he was in a slim shaft of sunlight sneaking in through his window. He was so vital, so strong and self-contained.

And it wasn't the way he dressed especially. He wore only the slacks and shirts he usually wore, but somehow he was riveting.

Forcing herself, Dusty walked down the hall toward the bathroom. To think that such a glorious specimen had been wounded and could be wounded again she now found was a growing worry for her. After all, that inevitable day, the day when it would all "go down" had to arrive eventually.

That her response to Tag could mean more than that, she wouldn't allow herself to think. She had promised herself from day one that she wouldn't get personally involved with Tag, and she fully intended to keep that promise. It was, in fact, easy to remind herself of that when she recalled her experience with her father.

Dusty's odd day didn't straighten out as it went along. She painted until she was bleary-eyed with it and, following supper, she couldn't wait to relax.

As on her very first night, she took a long, hot bath and climbed into bed with a book. She was reminded in other ways of her first night here, especially in her longing to see her sister, Leslie. And, as well, she experienced the same strange sense of isolation she'd felt the first night. The status quo she'd established had been broken, and she felt all the more cut off from her old life.

Again she was aware of the limited pools of light and the night sounds. Despite her hours of work, nothing about the apartment had changed. Except for the bathroom, it was still a barren, deserted shell.

Slipping under her covers, Dusty switched off the metal lamp. The same blue patch of light from the streetlight stretched across the ceiling. She hadn't noticed it much since the first night. After her days of renovating, she'd been crawling into bed bone-tired—even with a sense of satisfaction. Tonight there was none of that.

She heard again the clunk of the radiator, but turned her back to it. She knew it wouldn't clank again until after she was asleep. Sighing wearily, praying for it all to be over soon, she began to drift off. Then the pop of the water heater switching on rose to the surface of her drifting thoughts.

After another hour she admitted that the sound wasn't easy to ignore. It was as regular as the water cooling, that being the signal for the heater to switch on again. It seemed as if her thoughts were centered on listening to it, and it became every bit as annoying as the dripping of the kitchen faucet had been.

Finally it got to the point where she was unable to drift off because she was waiting for the water heater to switch on again. She couldn't stand it. Maybe she could do something. Even shut it off.

Pulling on a rosy robe over her flannel pajamas, Dusty padded to her door. Leaving that ajar, in order to give herself some light, she crept into the hallway. Except for the again seemingly loud crackle of the water heater, which coaxed her on, all was silent.

Passing Tag's room, she could barely make out his sprawled form on his cot. She was momentarily stopped by the fact that he still wore his shirt and pants. He looked uncomfortable—certainly not in a state that was conducive to sleep.

Going on, she reached the small closet holding the water heater and eased open the door. Then she stood staring at the heater, trying to figure some way to soundproof the closet or—

"Freeze!"

Scared half out of her wits, Dusty let out a squeak but retained just enough sense to do precisely as ordered.

"What the hell!" Tag exclaimed as he flipped on the hall switch. Then he let out a string of words Dusty had never even heard before—at least not all at once. "Dusty, what are you doing?"

"I'm checking the hot water heater. It was keeping me awake, and I—"

"Do you know what could have happened?"

Only then did Dusty think about what he was saying. Tag stood, his revolver in one hand, his eyes blazing. Even though it was lowered, the weapon was nonetheless frightening. But certainly he had been in control. Certainly nothing could have happened. He was too careful, too well-disciplined. Still, he must have come out of his room, creeping down the hallway with that gun pointed at her.

Dusty gulped, her gaze dropping to where Tag held the weapon at his side. The fine, strong hand that grasped the police revolver was visibly shaking.

Dusty lifted her unbelieving eyes to his. He seemed to be willing her to ignore his shaking hand, which was so badly betraying his cool composure. Indeed, his burning eyes and stance seemed to dare her to even mention it.

"T-tag," she began, sympathy evident in her tone and laid bare in her eyes.

Tag growled—an animalistic, inarticulate sound rumbling deep in his throat, warning her to shut up.

Without another word, he turned and walked sharply into his room, slamming his door behind him.

Dusty stumbled numbly back to her bed. Tag had not only been physically wounded, but emotionally as well. Worse, Tag was unsure of himself. Something had shaken his confidence in himself as a police officer to the core.

Dusty could imagine the agony he was going through. To love doing one thing, then to find himself no longer able to do it with confidence had to be tragic for a man like Tag. Maybe all he needed was time—time to heal inwardly as well as outwardly. Indeed, Dusty was sure he was banking on that.

THE NEXT MORNING when Dusty brought Tag his breakfast, she guessed that he hadn't been able to sleep any better than she had. He looked as worn as she felt, with dark smudges outlining the crisp blue of his eyes.

He watched her closely. But he didn't need to worry about whether she'd say anything. She didn't know what to say.

Over the next few days their relationship lapsed into nothing but a grim game of evasion. She painted until she was exhausted, while Tag, once again, remained behind closed doors. She saw him when she took in his meals, but he was eating less and with less enthusiasm.

Her single consolation was that the bathroom was now as clean as she could get it and that the hallway and her room were finished, as well. She had also soundproofed the hot water heater closet, as Mr. Cooms at the hardware store had suggested. Now only the faintest popping noises could be heard at night.

On Saturday when Pam burst in on Dusty for their planned visit to the park, Dusty almost fell into her arms. She had forgotten their arrangement, but luckily wasn't so sticky with paint she couldn't quickly wash up and go.

Pam, of course, had to see the bathroom and stood looking on as Dusty scrubbed away.

"The pale yellow paint and bright yellow towels look great together," Pam said, though with a bit of hesitation.

"What you're really trying to say is that it's too bad about the tile."

"Yeah. Only I didn't know how to put it nicely. I don't think I've ever seen an uglier shade of green."

"If I . . . I mean, if *we* were going to stay here, I'd chip it off and replace it."

"*If . . .?*" Pam repeated. "What are you almost saying? Are you moving? Are things bad between you and Tag?"

"No, of course not." Dusty pushed past Pam and headed toward her room. "I saw a new shower curtain that'll pick things up. Mr. Cooms has it on order. You won't even notice the tile when you see it."

Pam followed Dusty into her bedroom, checking out the new paint job in there, as well. The white chenille spread and white sheets looked as fresh as the paint. "Why don't you and I make some café curtains for in here?" Pam suggested.

"Café curtains?"

"Yeah, you know. They're real easy. And cheap."

"You have a sewing machine?"

"Yeah. We could whip some up in a couple of hours."

"That sounds great."

Dusty stopped in front of Tag's door on their way out. She didn't dare open it with Pam standing next to her. She'd be sure to see Tag's equipment. "I'm going to the park with Pam and Brent," she called out after giving the door a brief rap.

"Fine."

"He's having trouble with his plot line," Dusty said lamely, noticing how Pam was watching this very un-newlywed-looking procedure.

"I wouldn't know about plot lines, but I do know about trouble with new husbands. Come on. I'll tell you *all* about it." Pam's know-it-all inflection made Dusty chuckle.

Indeed, as the trio of Pam, Brent and Dusty talked and teased their way to the park, Dusty could have hugged Pam for the sense of release she was feeling.

The day was bright and warm. It would probably be one of the last nice fall days of the season, and everyone was out taking advantage of it. The park was lovely with the remnants of the colored leaves of autumn—now mostly red and gold running to brown—clinging tenuously to their branches and rattling dryly in the light breeze.

Dusty could see why everyone was delighted with the park's reclamation. It was old, probably turn-of-the-century. The large wrought-iron gates, which were freshly painted black and stood sentinel at the four main entrances, were all that was left of the original fence around the park. The trees were magnificent, as were the graceful plantings and planned walkways.

The boy ran off with some friends, and Dusty breathed the fresh air deeply, her eyes following a pair of cyclists with their loping dog as Pam told her about her first husband, Brent's daddy. When she stopped, almost in midsentence while describing her second husband, Dusty looked at her questioningly.

"You don't need to worry about you and Tag," Pam announced.

Dusty was, in fact, too tongue-tied by the unexpectedness of this comment to answer cogently. "I don't?"

"No. I can tell by the way he watches you," Pam insisted. "He loves you too much to let things go bad."

Dusty couldn't think how to reply. She wanted to be honest with this woman who she was coming to like, and felt badly because she couldn't. What a release it would be to pour the whole story into Pam's ears.

"I don't know whether he loves me or not," she finally mumbled.

Putting a reassuring arm around Dusty's shoulders, Pam coaxed her toward the children's playground. They seated themselves on a bench, and Pam watched all the activity with a smile on her face. But the familiar sight of the children at play tore nostalgically at Dusty's heart, and Pam must have sensed that.

"Do you miss teaching?"

"Do I ever. I love children. Especially the little ones."

"Yeah, I know what you mean. My mother taught school for years, and she loved it, too. It seems a shame that she, of all people, has never seen Brent."

Dusty was startled by Pam's statement and sensed that Pam was now feeling sad, as well. But should she ask Pam about the specifics of her situation? Dusty didn't know. "I'm sure your mom gets a good idea of what Brent is like from what you tell her," she finally suggested. "And certainly you send pictures, don't you?"

"Oh, I do that. It's just that I've felt time passing of late. I know my parents are growing older, and, well, I only moved to St. Louis because my first husband was in dentistry school at Wash U. Now he's gone, and there's no real reason for me to stay. No reason except, well, for the money it would cost to make the move."

Dusty suspected Pam wasn't telling her everything, but she turned again to watch the playing children and changed the subject. "I take it Brent's too old for all this fun stuff," she said with a nod toward the swings and slides.

"Oh, sure. He's involved with the big boys now. At least I can feel okay about where he plays and who he runs with when he's over here. It's especially good in the summer because they sponsor all sorts of programs. I'm a jogger myself."

Dusty's eyes lit up. "Are you?"

"Sure am. We jog year-round. Nothing monumental. Just for the exercise and fresh air. Why don't you run with me? I go out every Tuesday and Thursday before work and Sunday afternoon for twenty or thirty minutes. It's fun. Do you have a jogging suit?"

"Yeah! I have a jogging suit from my college phys ed—" Dusty caught herself up when she remembered her jogging outfit was still in her drawer at home. "I didn't pack it, though."

"You do have a couple of sweatshirts. I've seen you painting in them."

Dusty had to chuckle. "Now *those* shirts are in really rough condition. I'll break down and buy a new sweat suit."

"Great! We'll go shopping. I know just the place."

Dusty was glad the new subject had brought her friend back to being her usual self, even if it meant shopping.

TAG WATCHED JUAN ALVAREZ nudge his way through the crowded, smoky bar. He was coming in his direction, heading for the opposite bench seat in the booth he occupied. Tag knew what he wanted to say, but also knew to wait until they'd gotten past the amenities.

"How's your leg?" Alvarez asked, laying his coat down on the red plastic seat. "It's really cold tonight, so you gotta be feeling it."

"I am," Tag admitted. "Want a beer?"

"Sure."

The waitress was already standing over them, and Tag ordered another beer for himself and one for Alvarez.

"Thanks for meeting me after hours," Tag said when the waitress had left them.

His companion shrugged. "Goes with the territory. How's the case coming? I haven't gotten around to your recent reports."

"It's pretty much as we thought it'd be. There are a few visitors, a regular round of calls, but everything is at a standstill until they get their deal together."

The captain nodded.

"I want out." Tag hadn't meant it to be that abrupt, but he didn't feel like dancing around the problem, either.

His superior reacted as he'd expected—with incredulity. "You want out?"

"Yeah. Out."

Tag watched Alvarez's expression of surprise settle even more deeply into his features. He hated doing what he was doing. He'd never been a quitter, but . . .

"What happened?" Alvarez asked, really puzzled.

"Dusty got up last night. She was waltzing around, checking the water heater or some damn harebrained thing. I caught up with her in the dark hallway, with my revolver at her head."

The older man sank back against the rear of the booth, sighing wearily. "You know, Tag, something like that can hap—"

"Don't," Tag snapped. "Don't say it can happen to any of us until it happens to you." Tag was immediately sorry for his retort, but his patience was at an end. It had all been burned up in his last assignment.

"Look, Tag, I realize you didn't want to take Dusty on. But she knew the score."

"She was told about what's going on in the apartment next door, but no one told her she had to worry outside of her own bedroom door."

"You just need some time."

"And meanwhile?"

"And meanwhile, you can handle it."

Tag felt a renewal of the pressures he'd been living with for a long time, especially over the past few weeks. He lowered his eyes to the foam trickling down to rejoin the last of the beer in the bottom of his glass.

The waitress intruded once again but, since neither man wanted anything, she went on to more fertile ground with a neat sashay of her wide hips.

Tag allowed his gaze to roam the small hole-in-the-wall bar. It was the usual scene—neon lights overhead, a clock with a beer advertisement on its face hanging on the wall, a long shining bar that reflected all the rest. In a corner a jukebox played tunes that were barely decipherable above the din of conversation, while a group of regulars—who were feeling it—squabbled amicably over the well-used dart board.

Tag knew what Alvarez was doing. He was waiting for Tag's pride, for his sense of duty, to take hold, and Tag resented Alvarez because, although he recognized what the other man was doing, he still had no defense. And at the same time he envied Alvarez because he was so well adapted to the work they both did. Tag wondered if he'd ever adapt so well.

"You mentioned one time that Dusty's mother died," Tag said at last. "Did you know her?"

Alvarez seemed surprised at Tag's question, but was willing to answer. "My wife knew her better than I did. Dusty's mother was a pretty little thing. Quiet. Blond. The feminine type who would interest a guy like Ox, but the sort who wouldn't really suit him. She needed more than he could give.... Oh, hell, he wouldn't have done any better with anyone else, either."

"Dusty was really young?"

"Uh, pre-teen. Her mother had been ill for a long time, and Dusty had taken over even then. She was already both mother and father to her sister Leslie, and, well, she was used to running things. But when

Dusty's mother died, my wife stepped in for a while because Dusty seemed so young. Marge hired a housekeeper and dropped by all the time, saw to it that the girls went to Girl Scouts, that sort of business. Anyway, as I said, Dusty was used to taking care of Leslie and the house and her mother, as well, and, as it turned out, she didn't need the housekeeper. Dusty's smart like that. Smart and resourceful.''

Tag felt defeat seeping into his bones and he, too, leaned back against the booth, sighing a reluctant concession. He'd already been tied up in knots, and now Dusty had come along. She was everything Alvarez said she was—and more. Alvarez hadn't mentioned her looks. She was exactly what he didn't need. His emotions were already precariously balanced. He didn't want them toppled.

But what was he going to do? He'd tried to avoid her, even to ignore her. It was just that her cheery nature was so invasive—and her petite form so inviting.

"I'll stay," he heard himself mutter.

Alvarez's relief was even more irritating. "You won't be sorry."

Tag snorted. "I know I'll be sorry. One way or another. I'll for sure be sorry." Experiencing a sudden need to escape, Tag pulled himself to his feet. "I'd better get back."

"You getting out enough?"

"She all but shoves me out the door every night at just about this time."

"Good. Good."

Alvarez also stood up and followed Tag to the bar, but he was surprised when Tag pulled the check from his hand. "It's on me," Tag explained. "It was bad enough to get you over here off hours, much less to put you through that.''

Alvarez smiled. "Like I said, it goes with the territory."

CHAPTER SIX

OVER THE NEXT COUPLE WEEKS, Tag's silent treatment began, once again, to break down under the pressure of Dusty's constant cheerfulness. She had decided to go on as positively as she could and, damn it, she was going to do it.

The swarthy little man who had visited Syd Desota had been identified. She'd been told he was of no importance in the scheme of things, and that bolstered her spirits—and so did Tag's news that the single other regular visitor, a man in a Cardinals' baseball cap, was also a lesser gang member who only hung around Syd's to take advantage of the free phone.

At last Thanksgiving Day rolled around, but it turned out to be another strange day for Dusty. She loved the yearly cycle of seasons and holidays, and had never missed a headlong participation in them. Pam cooked a turkey, Dusty joined her and Brent for dinner, but Tag remained stubbornly in his room. Even the plate of food she brought him went unappreciated and, once again, she found herself trying to make excuses to Pam for their odd relationship.

Fortunately Brent dropped by the next afternoon, and Dusty was always happy to see Brent.

"Come on in," she called. "I'll fix some hot chocolate. I'm glad to see you, too, Roger," she added, noticing that Brent had his little friend with him.

Leaving the door for the boys to close, Dusty turned abruptly into the kitchen. Roger's face was bruised, and Dusty was afraid to reveal her reaction to this evidence of possible maltreatment. Rather than stare at him, she busied herself at the stove, while the boys shrugged out of their winter gear.

"I take it your mom is back at work," Dusty said to Brent.

His reply was immediate, of course. There was no shyness in Brent's makeup. "Yeah, she's gone off to the rockpile. She said I could come down, though."

Dusty chuckled. "Of course, you can. I've told you there's a standing invitation for hot chocolate, and you know that."

Just then Tag came in, and Dusty was surprised at the big smile on his face.

"Hi there, Brent," he said, seeming genuinely glad to see the boy.

"Hi, Tag. Did you see the game on TV yesterday?"

"Yeah. Some great plays. I enjoyed it."

"It was too bad you couldn't come up to have your dinner with us."

"I was sorry, too, but I was in a bad spot for stopping yesterday. How come you aren't in school?"

"We always have the day after Turkey Day off."

Dusty noticed the way Tag's eyes kept running to the small blond boy who was hovering just behind Brent's larger, well-built frame. "Who's your friend?"

"Oh, sorry, Tag. This is Roger."

"Hi, Roger," Tag said, taking the opportunity to really look at the boy.

When Roger didn't say anything but instead just dropped his eyes, Tag also knew to go slow.

"Can I help?" he asked, turning to Dusty.

"You want some hot chocolate?" she asked, the surprise in her voice evident.

"Of course I want some. As long as you've got marshmallows, that is."

"Great. I've got 'em, if you'll reach 'em down from the cupboard in the corner."

Dusty's next surprise came when Tag sat down on the kitchen floor with their visitors and discussed the football game that Brent seemed so interested in.

But when Tag asked Roger if he'd seen the game, the boy dropped his eyes before he mumbled a negative that tore at Dusty's heart.

When Tag reached out to ruffle his hair in an odd sort of sympathy, she couldn't believe it. Not only was Tag's unexpected friendliness to these children amazing to her, so was the evident ease the boys felt in his company. No, forget "ease." In Brent's eyes she could clearly see admiration, while definite hero worship marked the fleeting looks that Roger allowed himself.

BY THE NEXT DAY, the scene in the kitchen seemed almost forgotten. Dusty and Tag were again entrenched in their same old grooves. Except for his occasional forays into the fresh air, Tag stayed in his room, while Dusty went back to her redecorating. She was glad when the end of the week rolled by. Not only was the final coat on the woodwork finished, but her muscles were adjusting to her new regimen of jogging with Pam.

"This is all your fault," Dusty accused her friend Sunday afternoon when the two of them were going for their daily jog. "I owe my sore calves to you, Pam."

"I know," Pam agreed, laughing. "I love watching people suffer." Pam's breath expanded as a chill puff on the cold air. "Same time Tuesday?" she asked as an additional gibe.

"I guess so," Dusty conceded, unable to help her chuckle.

Staggering into her apartment, she headed straight for the bathroom. *Hot water,* she thought to herself. *My sore muscles want all the hot water the heater can handle.* Finding the bathroom door ajar, she went straight in and almost walked into Tag. Her eyes focused automatically on his naked back. Then her gaze dropped to the yellow towel slung low on his hips.

"It was inevitable," he said, continuing to shave as he looked at Dusty in the mirror.

"Not if you'd kept the door closed," she said archly, standing and staring at him instead of leaving. "We agreed that a closed door meant the bath was occupied."

"Since when do you observe a closed door? In any case, you were out jogging, so I didn't bother." Tag wiped the last of the lather from his face and turned to smile at her. "Actually, I don't mind. And from the looks of it, you don't seem to be so anxious to leave, either."

Tag's eyes made a quick trip up and down Dusty's bulkily layered form. Although she was embarrassed, she wasn't about to admit it to this grinning jackal. Pushing around his large frame, she turned the faucets on the tub to full force.

"You are finished, aren't you?" she asked in clipped tones.

"Yeah, I'm finished. And I'm afraid your noisy friend in the hall closet is finished, too." His eyes ran to the water that was pouring, stone-cold, into the tub.

Dusty no more let her disappointment show than she displayed her discomfort with his near nudity. Stalking into her own room, she closed the door and stripped out of her clothes. A picture of a grinning Tag in a foggy yellow bathroom wasn't so easily shut out.

Okay, so any female with half an eye would find him attractive, she finally admitted to herself later that morning. She was sitting on top of Jake's big, shaky ladder for what she hoped would be the last time, replacing the light fixture in the middle of the kitchen ceiling. Although the fixture was old, it was clean and it looked nice against the freshly painted room. Her next project would be to—

"Dusty!" Tag shouted from the hallway.

Her start caused the unstable ladder to sway, and she hastily pressed her hand against the ceiling to steady herself as Tag came into the kitchen.

"Have you shut off the electricity? My equipment's dead!"

"It'll only be off until I get this fixture screwed in. Jake's waiting in the basement at the power box to switch the electricity back on as soon as he hears my thump on the floor."

"Well, get to it."

Dusty could sense Tag's eyes running over Jake's ladder with his usual disapproval. And then, of course, his gaze moved to her. To her annoyance, she discovered that the pressure of his impatient stare had an effect on her ability to use her screwdriver. Her fingers fumbled, and that, combined with having to work over her head, made the last two screws take twice as long as the first two had.

Drat, she thought. Tag was still watching. Even when she began to climb down he was watching. Unfortunately her shirttail caught on the nail she used for holding her paint bucket handle.

Before she knew what was happening, Tag had her fast in his hands and was lifting her down. This also meant that the worn fabric of her old shirt gave way, the ripping noise sounding loud in the hollow rooms of the apartment. She was glad the rent was a vertical one up her back, which meant she could go on trying to ignore it.

"Thank you," she said when her feet touched the floor. "Now all I have to do is stomp—" which she did "—and voilà."

On cue the light switched on, the refrigerator began to hum and the hot water heater uttered a familiar pop as it, too, came to life. Everything seemed to be back to normal—everything but her heart, which was racing. Tag hadn't released his hold on her, and the look she read in his usually cool eyes told her that she wasn't the only one who wasn't back to normal.

"Dusty," he said huskily.

She could feel his fingertips, tentative at first, moving slowly up her spine, guided by the tear in her shirt. When he sensed she wouldn't resist, he flattened his hand and smoothed it, warm and hard, down the curve of her back. She didn't need to answer his repetitive whispering of her name, and couldn't have in any case. His seductive chant was both a declaration and a plea, and she yearned to answer it outside of words. Her smaller frame yearned for his larger one, his flesh a magnet with an irresistible pull.

"Dusty," he said again, bending forward until his mouth tentatively smoothed over hers.

Dusty didn't know which made more of a claim on her—his hands searching her back or his insistent lips at the seam of her mouth. Her reason fled. She wanted to give to him, to kiss him back and yes, to allow him the entrance to herself that he sought with his tongue.

Dusty was so surprised when Tag dropped his hold and stepped away from her that she nearly fell forward.

"God," he said, his voice ragged. "Let's get out of here."

"Out?"

"Yeah, out."

Since he was already heading into his room, Dusty could only think to follow and go into hers. When he reappeared in the hallway outside her door, already dressed in his sheepskin coat, she was putting on her powder-blue knit cap. Her glance at him caused him to look away.

"We should be seen together once in a while, and now's as good a time as any," he explained brusquely.

"Okay."

"We'll simply do a round of the block and the main drag, and then we'll come back. It won't take long."

Dusty lifted a shoulder. "It sounds fine to me. I'd like to get out, too. But what about your equipment?"

"Today is Syd's day at the clinic, and headquarters can take over on some of it."

The truth was that Dusty was as relieved to escape as he seemed to be. Their little encounter had shaken her as badly as it evidently had him, and she could guess why. Even while the word *Taggertitis* whispered wickedly through her mind as her excuse for what had happened, she knew that his problem had to do with the restraints he'd put on himself. It wasn't very flattering, but Dusty had to admit that what Tag was feeling was just what any man would feel after being locked up with a woman for weeks. Nothing could be better than for him to get out.

Brilliant winter sunlight greeted them on their stoop, and Tag took Dusty's hand in his. "We have to look like lovers, babe, so let's do it," he said.

Dusty pasted on a smile. "I'm ready."

Actually it was the best thing yet to be outside with John Taggert, to feel her gloved hand in his. They walked their first few blocks in silence, both of them drinking in the brisk air and enjoying the simple pleasure of being free. Tag looked good out-of-doors. His black hair was ruffled by the wind, his darker complexion turned ruddy rather than pink like hers, and his step quickened as his leg seemed to loosen up.

"This isn't bothering your wound, is it?" Dusty asked, just to be sure.

"It feels great. If I move fast enough, that is. Of course, I'll pay for it later. I don't walk regularly enough."

"I've known that all along," Dusty said, but didn't dare to go further. His leg was his business.

She was surprised when he was the one to reopen their conversation. And especially with his choice of topic. "After that night...when your dad was killed...I suppose you went through all the mug books."

"What an experience that was," Dusty admitted. "I'd never dreamed there were so many bad men."

"You better believe it," Tag told her. "And our books are only part of it. By the way, I've seen the computer composite picture you put together with the police artist. Alvarez said that you felt you came up with a pretty good likeness. It's too bad there hasn't been any luck with it."

"It amazes me," Dusty said, "but I carry a picture of that guy in my mind that's as clear as any photograph. In fact, it almost has the same still quality of a photo."

"Alvarez said the guy was lighting a cigarette."

"Yeah. In my mind, I can still see the way the glow of the lighter lit up his face." Dusty looked up at Tag and smiled. "It feels okay to talk about it. I thought I'd never be able to without getting the shivers."

"That's a good sign," Tag said, glancing quickly away.

"But then there are the bad dreams," Dusty added. "In some ways they're the worst. You can't just experience something once, but you have to go over it again and again when you're trying to sleep."

"Yeah," he said softly. "I know all about bad dreams."

They walked on in silence for a few minutes. Then Tag spoke again. "Alvarez says that you don't think this guy would recognize you."

"The murderer?"

"Yeah."

"He wouldn't. My rain hat fell over my face just as our eyes met."

Tag looked down at her, more seriously now, his hand even giving hers a gentle squeeze. "Don't count on that, babe. Don't count on it for a minute."

Switching her gaze back to the sidewalk, Dusty nodded. She couldn't figure Tag. The thing she remembered best about his kiss was its gentle insistence. He hadn't forced her, but . . . well, he'd been coaxing, and that, just like this moment of tenderness, was surprising.

Not wanting to think about it any more than he obviously did, Dusty tried to force herself to pay attention to their surroundings, but without success.

His kiss had simply happened, she told herself for the hundredth time. It had been a result of their days of being closed in with little other human contact. As humans, they needed contact. Even John Taggert.

"I heard," Tag said, "that you repeated the assailant's license number and the make of the car as well as any professional could have."

Dusty snorted in an imitation of him. "A fat lot of good that did. The license plates were stolen from a car that was sitting on a gas station lot waiting to be repaired. As for the car itself, pieces of it were found in a chop shop just south of St. Louis. My little effort earned us nothing."

"It happens that way sometimes. This guy's been lucky so far, but he won't elude us forever."

"Do you think he'll come to visit Syd?"

Tag's hesitation indicated that he doubted it. "You can never tell what'll happen on a stakeout like this. We might never get much more than we have. And then again, your creep could show up or the Desotas could come back from Florida and divvy up their goods right under our noses."

At least he was trying to be positive for her sake, Dusty thought.

They'd reached the main street of their little neighborhood, and Tag tightened his hold on her hand as a warning to play her part. Several people passed by and, while a face or two looked familiar, no one greeted them. They were observed, however, and that, after all, was Tag's purpose.

As they headed home, Dusty thought he seemed pleased with their little jaunt. Until they were inside the apartment, that is. Once he reached his room, she heard him collapse on his cot. He obviously tried to suppress the groan of pain that followed, but she heard that, too. And automatically her heart filled with sympathy for Tag. But she knew enough to hide it by going cheerfully about her business. No matter how much he had opened up with her on their walk, and even despite his kiss, things hadn't changed between them.

CHAPTER SEVEN

TAG SAT IN HIS DINGY BEDROOM feeling as gray as the morning outside. He was listening to her again and thinking about her, picturing what she looked like as she bent over, scrubbing the kitchen floor. Wasn't that her little hum he heard? How could such a simple sound suddenly seem so...well, damn it, alluring? He wanted to talk to her. No, he wanted to kiss her again. How had he ever let go and done that crazy thing? Thank goodness he'd come to his senses before he'd gotten an even better taste.

He tried again to concentrate on the report he was writing. It was all so damn boring, and her chatter was so sweet. Hell, he'd come all the way to St. Louis to make a change, and he was in bigger trouble than ever. What a stupid business. He'd known all along to refuse Alvarez. Yet here he sat with her in the other room driving him up the wall.

Oh, he knew it wasn't just her. She was simply the last straw. But she was fast becoming his major problem. He wanted her. But then who wouldn't? Especially in these circumstances? Living with her was like having her dangled under his nose, and he was being driven to the point of madness.

Still, it wasn't just her. The emotional pack he was carrying had been on his back for a long time. His job had always been a burden, but nothing he couldn't handle until . . . until that night when he . . . Damn it! He would *not* think about that night.

Hearing the doorbell gave Tag a good excuse to get out of his room. "I'll get it," he called out as he limped quickly past the kitchen. Then he stopped abruptly as he caught a glimpse of Dusty's rump as she worked over her scrub brush. "Damn," he muttered, and hurried on into the living room.

He was expecting his partner Ellen Daniels to be at the door and was surprised to see an elfin old man instead. Right away he knew he had to be facing one of Dusty's "buddies." He was beginning to see that Alvarez was right. Dusty Landry could win over almost anybody. The bright smile in the pointed features of the elderly gentleman before him proved it.

"I'm Jake, your neighbor from upstairs. And you must be Tag. I've heard all about you."

"Knowing Dusty, I'm sure you know everything she knows."

The old man chuckled. "Perhaps not quite. Actually, I've come to get my ladder."

"It's about time," Tag said, pushing open the screen door and sounding more surly than he liked.

The old man chuckled yet again. "My sentiments exactly, Tag. I told her that ladder should have been tossed onto the trash heap years ago, but she insisted she didn't want to buy a new one. We're lucky she hasn't broken her neck. But now that she's done with it, I thought I'd haul it off to the curb for the rubbish pickup. That'll keep her off of it, if nothing else has."

The spry fellow's wink coaxed a smile from Tag. He couldn't help his immediate liking for the man. "I'll take it out. To the curb, you say?"

"Yeah, to the curb. The garbagemen should be around soon."

Once again Tag smiled. Then he invited the fellow in.

"No, no, that's all right," Jake said. "I'll just wait here."

Dusty passed Tag in the kitchen doorway, the damp knees of her jeans evidence of what she'd been doing.

"Jake," she called out with a ready grin. "Come on in."

"No, not now, Dusty. You're busy and this strappin' husband of yours is going to haul off the ladder. I think I'd better watch him so he doesn't pull something. In fact," he added when Tag limped by, "you don't look like you should be carrying that thing, after all."

"I'll help," Dusty said. "Don't worry."

Tag was reluctant to let her, but she grabbed one end of the ladder, anyway. In a minute the rickety old thing was lying next to the curb. Tag went back to his room while Dusty resumed her work on the tile of the kitchen floor. Then yet another rap sounded at the door. Once again Tag called out that he would get it as he passed her by and, shortly after, Dusty got up, swiped at her damp knees and walked into the living room.

She didn't know who she'd been expecting, but certainly not the person she saw. The new arrival was nothing if not lovely. And she was tall—almost as tall as Tag, with a long, slender body that accentuated her height. Beside her, Dusty felt like a dwarf.

"My partner, Ellen Daniels. Dusty Landry," Tag said by way of introduction. "I appreciate your running over, Ellen," he added to the ash blond beauty with the green eyes.

"I don't mind," she replied, her eyes running quickly over Dusty's diminutive form, and Dusty could see that in Ellen's eyes she didn't measure up.

"It was nice meeting you," Dusty lied, smiling sweetly as she turned to leave.

"Don't go, Dusty," Tag said. "Ellen's brought some stuff we need to examine."

Turning back, and shoving her fists into the pockets of her worn jeans, Dusty nodded.

Ellen was dressed attractively. Her soft knit dress was the color of her green eyes and emphasized their unusual, fascinating shade. Wondering if Tag also admired his partner's natty presentation, her gaze switched to his. He, however, was moving toward the hall.

"Why don't we go to my room? At least there's a couple of chairs back there."

With murmured agreement, the women followed and made themselves as comfortable as possible in his small space. Inhaling a deep breath, Dusty told herself to pay attention. No matter what conjectures were running through her head, this was important business.

Fingering a packet of some sort, Tag assumed the pose of instructor. "Ellen's brought some photos and tapes that were collected on the Desotas in Miami. It'll take me a couple of days to listen to the tapes, but I'm told not to expect anything. It seems the drug deal they were working on fell through and they plan to stay in Florida until after Christmas.''

Dusty was sure that the disappointment she was feeling showed in her eyes. She'd known that they'd been waiting for the Desotas to get a drug deal together—drugs that they would hopefully be caught in the act of selling. That the gang's deal had fallen through meant, not only that they would remain in Florida, but that she and Tag would have to stay in the apartment. Especially since the man who had murdered her father had neither resurfaced nor been identified.

Dusty forced herself to nod as nonchalantly as she could. She wasn't about to reveal her true feelings in front of a cool number like Ellen Daniels.

Fortunately Tag was intent on his purpose. ''As I said, I'll be the one to listen to the tapes, but we want you, Dusty, to check these photos taken of the gang around their pool in Miami. I know you've seen their mug shots, but these enlargements have people in the background, and you might just catch something we wouldn't. So take your time and examine each one carefully.''

''I understand,'' Dusty murmured.

As she took the eight-by-ten glossies from Tag, Dusty tried not to betray her uncertainty. If she could tell anything about both Ellen and Tag, it was that this was normal for them—that they were professionals.

After ten minutes it was clear to Dusty that there was nothing in the photos, and she returned them to Tag.

"We didn't think you'd see anything," he said. "We'd already identified almost everybody, but thought it was still worth the try. Thanks, anyway." Turning to Ellen, he added, "Well, that's that."

"That's that," she agreed.

Dusty couldn't help the way her mind kept evaluating Tag and Ellen's relationship. Obviously they liked and respected each other. Ellen was Tag's partner and shared his world, while Dusty was just an unwanted responsibility. That summation was surprisingly painful.

And Dusty knew that the brief whatever-it-had-been that Tag had indulged in in the kitchen just yesterday afternoon didn't give her any edge over Ellen Daniels.

No, indeed, Dusty thought. While Tag thought she was worth a convenient little physical fling, Ellen Daniels was above that. Tag treated Ellen Daniels as an equal.

"Well," Tag said, sounding a little anxious to be rid of both of his female companions. "If that's all, Ellen, I don't want to keep you."

The blonde, however, appeared reluctant to leave. "Are you sure you don't want to get out more often?" she asked, reopening a subject they had evidently discussed before—presumably on the phone. "I'd be more than happy to work something out and come by to relieve you."

"No. Dusty takes over for a while each night. I can't go too far, anyway. Not with this leg."

"Well," she conceded reluctantly, "I guess I'll go then." She sent a final evaluative look in Dusty's direction. And Dusty could see that in Ellen's mind she still didn't measure up. "If you change your mind—"

"Yeah. I'll know where to call," Tag said, walking Ellen to the front room.

Dusty stayed where she was but, even so, heard Ellen's parting remark.

"I still can't imagine what sort of assistance she can be," Dusty heard her say, her crisp voice carrying clearly.

"She's enough for me."

Dusty walked into her room. She wanted to get back to her floor scrubbing, but she needed a minute to get herself together. All sorts of emotions were tumbling around inside of her.

Tag's impatience bothered her. She could never get used to it, no matter how hard she tried. On top of that, Ellen Daniels's visit had shown her clearly that Tag didn't respect her—not in the way he respected his gorgeous partner, and that also stung. Finally Ellen Daniels's little snub had been an unexpected zinger.

Of course, there was nothing unusual about the woman's pride in sharing Tag's life and his main interest, nor in her evident desire to have those aspects of him to herself. Still, Dusty wished Ellen would have concealed her dislike a little better.

But, worst of all, how would Dusty forget the feel of Tag's embrace?

At last she heard the front door close. Ellen had left. Waiting until she also heard Tag return to his room, she went back to the kitchen.

It took a while before her favorite apartment activity of "fixing up" worked its magic on her spirits. Still, it was inevitable that it would. She was an optimist, after all, and wouldn't let her feelings stay hurt, especially not when she knew the hurt had been given unintentionally.

When Tag walked in sometime later, she was back to normal and could see him for what he was. He was a professional—a wounded professional who resented being cooped up and kept from doing what he did well. That, too, was understandable, and Dusty decided to let his obvious struggle with himself go by her. She had known all along not to indulge the attraction she felt for him—that dratted Taggertitis could be the death of her, if she let it.

"Well, what do you think?" she asked, almost cheerfully as she stood up.

Her eyes followed Tag's over the freshly scrubbed floor as she stripped off her rubber gloves and dropped them next to her bucket. Unsticking her jeans from her knees, she reached to readjust the twisted yellow scarf that was holding the mass of her rust-brown curls at bay.

"It looks better," he said. "Anyway, you've certainly done the best you can with such an old floor. And the tan tile doesn't look too bad against the yellow paint."

"I think you're right," Dusty said with a pert smile. She saw him looking at her then, his eyes making their usual quick search of her appearance. She could feel them on the tumble of her curls, the pink of her cheeks, the curve of her lips, and she experienced the stun his pale blue stare could deliver.

Oh, no, she thought. He's going to do it again. Still, even as he reached for her she knew she wouldn't resist. In fact, she longed for him and lifted herself onto the toes of her sneakers, anticipating his kiss. He was gathering her into his arms, and she was aiding and abetting him. *Drat,* she thought—or thought she thought—before all thinking was suspended.

His kiss was long and lingering, stunningly gentle for such an impatient male. She could feel the desire behind it, the yearning that matched her own. It was his warmth, however, the physicality of him that was irresistible, and she simply had to respond . . . simply had to hang on to him and kiss him back.

The trail of his kisses lead to her ear. He whispered to her intimately, softly, calling her name as a plea. She knew what he was asking, because she wanted what he wanted. His hand skimmed the side of her breast and, when she sighed, cupped her through the double knit of her sweatshirt.

"Dusty," he said, his voice thick with desire, "let's go back to your room."

Dusty wanted to. The warmth of his hand, insistently rubbing at her breast, teasing her nipple to an aching hardness, was setting off a deeper thrum deep in her abdomen. Still, somehow, some very small and remote spark of resistance forced itself to the surface.

"No," she whispered, half hoping he wouldn't hear her.

But he did. Indeed, her little "No" caused a drastic reaction. He loosened his wonderfully warm embrace, releasing her in order to frown into her face.

"What do you mean, no?"

Dusty returned his stare. The only contact between them was the grasp of his hands on her upper arms, but even that touch made her desire far more irresistible. She wanted to push the button that would make him reverse his actions, make him step up to her again, enfold her in his arms again. . . .

"I mean no," she said, sounding sure when she wasn't.

Of course, she could have expected the immediate irritation that clouded his blue eyes. "No doesn't make any sense, and you know it."

"No is the *only* thing that makes sense." Her words sounded even more firm.

"You don't believe that."

"Yes, I do."

"But why?"

"Because I don't want to be the little fling you have on your Desota gang stakeout."

Tag's hiss as he dropped her arms and turned away was actually a tempered, nasty word. But Dusty had known to expect that, as well.

"All right, then," he said sarcastically, "I'll go back to my room and you can go on with your floor scrubbing and we'll pretend there's nothing else going on here."

"Good."

"Good? You don't mean that."

"I mean it as much as I mean no."

"Are you saying that you're going back to floor scrubbing and me to my room, and that'll be that?"

"Actually, I'm pretty much finished scrubbing the floor. I'm planning on doing a little shopping."

"Ha! Shopping. The woman's cure-all."

Dusty remained fairly calm, considering how she was feeling. "Don't you think it would look strange for me to go to all this trouble only to live in empty rooms? Anyway, you said there would be a little money for furniture. Secondhand furniture."

Tag rubbed his forehead. "All right," he said at last, his frustration evident in his voice. "I'll get the money."

Soon Dusty was browsing through the string of secondhand shops she'd been dying to stick her nose into for weeks. She'd allowed herself glimpses in the windows but had decided to do her painting and planning first. She wanted to keep the costs down and, knowing she had plenty of time, she carefully picked her way through them.

It was funny how one shop looked like the next. Single kitchen chairs, lost from their mates, were hung on nails high along the walls, while better, smaller pieces such as jewelry and dishes were stashed in old glass cases to be watched over by the owners. Nicely dressed women from the suburbs wove their way through the narrow paths between the piles of furniture, looking for a "good deal," while less well off people competed for the same bargains as necessities.

Most of the stuff was utter junk, and all of it was dust-covered. But somehow it was fascinating to rummage through it, and the occasional "real find" was truly exciting.

When Dusty got home, she took her carefully thought out floor plans, furniture lists and prices and walked to Tag's closed door. She stood there for a minute, unable to make the first move. Sliding the paper under the door seemed silly, and she couldn't bring herself to knock.

Finally she went back to the kitchen and put her supper on the stove. She was glad to settle for leftovers. The days were shorter now, narrowing down to the darkest day of the year, and Dusty stared out the kitchen window while waiting for her single serving of stew to warm. She could make out the dark plot of Jake's little garden, the almost naked sycamore beyond that, the alley that was even farther away. She felt lonely and isolated and was glad she would see Pam tomorrow night for a movie.

After finishing her own solitary meal, she put a little something together for Tag and, covering it with plastic wrap, stuck it back in the fridge. She didn't want to be enemies with him, after all, and saw her actions as a bit of a peace offering.

She also put her little paper-clipped packet of notes on top of the sandwich and next to a salad she whipped together. After taking her usual long bath, she went to bed with a romance paperback.

That Tag hadn't asked her to watch over his equipment tonight nibbled at her conscience. She was debating whether she should get back out of bed and go offer her services when Tag stuck his head in the slightly opened doorway.

"You dressed?" he asked.

"Yes." Dusty was wearing her flannel pajamas, and when he walked across the floor, she sat up straight in bed.

He was tapping her notes against the finger of one hand, his eyes briefly racing over her in the bed before he brought them under control. "Everything looks fine," he said, standing above her.

She felt off balance with him staring at her.

"Your furniture purchases look fine," he repeated.

"Oh."

"Do you need help in getting it all here?"

"No, most of the shops will deliver for a small charge, and Pam and Brent will help with what's luggable."

Tag reached into his pocket and removed a wad of bills, which he placed on her blanket. "There's a little extra there, but if you need more it's no problem. I didn't expect to get by this cheaply."

"Fine."

He seemed to hesitate before he went on. "I'm sorry about what happened today. I was just blowing off steam."

"I understand."

When Tag's face broke into his sweetest smile, Dusty couldn't help but stare. He was nothing short of amazing in this guise. Truly his tenderness was the hardest aspect of him to resist. "Does this mean that you'll keep cooking for me?" he asked.

"Sure. I hadn't planned on letting you starve. I guess the way to reach a man is through his stomach, after all."

"The way to a man's heart," he corrected.

The pair of them remained stationary for a moment, both of them smiling.

"I'll see you tomorrow, then," Tag said, moving away from the bed.

"Good night, Tag."

"Good night, babe," she heard him murmur just before he closed the door behind him.

CHAPTER EIGHT

THE NEXT DAY was a busy one. It was Saturday, and Pam and Brent were able to help Dusty with her furniture from the secondhand stores. They carried what they could to save delivery charges and had fun besides.

Dusty stood, counting out her final precious dollars. She had actually been able to buy the little cabinet she'd thought would be beyond her means. That cabinet, plus a drop leaf table and two chairs, were all that would fit into the kitchen—those and a big plant, which she planned to place in the sunny eastern window.

"Will that do it, Mr. Getty?" she asked the shop owner.

"That'll do it, girl." Mr. Getty had the same twinkle in his eye that Dusty had in hers. The dickering had been fun. "I'll send it over on the truck. No sense in you two trying to carry it five blocks."

Dusty sent Pam a covert look of surprise. This offer of help was unexpected, coming as it did from the cunning Mr. Getty. Pam winked at Dusty. The pair of them had often chuckled over the shopkeeper's stingy ways. He and Dusty had bargained over the price down to the last dollar seventy-five.

"I've got something else you might be interested in, girl."

"Oh?" Dusty was curious despite her empty pockets.

"Yeah. You look like the kinda girl who likes pets." The old man was moving toward the curtained door behind him.

"Pets?" Dusty echoed.

"You've got Dusty all wrong, Mr. Getty," Pam cut in, sending Dusty a warning glance.

"I don't think so," the old man called from beyond the curtain, his voice almost inaudible above all the clanging and banging noises he was making. Mr. Getty was obviously looking for something very specific.

"Let's go," Pam whispered. "Heaven only knows what he's got in there."

"It wouldn't be polite to just walk out."

"Any pet he's got is bound to be something reptilian," Pam muttered, rubbing her hands together against the cold of the dirty shop. "What else could survive at the temperature he keeps this place?"

Dusty pulled her own coat collar a little more tightly around her neck. Finally Mr. Getty parted the stained curtains and came toward them carrying a beat-up bird cage. The cage's occupant was equally beat-up, and the poor creature took one more jar when Mr. Getty bumped his cage on the counter.

"A parrot," Pam gasped, her eyes looking enormous in her dark face.

Both the parrot and Mr. Getty nodded that that was what the mangy fellow was. And while the man took up an expectant pose, the parrot fluffed what was left of its feathers.

"Does he talk?" Dusty asked.

"Honey, it doesn't matter if the thing talks or not," Pam pronounced, nudging her in the direction of the door.

"I'll be truthful with you," the old man said, ignoring Pam and beginning to make his pitch. "I don't know if he talks or not. I simply bought all the furniture in an apartment last week, and he came along on the truck. The cage has still got all its cups," he declared, as if that should be an added inducement. In the eyes of the penny-pinching Mr. Getty, it probably was.

"Well, I don't know," Dusty said hesitantly.

"Well, I do," Pam said crisply. "You have no idea where that thing's been."

The parrot cocked his head and blinked. Dusty, who had always been a sucker for animals, was clearly fascinated, and Pam had a premonition that Mr. Getty—the sly old devil—was going to make a sale no matter how well Pam played the part of a good angel.

"I can make you a good deal," Mr. Getty cajoled. "Seeing as how you've been such a good customer."

"She's not interested," Pam stated, pushing at Dusty's arm.

"Parrots are worth a lot of money nowadays," the old man suggested.

"Not that one," Pam argued.

"I'll tell you what. Since I don't have any way to keep him, I'll let you have him for twenty dollars."

Pam didn't even dignify this offer with an answer.

"Okay. Say fifteen dollars, and I'll throw in his box of seed."

"What'll you do with his seed in any case?" Pam scoffed. "Sell it to the next peg-legged guy who walks in here with a parrot on his shoulder?"

"All right," he conceded, making the grand sacrifice. "Eight dollars. The cage alone is worth eight dollars."

Pam snorted while Dusty reached a finger out to the bird.

"Don't touch him. With all those bald spots, he's probably got something dreadful. I wonder if parrots can give people things."

"Five bucks," Mr. Getty offered.

"Five bucks?" Pam repeated innocently.

"Yeah, five bucks. I'll put the bird in the cab of the truck when my boy brings over the cabinet. It has to be kept warm, you know."

"*And* you'll pay the vet's bill if he needs some sort of treatment, *which* he undoubtedly does," Pam insisted.

"You've got yourself a parrot, lady."

"I . . . I've got it?" asked Dusty, coming awake.

"You sure do, honey!" Pam's grin celebrated her victory over Mr. Getty. "For just five bucks, which I'll pay. Just consider him my Christmas present to you."

"But what about Tag?"

"Tag loves you. He'll want you to have the bird if it'll make you happy."

Dusty couldn't figure how this had happened and switched her questioning eyes to Mr. Getty.

"He's even got a cage cover" was the shopkeeper's final bit of good news.

Pam and Dusty made it to the door before Dusty stopped and took one last look at the green beastie, which at that minute was stretching its beak.

"D-does it have a name?"

The old man shook his head. "Naw, you can name him any—"

"Louie-Louie," called the green parrot.

The old man quickly reversed himself. "Yeah, that's it—Louie."

"Louie-Louie," the parrot insisted.

Mr. Getty nodded sagely. "I'll send him over right away."

"You'll have your boy take him to the vet first," returned Pam, getting in the last lick, then closing the door behind her and Dusty. "That'll give us some time to break the news to Tag," she added as they stepped onto the sidewalk.

"I don't think this is a good idea, Pam," Dusty said, now that they were out in the clear light of day. "Tag—"

"Tag'll be the one to take to Louie-Louie. Just wait and see. Now where's our next stop?"

Dusty continued looking dubious. "We're finished, except for the area rug I'm supposed to check on."

"That's at that cheap little import shop, right?"

"Right."

"You're getting the bookshelves there, too, aren't you?"

"If Tag gives his okay. Those weren't on my list, but he has so many books."

Pam was in the mood to steamroller over any and all of Dusty's fears and trepidations. "We'll get 'em," she announced, linking her arm in Dusty's. "Brent has basketball practice, so I can go with you."

Dusty was beginning to think that jousting with Mr. Getty and coming out the winner was some kind of cure-all. Pam's eyes were sparkling, just like hers had when she'd won the cabinet for a measly dollar seventy-five. But now she wasn't so sure that Pam had "won" anything. It was more likely they'd been soft-soaped and maneuvered according to Mr. Getty's designs. The old man was wily. And experienced. She hated to admit it, but he'd taken both she and Pam for a buggy ride. Didn't the fact that Louie-Louie was on his way to her apartment prove that? Gulping at the thought of Tag's reaction, Dusty tried to focus her attention on the bustle of the street scene around her.

It was good to be out. She'd made other purchases below budget, and appreciated having a friend. Matching her stride to Pam's, she sent her a tentative smile. She'd deal with Tag later. Even if that meant dropping Louie-Louie on Pam's doorstep after midnight.

The crisp December air stung Dusty's face and lungs. The neighborhood was becoming a familiar one. Dusty realized she was sort of fitting in. The woman carrying her bright orange basket of clean clothes from the Laundromat was recognizable and sent her a friendly hello. Mr. Cooms waved when she passed the plate glass window of his hardware store, while three kids whizzed by on skateboards, shouting out, "Hello, Mrs. Peters," and "Hi, Mrs. Taggert."

"Wasn't one of those boys Roger?" Pam asked, craning her neck.

"Yeah. Did I tell you that Brent brought him around for hot chocolate again?"

Pam nodded. "I hope you don't mind. That's the problem with a latchkey kid. While I'm slaving behind a department store counter, he's out scrounging around the neighborhood looking for company."

"It's not like that, and you know it. Anyway, I'm glad they dropped by. Though I don't kid myself about who they're really coming to see. Tag sits around on the kitchen floor discussing baseball scores with Brent and Roger. Who can compete with that?"

"I know what you're saying. Brent took to Tag right off. But that's the way it should be with little boys and men like Tag. Tell Tag thanks, will ya?"

Once again Dusty felt an odd sort of happiness. It didn't last long, however. When the pair of them got back to the stoop in front of the flat, Pam deserted her at the door. Her friend was obviously leaving her to face Tag with the news about Louie-Louie on her own, and Dusty actually found herself experiencing the same guilt she'd felt in the past when facing her father over some misdemeanor she'd committed.

How silly, she admonished herself, going into their apartment. I'll take care of Louie-Louie and Tag won't be bothered. I'm a free woman. I can have what I want.

With this determination fresh in her mind, Dusty moved down the hallway toward her bedroom.

"Dusty," Tag called just as she was passing his door.

"Hi," she said, popping in, still unwinding her scarf. She couldn't believe how much she felt like a kid being called on the carpet.

From Tag's expression, he looked as if he was playing his part, as well. "Mr. Getty's grandson made a
delivery this afternoon."

"Yeah, I know." She remained cheery. "I bought
a cabinet, a pair of lamps and I got a—"

"A bird," he finished for her. "At least the kid
claimed it's a bird. I have my doubts. He also insisted
you actually want it."

"I didn't buy it."

"It's says here on the bill of sale that you did," he
replied, dangling the yellow slip under her nose.

Dusty stiffened her back, straightening herself to
her full height. "You can at least give me a chance to
explain."

"Fine. Explain."

"Pam paid for the bird. It didn't cost me a single
cent."

"Yeah. One bird, five dollars. One cage, no charge.
One box of seed, no charge. One vet fee, no charge.
Delivery fee, no charge. And 'All sales final. No re-
turns accepted.' Those are underlined in red pen."
Tag's eyes lifted from the yellow slip to focus on
Dusty.

"I'm surprised he didn't mention the newspaper on
the bottom of the cage," she said with a nervous little
laugh.

Tag remained stony. "Whether you paid for the bird
or not isn't my concern. The bird is here and can't be
returned. *That's* what we're discussing."

"It's not much of a discussion, with you jumping
on my every word."

Again Tag was silent, his eyes demanding that Dusty
have her say so he could pounce again.

"It was a question of the thing needing a home. You know how cold it is at Mr. Getty's. No, you wouldn't know that. But it's cold. I think even Mr. Getty was worried, or he wouldn't have thrown in a vet's examination at no charge. It might have taken him days to find the creature a place, you know."

"And so we're it," Tag muttered, tossing the yellow slip on the table.

"No. *We're* not it. *I'm* it. I take full responsibility." When Tag didn't answer, Dusty relaxed a bit. "Where is he?"

"Somewhere in the pile of junk in the living room. I've been answering the door all day."

"Sorry." Dusty knew both that Tag didn't like being disturbed and that she was a constant upheaval in his usually solitary life. "I'll get it all straightened out."

"Is there anything you need help with?" he asked grudgingly.

"No. I purposely bought things I could handle. The old TV might be a little heavy, but there isn't a couch or a large kitchen table or anything."

Tag already had his nose in his paper, and Dusty went to get into some jeans. She was looking forward to setting up the furniture.

Louie-Louie was first. He required a change of newspaper on the bottom of his cage. Although he didn't make a fuss while she worked with him, he eyed Dusty warily. She hoped he'd talk again, but mum was the word, even when she introduced him to the sunny window in the kitchen.

"I had planned to put a plant here," she told him, placing his clean cage on the small cabinet Brent had brought in earlier. "But you're green, so you'll do."

Dusty was delighted when everything began to fall into place. Pam and she had bought a yellow-and-white patterned fabric for making café curtains, and Dusty hoped to sew up a storm on Sunday after their jog around the park.

Dusty thought Tag might stroll in to have a look and, perhaps, even offer to eat with her. But, since he didn't, she took in the usual tray.

When he hardly glanced up from his book, she realized she was getting used to ignoring his impersonal treatment. He held to his part of their unspoken bargain of keeping a courteous distance, and so did she. In any case, she was afraid to let anything else develop between them. She realized Tag only wanted a physical thing and that wasn't for her. Although she had to admit she was drawn to him, she wasn't capable of a casual affair. For her it had to be all or nothing, and she had always known that.

The following morning Dusty was up bright and early. She talked to Louie-Louie while she got breakfast together. However, he would only look at her with a certain amount of curiosity after first shuffling over on his perch to the farthest end of his cage. Still, she talked—even when he cocked his head and gave her the gimlet eye.

"I thought you liked me when we were at Mr. Getty's store. You even said your name."

Louie-Louie merely blinked.

"Oh, I see. You simply saw me as a way out of Mr. Getty's storeroom. Still, I guess I don't blame you."

Dusty fetched Tag his breakfast, jogged with Pam, cleaned up and then she and Pam whipped together three pairs of café curtains, two for the kitchen and one for her bedroom.

When she got back from Pam's, it was too late to hang her curtains, however, and she wanted to wash the windows first, anyway. Finding Tag's dishes in the sink, she also saw that Louie-Louie's cage had been covered. His cage cover was a hideous thing made from a floral-patterned fabric that definitely didn't fit in with her decorating plans. She had to smile at its neatly tied strings, however. It was nice of Tag to have taken the time.

It was on the following day that everything came together in a major way. The curtain rods were a struggle to install, but once that was accomplished, the crisp curtains and sparkling windows finished everything off. The rooms didn't look raw anymore, and the area carpet in the living room, with its gay pattern, muffled the hollow sound of people's footsteps. Dusty set up the TV and relaxed in one of the pair of large overstuffed armchairs she'd chosen.

She decided to sew rings on the café curtains that would go over the sink. The living room chairs were worn but comfortable, and leaning back, she picked up one of the plastic rings for the curtain.

She was always startled when the doorbell rang. Spilling half a package of rings on the floor in getting up, she finally answered the door and was surprised to find their caller was Ellen Daniels.

"Come in, Ellen."

The crisply attired woman stepped in, offering an equally crisp greeting. "Hello, Dusty."

Stopping just inside the doorway, the woman's green eyes flickered over Dusty's half-finished room, taking in her little pile of sewing next to her cup of tea. Dusty felt a zing of pique along with a slower flush of pride. The decorating was definitely low-cost, but the result was homey.

"How cozy," Ellen Daniels said neutrally, turning a disapproving gaze on Dusty.

"Thank you."

"Very unusual for a stakeout, however," she added as a cool judgment.

Realizing that Ellen was the type who would have made do no matter how bored she became, Dusty forced a smile. By God, she was going to do this right. "I'm the sort who needs to be busy," she said.

Ellen didn't smile in return but fortunately Tag came, saving Dusty from some neat little reprimand she might otherwise have gotten. Dusty saw, however, that Tag didn't notice the now-comfortable TV area or the high sheen on the hardwood flooring.

"I've brought the rest of the tapes," Ellen told Tag. "There's one more photo, as well."

"Good," he said perfunctorily. "Come on back to my room and I'll have a look."

"Don't we have to be quiet back here?" Ellen asked as they started down the hallway.

"Luckily for us, the construction is old, the walls are thick and Syd's hearing is impaired. He's also as blind as a bat. Dusty," he added over his shoulder, "you'll need to see this last picture."

Reluctantly Dusty gathered herself and followed the others. Once again she was given the metal chair by the card table, while Ellen and Tag remained standing in the small, grubby room. The photo meant nothing, and she put it on the table with a shake of her head.

"And how'd you do with the tapes?" Ellen said to Tag.

"I'd hoped they might spark an idea, but so far it's not much better than listening to old Syd snore day and night."

"And the guy in the red baseball cap?" Ellen queried.

"He's here a couple of times a week, but he only calls his various lady friends. I'll take Syd's snoring any day over his gibberish."

Ellen nodded sympathetically. "And, other than that single visit by that no-account Joe Potts, there's been no one else?"

"No one."

"Nothing to do but wait, then."

"And read."

"Yeah, well, you've always been a big reader. Even when we were holed up together downtown, you found time to read."

Dusty felt like a fifth wheel. "Can I get you some coffee?" she asked, starting to rise from her chair.

"No," they both said in unison.

Since Ellen remained all but blocking the doorway, Dusty was forced to sink back into her seat and listen as the pair went on with their conversation. It was just as irritating now to see how professionally Tag treated his partner in comparison to her as it had been the last time.

"It's a shame about the tapes from Florida," Ellen was saying. "I'd thought they might be encouraging, might give the D.A.'s office some real evidence."

"The Desotas are taking it easy, at least for the time being. Their families are down there with them for the holidays, and there's a lot of sitting around the pool. Except for the younger brother's wife. He's still having trouble with her. She's kicking up her heels, and it's got him mad as hell.''

"Well, I guess if that's all, I'd better be getting back. Only I'm supposed to tell you that Alvarez thinks I should come by more often. He says it would look better if there was more activity here.''

Tag snorted. "Tell him he doesn't need to worry about that. Dusty is the neighborhood gadabout. Somebody's always dropping by. In that respect she's a good cover.''

This was high praise to Dusty's ears. Tag usually treated her as little more than a nuisance, and she'd often wondered if he didn't disapprove of the cheerful way she was trying to get them through this sticky situation. But though she felt better, Dusty saw that Ellen had stiffened at the remark. Ellen was, after all, Tag's partner and obviously felt that Dusty was taking her rightful place.

"Dusty's working out fine,'' Tag added, obviously oblivious to his partner's feelings. "Besides providing us with a good cover and taking over for me once in a while, she's handling it all with a sense of courage that's unusual in a civilian.''

This remark didn't sit well with Ellen Daniels. Dusty could tell by the way the other woman's slender back suddenly stiffened.

Fortunately Ellen didn't stay much longer. After a little more conversation about the case, she left and Dusty went back to her café curtains while Tag went on with his tape listening sessions.

CHAPTER NINE

THE AFTERNOON FOLLOWING Ellen Daniels's visit, Dusty added the decorating touches that were the most fun of all. A pot of chives on the kitchen windowsill, a Boston fern for the living room window and a flowering plant in her bedroom made dramatic changes that brought life to the rooms.

She also assembled her bargain lamps and by evening saw that they, too, made an enormous difference. Soft light suffused the small spaces, and it was a pleasure to turn them on and walk from one room to the next.

When she discovered there was a movie she wanted to see on the late late show, she spent the evening getting ready for it. After Tag returned from his hour out, she had a leisurely bath, put on her pajamas and went to the living room. Cuddling into a warm blanket was almost good enough, but finally she succumbed to the knowledge that there was a bag of popcorn on a kitchen shelf.

Dusty knew that Tag's closed door kept the delicious aroma from invading his sanctum and didn't think he'd be interested in any case. Fixing herself a soda—glad that Pam couldn't tut-tut over what she was eating—she padded back into the living room and settled down to watch Bogie do his stuff.

Somewhere around the middle of the movie, she began to wonder if she'd be able to stay awake. The commercial breaks were getting longer and more frequent and her eyelids were feeling droopier.

"That popcorn sure smells good," Tag said from just behind her.

Scrambling into a sitting position, Dusty automatically checked the blanket she was wrapped in. It was a silly concern because she wore her flannel pajamas with pink rosebuds and her rose-colored robe over those.

"I hope I didn't wake you," she managed.

"Naw. I don't sleep much."

Tag's eyes slid to the bowl of popcorn.

"Would you like some?" Dusty asked.

"Yeah, it looks good."

"I'll make a fresh batch."

"No. This'll do."

Taking the bowl from her lap, Tag walked around to sit on the armchair that was separated from hers by a table with a lamp. Dusty slid her eyes back to the screen, but she'd lost her concentration. A black-and-white Bogie had nothing on a real-life John Taggert.

"I haven't had popcorn in years," Tag said. "I'd forgotten how good it tastes."

"You want some soda?"

"I'll share yours."

Adding more cola to what was left in her glass, he took a big swig. When he found Dusty's eyes still on him, he smiled. "You've done wonders with the apartment."

"Thanks."

"It comes close to feeling like a home."

"And the chair?"

"What chair?"

Dusty chuckled. "The one you're sitting on."

"It's okay," he said, putting a fistful of popcorn into his mouth. "I'd rather have a couch. I used to love to stretch out on the couch at home and spin stories in my head. My mom said she always knew where to look for me. I'd either be following my dad around, watching a baseball game or reading a book."

Dusty noticed that he didn't mention an interest in sports or, more particularly, in girls.

"Why are you looking at me like that?" he asked suddenly.

"L-like what?" She had been staring at him, studying him.

"I don't know. Like I'm under a microscope or something."

"I was thinking about what you said. About liking to read."

"Yeah. It's a good thing I do, or I'd go nuts in this kind of situation."

"I notice you read almost anything."

Tag nodded.

"I thought I'd haul your books in here and fill some of these shelves."

"Fine." Tag refilled her glass and took another drink.

"You said your father was in law enforcement," she coaxed.

"Yeah."

"I take it that's where you got your interest in it."

"It was all I ever thought I'd want to do. I sloughed off any schoolwork that would have prepared me for

anything else and got into it as soon as I could."
Looking at Dusty, he smiled ironically. "I found out
too late that I could have emulated my dad without
taking up his vocation."

Dusty looked puzzled.

"My dad was a good man. We all loved him, and I,
being the youngest, adored him. That's how I got my
nickname, Tag's not just short for Taggert. It's short
for tag-along, too. Naturally my wanting to be just like
my dad included doing what he did. But I don't know
how he did it and stayed so good. He never soured. He
never got tired of the...the..."

"The grubbiness of the job?"

"Yeah," he said, looking at her with a new appre-
ciation.

"My dad never became disenchanted with it,
either," she said, "but for different reasons. He loved
the scuzziness, dealing with the dregs. He didn't see
himself as a knight in shining armor, standing for the
law. He glorified in the glory of it, in the exercise of
authority. I never really understood, but, well, he
loved it and I'm here because I loved him."

Tag, who had been listening intently, switched his
eyes to the TV. How good of him, Dusty thought. He
refused to stand in judgment, although he obviously
understood—obviously knew other lawmen who were
the same.

"I'd give anything to get out," he murmured,
amazing her.

"Can't you?"

"God, I don't know. I'm good at my job. I'm certainly needed, but..."

That was it. He'd gone as far as he could and Dusty saw that. She also saw the struggle that she knew was going on inside of him.

"In any case, I honestly don't know another thing I'd be as good at. I had a certain facility for writing when I was in school, but that was only high school. I guess the job's not so bad," he finished. "Anyway, Bogie makes it all look so easy, so cut and dried," he added, indicating the TV with a small smile.

"The times were simpler," Dusty murmured.

Tag stretched. "Yeah, I guess." He looked at her. "It's hard for me to discuss my job, not only because of my own questions concerning it, but because everyone I run with is on the force and can't think of doing anything else. I wouldn't dare to question it in front of one of them. It's good to be able to talk to someone like you. You've had enough experience through your father to understand, and yet you aren't so enamored with the idea of being a policeman that you can't criticize what's wrong with it. God, I wouldn't even frown in front of Ellen. But you're different."

"Yes. I'm definitely different from Ellen," Dusty said, coloring at this comparison to the woman he obviously respected.

"Hey. I didn't meant to upset you."

Damn my translucent skin. "You're not upsetting me."

"Yes, I am. I can see it. But why?"

"I don't suppose there are many women who compare well to Ellen Daniels. It's obvious that she's very good at what she does and, while I think I'm pretty good at what I do, teaching is a far cry from having the courage to be a cop."

"That's true. Ellen's an excellent cop. And very dedicated. I know I can count on her."

Dusty sighed. "Well, I guess I'll go to bed." Standing up, she rewrapped her blanket more tightly around her.

Tag stood, too. He evidently sensed her turmoil, because he placed a large hand on her arm. "Hey, babe, I didn't mean anything."

He was obviously at a loss as to what he'd said to make her uncomfortable, and she was too worn out to explain. "I know you didn't mean anything," she said. "I'm just tired. I'll cover the bird and go to bed."

"I've already covered him."

"Oh?" Dusty was again surprised at Tag's consideration for their disliked border. "Well, good night."

"I don't suppose you'd go for a good-night kiss," Tag said lazily.

"I don't think it's a good idea."

"It's definitely not a good idea. Not with our little history. Still, I want one awfully bad." Tag had Dusty in his arms before she could protest. "God, but you're a sweet little bundle," he whispered, pushing his firm mouth against her softer, more pliant one.

Just as before, Dusty gave in. She couldn't help herself, and Tag felt her surrender. He groaned deeply in his throat, pulling her even more comfortably against him.

But Dusty was already resisting, already pushing at his chest.

"Oh, God, Dusty, why not? Is there someone else?" he asked, suddenly stiff.

"No."

"Then who's it going to matter to? It's just you and me here in this little apartment. No one else exists."

"It matters to me."

"You want to as much as I do," he stated knowingly.

Dusty looked unflinchingly back. "Yes, I do."

"Then why? You aren't holding out for that June-moon-spoon garbage, are you?"

"That what?"

"You know. Love, romance—that kind of stuff."

"Yes, that's exactly what I'm holding out for."

Tag's smile was sad. "It doesn't exist, Dusty. Take my word for it."

"It exists for some people."

He shrugged a wide shoulder. "Maybe half a dozen."

"Well, I'm one of the half dozen."

Dusty turned away and headed for her room. But Tag was too quick for her. He had her pressed against the wall in the dark hallway before she was barely into it. She could hardly make out his face in the much dimmer light. Even so there was enough to see his desire.

"If I were to kiss you again," he whispered, "how long do you think you could hold out? How long do you think it would be before you'd be clinging to me and making those soft, whimpering noises you've made in the past? I've dreamed about those sounds. And about you and me. You want to hear my dreams?"

"No."

"Why not? Are you afraid to hear them? Afraid that what I say will get you as steamed up for me as I am for you?"

Dusty stared into Tag's pale blue eyes. All she needed to do was protest, and he'd let her go. Still, for a moment she hesitated. His threat smacked too much of the truth. "I told you before that I don't want to be your stakeout fling. Go out and find someone who's willing."

Just as she thought, Tag released her. "Don't try that, babe. You're plenty willing."

"Not as willing as someone who doesn't mind a fling," she pronounced, not quite so collected anymore.

Taggertitis, Taggertitis, played mockingly in her brain as she walked toward her bedroom.

"I've been told there are women by the dozens who are more than willing where you're concerned," she added, turning the knob on her door.

Tag stood where she had left him, watching her. "But it's your sweet, speckled hide I want."

Dusty pushed her door ajar. "I'm sure any speckled hide will do."

"Don't be so damn naive. I'm telling you that what I want isn't that sort of thing."

"Whatever *thing* it is, I don't want it."

"Oh, right, you want the June-moon-spoon bit. Like I said, don't be so damn naive."

They both stepped into their rooms and closed their doors behind them simultaneously—but not too loudly. It was more as if they'd agreed to disagree rather than argued. They were coming at their mutual desire from two directions.

Dusty wanted to be courted and loved, had always wanted that, while he admitted he wanted no more than an affair without commitment. Their differences had been aired and, though Dusty thought Tag might not give up, there was no rancor between them. She was surprised, however, when she heard him at her door not ten minutes later.

"I'm going out," he said, his voice tight. "I've notified headquarters and, if you aren't too tired, I'd appreciate your keeping an eye on things."

Dusty didn't dare open her door. She was afraid he'd read her automatic concern. "All right," she said.

TAG OPENED THE TOP BUTTON of his sheepskin coat. It wasn't quite as cold as it usually was this late at night, and the coat would get hot. Before starting this assignment he had never done much walking but, what with doing so much of it lately, it was becoming a kind of pleasure. At least he was alone, and what he wanted second only to Dusty was to be alone.

The streetlamps that marked the slim trail of broken vegetation between sidewalk and street, the houses that lined the way—some with lights and some not—were growing familiar.

Still, it wasn't all pleasure. His leg hurt like hell, and any time alone stirred up his usual train of thought.

To hear a car come up behind him, slowing down as it blinked its headlights from high to dim, was surprising. It had to be . . . well, at least one in the morning. At last the vehicle got close enough, and he recognized it as Alvarez's battered car.

Pulling up alongside of him, the older man rolled down his window. "What're you doing out?"

"I had to get away for a while."

The captain smiled his understanding. "Get in and I'll take you for a spin through the park."

"Forest Park?"

"What other park do you have in mind?"

"It's late."

"Hell, I know that. I'm on my way home after one unbelievable day."

"You sure?"

"Get in," the older man ordered.

Forest Park was beautiful at night. It was a full-size park complete with dense woods as well as open fields and it was plunk in the middle of the city. Its meandering lagoons, reflecting its trees and quaint bridges, spoke of more gracious times—of the summer when it had been the grounds for the 1904 St. Louis World's Fair.

That all of this was lost on Tag would have been obvious to anyone, and Alvarez peered at him speculatively in the dim illumination of the dash.

"How's the case going?" was the inevitable question. "I've read your reports, and it seems that everything's slowing down both here and in Miami."

Tag nodded.

"Is your leg bothering you?"

"Some."

And then, of course, Tag knew to expect the usual lecture. "You need to exercise more. I can get someone over to the apartment to watch things for a couple of afternoons a week. You can get away, exercise with that bunch you played ball with in the summer, get back into your group therapy."

Tag could feel the automatic resistance building in his gut. "I'm not interested in any of that."

"The therapist said you quit the group too soon."

"I didn't find it helpful. I'm not the sort to lay everything out on the table like that. You've got to let me work through this in my own way."

Alvarez turned his ever-complaining car into the extra quiet of the winding lane that ran behind the Art Museum. While Tag hoped that that would be the end of the usual inquisition, he also knew his was a faint hope.

"You could use your time off in other ways, you know."

Tag smiled at his superior's unlikely try at tact. "I'm used to long stretches of celibacy."

The next spate of quiet only led to the next question. "Look, Tag, I'm not going to bring up your last case because I know you don't want me to."

"Thanks for that at least."

"But what else is it? Is it being responsible for Dusty that's getting to you?"

"Some of it."

"The two of you get along, don't you? I mean, you're not at each other's throat?"

"Not exactly. No, we're not at each other's throat. She's too nice for that."

"She's a great little gal."

Tag couldn't help smiling. "So you've said."

"What is it, then? Ellen told me that you said she's doing a great job."

"She is." Tag didn't want it to, but his ready irritation bubbled up to color his voice. "How can I get upset when she keeps coming at me with an unrelenting good cheer and home-cooked meals?"

"She's a good cook," the proud "uncle" bragged.

"Yeah, and that's not all. Everywhere I look she's bent over some piece of molding, sanding away...hanging on to a ladder just within my reach."

Tag didn't turn his head, but he could tell that Alvarez had shot him another speculative glance. "You need an afternoon out."

Tag experienced another rise of impatience. "And I'm telling you I don't need an afternoon of *that*. What I need is out altogether, and I can't get out. What I need is sleep, and I can't sleep."

For what felt like the thousandth time, Tag regretted his lack of patience. He knew that this man cared about him and wanted to help.

"It's just that little room . . . and that Syd Desota does nothing but snore. I mean, the guy falls asleep in the can, for cripes sake. I usually take this sort of situation in my stride, but I can't seem to pull myself..."

When Tag fell silent again, Alvarez gave him a quick, sympathetic glance, and Tag continued. "It's just a matter of time. I just need some time. Of course, if she weren't so damn cheery it would help. And it might help if she weren't so damn into everything. So damn everywhere I look. So damn energetic. So damn...charming."

Now how had all of that come pouring out when he'd never intended to say anything? he asked himself.

They had returned to the apartment, and as Tag got out of the car, Alvarez just smiled and said, "We'll talk some more." Then he pulled off.

"Yeah," Tag muttered under his breath, watching the car move off, leaving a blue haze in its wake. "Just what I need—more talk."

CHAPTER TEN

DUSTY'S SINGLE DISLIKE was going to the Laundromat. Still, she had to go on the following wintry afternoon. Flopping down on one of the orangish molded plastic chairs that stood in a row along at the front, she watched her laundry tumble around with Tag's in the suds. She couldn't believe she'd forgotten to bring a book, and her eyes drifted over the well-used room with its garish paint and lint-filled fluorescent light fixtures. There were only a few people using the machines at this hour, and no one to talk to.

When a tap sounded on the window behind her, she turned to see Brent's smiling face. He was with his smaller, quieter friend, Roger, and Dusty motioned for the boys to come in and see her. She had found herself thinking of the smaller boy often over the past few weeks and wasn't surprised when he hung back. But as soon as they exchanged greetings, she read a better reason than shyness for the hesitation. The child had a large bruise on his cheekbone, just below his eye. It was obviously a few days old because the swelling had gone down and the colors were fading to purple, green and yellow rather than being a fresher blue. Still, it was an ugly thing—frightening proof of what it had been in the beginning and even more frightening as proof of what she'd suspected since she'd first seen fading bruises on his face.

Dusty was a teacher. She had seen bruises before. She had, in fact, been instructed to be on the lookout for them. But though she was suspicious that the boy had been struck, she didn't know him well enough to ask him straight out. It wasn't that she was standing on ceremony. She believed adults should help children in Roger's position. It was the boy's attitude that kept her mouth shut for the time being. He was shy, and she wouldn't challenge him unless she felt he could be comfortable enough to confide in her. Otherwise, she'd seem as much a threat as whoever was abusing him.

Unfortunately the child appeared to sense some of what was running through Dusty's mind, and he excused himself. Brent remained with her, though, until the end of the dryer cycle. Then the two of them made their way home, carrying a mix of schoolbooks and wash baskets.

"How many more weeks of school do you have until Christmas break?" Dusty asked, readjusting her powder-blue scarf against the lateness of the gray day.

"Three and a half."

"I'll bet you'll be glad for the time off."

"Yeah." Brent grinned. "Mom says if it gets cold enough this year, she'll take me ice skating on the lagoon in the park."

"Well, we have to have a really cold winter to get that kind of ice." Dusty trudged on, then asked casually, "Does Roger live nearby?"

"Not that close. But he's in my class. When he comes."

Absenteeism was another bad sign. "He's absent a lot, huh?"

"Yeah."

"Because he's in bad shape a lot, huh?"

Brent gave Dusty a sideways look, obviously anxious to protect his friend, to adhere to the kids' code. "Yeah," he finally admitted.

"Who does that to him? Has he ever told you?"

Again Brent hesitated. Dusty had expected that, however. She also expected that Brent would eventually answer her because they had become friends.

"He's never told me exactly, but he lives with his dad and nobody else."

"He probably loves his dad, even though he's scared of him. He's probably torn between not wanting to get his dad in trouble and being afraid of when he'll be angry again. It's a sad way for Roger to live."

"He told me he's scared. He's missed so much school that he thinks he'll get put back. But he's too embarrassed to come when he's hurt. Anyway, I don't think he loves his dad."

"He needs a friend like you, Brent. I'm proud that you're sticking by him through this bad time. But, Brent, something has to be done. It's not fair for Roger to live like he is."

"What can I do?" the boy asked, obviously aghast.

"You can't do anything but stick by Roger and trust me. This is adult business to be handled among adults. You don't have to explain to Roger that I know if you don't want to. Tell you what," Dusty said, thinking fast, "why don't you bring Roger to see me? You say he's behind in his schoolwork. I'd be happy to help him catch up. I'm a teacher, you know."

"You mean tutor him?"

"Exactly. That'll give me a chance to get to know him and maybe he'll open up to me. That'll also leave you out of it. In the meantime, I'll look into what's to be done."

"His dad is really mean, Dusty." Brent's comment was meant as a warning. "He gives me the creeps."

"You just stay out of it, be a friend to Roger and bring him to me. Okay?"

"Okay."

"And thanks for telling me, Brent. That took courage. Believe me, you didn't betray Roger's secret. You've simply opened a way for him to get out."

"Thanks, Dusty."

The pair had reached the stoop in front of their doors. They put down Dusty's baskets so that she could fish around in her purse for her key. When Brent reached out for a hug, she took him into her arms. Giving him a pat on the back, she looked into his smiling face.

"Remember. You bring him to me for tutoring. There won't be any charge. Have him tote all his books, and you come along the first time to help us sort out what he's missed. I may have to call his teacher in any case."

"Okay."

"Hey, you two!" Pam called, coming up the front steps. "What's going on?"

"Nothing really," Dusty said. She knew that now was the time to prove she could keep confidences. And so she said only what the boy would see as being all right.

"I've offered to tutor Brent's friend Roger, and Brent thinks that's a good deal."

"So do I," said Pam. "I've been wondering how Roger's been doing. I haven't seen him lately."

"He's doing fine," replied Brent, pushing open their door. "See ya, Dusty."

"See you, Brent."

"Is the boy really okay?" Pam asked when Brent was out of earshot.

"He had a bruise on his face today. Brent says it's not unusual and that his injuries keep him out of school."

Pam nodded knowingly. "I've wondered myself. I don't see Roger often enough to really know him, but he seems like a nice boy."

"Do you know anything about his situation at home?"

Pam leaned against the railing. In spite of the streetlamp, dusk was deepening to dark and Dusty could barely see her face.

"The only thing I can remember Brent saying is that he hasn't got anyone but his dad. I don't think Roger lives that close by. Oh, and some neighbor lady oversees his meals, but it's my impression that the boys don't like her."

"Well." Dusty sighed. "I'll start by getting to know Roger myself. I'm not sure how I should go about this, and I don't want to blunder in and get him on the defensive."

"You'll let me know if there's anything I can do, won't you?"

"Sure," Dusty said with a smile.

"How about going Christmas shopping with me tomorrow?"

Dusty stood for a moment, trying to switch mental gears. She hadn't thought about it, but she would probably end up spending Christmas here. She had always loved Christmas, and her thoughts automatically ran to her sister Leslie. She couldn't imagine a Christmas without her.

"Sure," she managed at last.

"You sure you want to go, honey?" Pam asked, a pucker of worry showing in her forehead. Her friend was obviously wondering what had been going through Dusty's mind to make her reply so long in coming.

"Sure I'm sure. I was just realizing Christmas is on the way. I hadn't thought about it."

"Well, it's for sure on its way. And knowing you for the little domestic thing you are, I would imagine you can come up with big plans."

Dusty laughed. "I do make a great chocolate chip cookie."

"Oh, no," Pam groaned. "I shouldn't have told you. I can see it now—me eating 'em as fast as you bake 'em."

"Hopefully there will be others who will want to arm-wrestle you over them."

Pam chuckled. "Well, I guess I'd better get supper on the table. But tomorrow I think we should start early."

Nodding, Dusty agreed and stepped into the warmth of her apartment. She was amazed to find Tag watching TV. The set was on low, and there was a book on the table next to his armchair. The whole scene looked comfortable and cozy—just the sort of situation a married couple would share.

Shaking herself from such an odd thought, Dusty put down her wash basket.

"The lamp in here just blinked and went out," Tag said.

Walking over to the guilty party, Dusty tried its switch. "I'll see what I can do with it," she replied.

"Are you all right?"

"Yeah, just a little tired. If it's okay with you, I'm going Christmas shopping with Pam tomorrow."

Tag's nose was already stuck in his book, "Yeah, fine."

Just as Dusty was setting Tag's supper on the card table, the sound-activated recorder clicked on. She nearly dropped her tray, and Tag's coffee sloshed over the rim of its cup.

The two of them exchanged a meaningful glance, listening as the noises of a newcomer in the apartment next door came through the little speaker. The exchange of voices, first between Syd and his guest, and then the ones picked up by the phone bug were crystal clear. The latter conversation was very long and was only the first of several that were made over the span of the evening. Dusty sat with Tag throughout, listening carefully between her quick trips into the kitchen to clean up and get more coffee.

"Who is this guy?" Tag asked time and again. "I can't believe that, after all the damn tapes I've listened to, I don't recognize this voice. You didn't hear Syd mention the guy's name when he greeted him, did you?"

Dusty shook her head.

"He hasn't had to identify himself in any of his calls, either. He's got to be one hell of a big fish."

Dusty watched Tag walk back and forth. She could hardly stand the tension, their need to whisper. The conversations that went on and on meant nothing to her, and Tag admitted, several times, that he had no idea what the guy was talking about, either. Some deal...in drugs, of course.

Dusty's urge to get out became urgent. She needed time to herself. She needed the space to calm down. The voices being piped in were frightening in what they represented—drugs and ugliness and her father's death.

"Why don't you take your bath?" Tag finally suggested. "You look exhausted."

"Are you sure?"

"Yeah, I'm sure. If this is the guy who murdered your dad, you've got to see him for identification, not hear him."

Dusty was hesitant. She felt as if she should keep watch with Tag.

Still, she wanted very badly to get away from the sounds echoing in his dingy little room.

"Go on," he coaxed, looking into her lingering gaze. "Take a long one and relax. Get into your pajamas and, if I have anything more, I'll play it for you. If he looks like he's leaving, I'll call you."

"You won't get out for a bit, then?" she asked, knowing his answer before she heard it.

"Not tonight."

Still, she sat.

"Go on. I'm fine."

Dusty got up with a sigh. She had to admit she felt leaden. That rainy night of seven months ago, the one she'd thought she was dealing with so well, had come back with a vengeance. Could the man they were listening to be the one who had killed her father? Oh, if she could only see him—identify him. How ludicrous it was that, for all the time Tag spent in his room, he hadn't been there when the guy had come up to the stoop. If only Tag had been where he should have been, he would have gotten a Polaroid and she would already know if this man—only a wall away—was the one.

Forcing herself to fill the tub and, adding a double dose of bubble bath, Dusty sank into it and leaned back. She had piled her rust-colored hair on top of her head and could already feel the curl getting even curlier. She wouldn't worry about the riotous tangle it was certain to end up in. All she wanted to do was to relax, to not think at all. That was impossible, however.

The idea of "the creep" being in the next apartment made her feel nauseated. And afraid. If that man were somehow to discover one of Tag's listening devices, he'd be looking to kill again.

"Dusty," Tag called softly, already pushing into the bathroom.

Dusty's automatic response was to sit straight up. Something flashed in Tag's eyes before his haste and concern again came to the fore. "The guy's leaving."

Dusty nodded.

Reaching for a towel, Tag stood and held it open. Dusty was already out of the tub before it flashed through her mind that she had nothing covering her rosy skin but bubbles. Tag, however, had her bundled up in the towel before she could think much beyond that.

It was his next move that startled her. Switching off the light, he spoke close to her ear. "I've got the Nikon set up for taking automatic pictures. It should get him in the light of the streetlamp. But I want you to observe from the window in here. Just in case. You'll be able to see better from in here."

Dusty shivered, knowing it was a result of her fear rather than her wet skin. She agreed automatically, and Tag lifted her up to the window set high in the wall. She remembered painting around it, but that incongruous thought was soon crowded out of her mind. Tag was hefting her to a seated position on a broad shoulder, balancing her there easily.

The hard part came next. The wait. Dusty saw, without really seeing, the sidewalk, the front yard, the streetlamp...

At last they heard the door to Syd's apartment open, and Dusty held her breath. The man was bidding his host a terse good-night. Then he turned and walked quickly down to the sidewalk. Dusty only caught a glimpse of the man's face. But it was enough.

"It's not him," she whispered, watching as the man got into a car at the curb.

"Are you sure?" Tag asked, not moving.

"I'm positive."

Finally he let her down, handling her as if she were only a child. After that she didn't know what happened. She began to shiver, and she felt her fear collect in her stomach and throat. Before she could think, she was sobbing—sobbing wretchedly, in a way she hadn't since the night of the murder. No. Not even then had she cried like this.

Tag enfolded her in his arms, patting her back and snuggling her damp form against the hard muscles of his chest. "It's all right, babe. It's been pretty awful tonight, but it's all right now. Everything's going to be just fine."

"I...I loved my dad. H-he wasn't easy to...to love, but I did."

"I'm sure you did, babe."

"I hope h-he knew."

"Of course he did. People know it when other people love them, even when it isn't talked about."

"But...but I don't know if he loved me. At the...end he said he did, but..."

"I'm sure he did. I'm sure he did. People can't help themselves when it comes to you. You've handled this so bravely, Dusty. I know it's been hell, but no one could have done better than you. No one would have managed with more class and goodwill than you have. There's no need to be ashamed of crying, either. We all need to cry at least once in a while."

Dusty disengaged herself from his grip and looked up into what she could see of Tag's face. "Have...have you ever cried, Tag?" she asked, wanting his understanding—wanting to know.

Wiping her tears with the pad of his thumb, he smiled as softly as he spoke. "Yeah, I've cried. One night not too long ago I sobbed every bit as hard as you have."

Dusty didn't know what to say and, leaning into him, let him lead her back to her room. Helping her into her robe, he knotted its ties at her waist and looked at her, still softly, but more seriously. "I have to get back. I've got to notify—"

"I know," Dusty said. "Go on. I'm all right now."

"You sure?"

"I'm sure."

"If you want, you can come sit with me."

"We'll see," Dusty said. "For some reason I'm exhausted."

"I know the reason. Do what you want. Whatever will help the most."

Dusty managed a weak smile. "Thanks, Tag. You've been..."

Nodding and giving her a quick kiss, he moved to the door. "I've gotta go. I'm just sorry we didn't catch our man so you could get out of here."

CHAPTER ELEVEN

DUSTY MOANED when her alarm went off. She'd only slept a couple of hours and wondered if she'd ever really sleep again. She couldn't forget the man who had visited Syd Desota the night before and hadn't been able to shake the creepy feeling she'd experienced ever since.

But Tag...Tag had been so kind. She had been right in remembering him as being kind on the night her dad had been killed.

After seeing that she was safely tucked into bed, he'd paid one more brief call on her in her bedroom. He'd said he'd learned the identity of the man who had visited Syd's apartment—the one they had thought could have been "the creep." Apparently the guy was a fringe member of the Desota gang who'd been on the verge of his own deal. Tag's news had obviously been meant to reassure her so that she could sleep.

Still, she hadn't slept, and now she felt an uncharacteristic reluctance to rise and meet the day. But she'd told Pam she'd go Christmas shopping, and Pam wanted to get an early start. Unable to think of anything she'd rather *not* do than face the Christmas shopping crowds, she dressed and headed into the kitchen where she found Tag.

Suddenly she didn't know how to act. She was slightly ashamed about her behavior the night before and wondered how Tag would treat her in the saner light of day. He seemed the same, however. Oh, maybe not quite as impatient as usual, but not really any different, either.

"I'm getting my own breakfast," he said, "so you and Pam can go."

Once again Dusty felt an odd sense that everything, including Tag, should be different this morning. "Are you sure I should leave?"

"Sure I'm sure."

"Did anything else happen last night? I could hear you up pretty late."

"Yeah, something did happen, as a matter of fact. We got the guy at Syd's. A good-size fish, too."

"But won't that tip off the Desotas?"

"This guy's too distantly connected to them for the Desotas to know exactly what happened."

"Well, that's something, then."

"Yeah. Alvarez was pleased. So you're going shopping for Christmas?"

Dusty had the feeling that he wanted to get rid of her. "I guess so."

"Get going, then," he said, walking out.

Things improved after that. Every store Dusty and Pam went into was packed, and each purchase took forever, but Dusty began to enjoy it. The old seasonal colors, lights and music finally got to her—as they always did. She had a number of people to buy for: people in her neighborhood, people at Brockham Elementary and her family, too—Leslie and Eric and her nephews.

Dusty knew that she wouldn't be going to New York for her holiday visit, and her heart tore at the idea of not seeing her sister. But she wasn't about to get on an emotional roller coaster again if she could help it and switched her thoughts back to Pam.

They were standing in line at the notions counter, their hands full of purses, gloves and packages. Dusty thought that Pam looked unusually wilted and nudged her with an elbow.

"Don't go to sleep on me now. We've got all this stuff to get home."

"I'm not sleeping. Not even Brent could sleep in here."

"Is something wrong?" Dusty ventured. "You haven't changed your mind about having Tag and me up for Christmas Eve, have you? I know it'll be a lot of trouble on top of working all day, and I'll understand if you renege."

Moving up one more space in the line and resettling themselves didn't change Pam's expression. "No," she said. "I want you to come. Really, I need for you to come. Most everybody I know here in St. Louis has a family they can spend Christmas with and, as I told you, my family is in Memphis. The fact is, I'll be missing them something awful but having you and Tag over will help."

Dusty didn't know what to say. It seemed that Pam was really upset, and that was unlike her friend.

"Well, you more than anyone should understand, Dusty. This is only your first Christmas away from home. You must be feeling it. It's something you never quite get used to, Dusty. Not even when it's been eleven years like I've been away, though, of course, in my case it's not of my choosing.''

Dusty's sympathetic expression coaxed Pam to go on. ''You told me that your mother didn't react well to your marriage, right?''

Dusty felt a slight start. Pam was catching her up in one of the fibs she'd had to tell her, and she hated the fact that she'd have to do it all over again. ''Yes...'' she finally managed.

But Pam, oblivious and trusting, was continuing to confide in her. ''The fact is, what happened to you happened to me, only it was worse. I got pregnant with Brent before I was married, and that upset my dad so bad that he told me to get out.

''Then the guy and I were divorced and I remarried and then divorced again. Those were all mistakes...my mistakes, and they made him all the angrier, all the more disapproving. He's at a point where he won't speak to me at all.''

''I'm sorry, Pam.'' Dusty said, not knowing what else to say. ''I really am.''

''I'm sorry for Brent. He's the one who's been deprived of a family. And then there's my mom. I know she's never thought that what my dad did was right, but she doesn't have anything to say because he's so autocratic.''

''You told me your family's a big one. Isn't there someone who can talk to your dad?''

''Almost every person in my family, and that includes my three brothers-in-law, have gone to my dad and tried to get him to change his mind. The funny thing is, he almost has a few times, but I keep messing up.''

"I don't think you're messing up. You're making decisions that you think are the right ones. It's not your fault they haven't worked out."

"I wish my dad could see it that way. I'd give anything to move back. There's nothing for me here, but I won't move until he accepts me. I can be just as stubborn as he."

Pam smiled, but Dusty couldn't. She felt too bad about her friend's situation.

By the time they got back to the flat, they were doing better, however. Better despite being tired. Dusty barely had her key in the door when Tag opened it.

"Hi," he said, relieving her of her shopping bags. "Looks like you were successful."

"Yeah. Is there any Christmas shopping I can do for you?" she added.

Tag closed the door on the cold night. "My family knows not to expect me until after the first of the year."

Shrugging out of her coat, Dusty followed Tag into the kitchen. She moved toward the bird cage to cover Louie-Louie for the night, but Tag was there first. He was poking a finger between the bars, trying to coax the parrot to come to him. Louie-Louie ruffled his feathers, cocked his head, then, instead of giving Tag the gimlet eye, as he would have given Dusty, the mangy critter inched a bit closer.

"Louie-Louie," the parrot said.

"Louie-Louie," Tag repeated.

The bird screeched and, amazingly, spoke. "Twinkle, twinkle, little."

"Star," Tag finished.

Once again the parrot replied, "Twinkle, twinkle, little."

"Star, damn it."

"You taught him that?" Dusty asked. She hadn't heard a single word from the parrot since their meeting at Mr. Getty's. In fact, she'd talked to him until she was blue in the face and had never gotten so much as a syllable from him.

"I didn't teach him," Tag replied. "He's said that much of the rhyme all the time we've had him. He's sort of nocturnal, like myself. He's talked a blue streak since his first night here. Still, he always stops at the word *star*."

"Twinkle, twinkle, little."

"Star, damn it. He loves crackers."

"He does?"

"Yeah, he goes through 'em like crazy."

"I didn't know."

"You wouldn't. He cleans up every speck, usually before I finish my coffee. I come out every night, around three, make a cup and give him a cracker. It's our little ritual, isn't it, old boy?"

Tag renewed his attempts at contact by again reaching a long finger through the bars toward the bird. "Louie-Louie. Louie-Louie."

Dusty was surprised. She would never have thought that Tag would take an interest in a beat-up fellow like Louie-Louie.

"I guess I'll go to bed," Tag announced in his usual abrupt manner. "Good night, Dusty."

"Good night."

Tag moved away, walking back to his room. It was funny how he seemed to fill rooms. It was funnier still that Dusty felt odd at being left behind. Tag obviously left her easily enough.

THE FOLLOWING DAY Dusty finally sat on the kitchen floor and took the broken lamp apart. As usual, Louie-Louie turned a cold shoulder no matter how much she talked to him. Only when Tag came in did the bird brighten and screech out a greeting. Dusty felt insulted on top of her irritation with the lamp.

Tag was coaxing the parrot to finish his singsong repetition of "Twinkle, Twinkle, Little Star" but to no avail. Louie-Louie balked with a quick blink and a cocked head.

"He doesn't do anything he doesn't want to," Dusty muttered. She stared at the lamp, which still wasn't working even though she'd had it apart and back together twice.

Tag came to stand over where she was sitting on the floor, the pieces of the lamp spread in an arc around her. "Take it back," he said.

"Ha! This is my bargain lamp from Mr. Getty's, remember?"

"It didn't cost enough to get all hot and bothered. Trash it and buy another one."

"But this one is so perfect."

"It's not perfect if it doesn't work."

"It worked the evening I first put it together."

"Get another switch from Mr. Cooms."

"It's not likely to be the switch."

"It's possible."

"But not likely."

Tag shrugged, obviously giving up on that little go-around. He'd just as soon leave Dusty in her tiff as not, his casual, uneven exit said.

Dusty's trip to the hardware store revealed that it was the switch that was defective. Her additional stop at Mr. Getty's also led to its usual trouble.

When she got home, she stepped up to Tag's door and knocked softly.

"Yeah," he called out unencouragingly.

"I'd like to talk to you."

"Um."

He was sitting in his metal chair, with his legs stretched out and his feet resting on the cot. He was reading and put down his book when she came in, at the same time lifting one foot from the cot. His wince, together with the way he had to assist his other leg, were precisely what she wanted to discuss. She only hoped he'd take her offer in the spirit she meant it.

"I was at Mr. Getty's shop today—"

"Oh, no."

"I bought a used exercise bike."

"Who for? You?"

"No. You."

She could see he was in a bad mood, probably because his leg hurt. He was always at his crabbiest when his leg hurt.

"Have you paid for it?"

"No. I've got him holding it for me."

"If there's three inches of dust on it, like there is on everything else, I don't think there's much chance you'll miss out. In fact, you're probably the exact pigeon he's been waiting for. No. You're his best pigeon."

"I wanted to ask you before buying it."

"Since when?"

"Since I had Captain Alvarez call your doctor and he said you should be exercising your leg. He also recommended a shoe weight, and I've got Mr. Getty looking for one of those, as well."

"How much do you want to bet he locates one by lunch?"

Dusty was encouraged. For all his remarks he hadn't said no. "So?" she asked.

"So what?"

"Will you let me have him deliver it?"

"I guess."

"Your doctor says—"

"I know what the doctor says. Get it and I'll use it." Tag lifted his book, indicating that the subject was closed and she should go.

But Dusty wasn't about to let the opportunity pass. "Don't you think he should look at your leg again?"

Tag softened a bit. "It's getting better. It's just all this sitting around."

"So the bike is a good idea," Dusty suggested with a smile.

Tag smiled grudgingly. "Yeah, it's a good idea."

Dusty nearly floated out the door.

"Dusty," he called after her.

"Yeah," she said, sticking her head back in.

"Don't get on my back about this. I'll do it in my own way."

"Okay." Still smiling, she turned to leave again.

"Dusty."

"Yeah."

Tag really smiled this time. "Thanks, I guess."

"You're welcome, I guess."

"You're seeing to it that I get out. You're fixing me regular, balanced meals, decaffeinating my coffee and now forcing exercise on me. What do you think you're doing?"

"Only what common sense would dictate."

"And what's your next goal in my reform?"

Dusty pulled her eyes away from his telltale, absentminded rubbing of his leg and laughed. She was delighted to fall in with his light tone. "Uh, let's see. I guess I'd like to end your middle-of-the-night ramblings so you'll sleep better."

"You'll have to sleep with me to fix that."

"I'll think of another way," Dusty said, still smiling.

"Yeah. That's what I'm worried about. I've learned how determined you can be. I expect to see you hovering over me with a rubber hammer one of these nights."

Again Dusty laughed.

"Did Mr. Getty take the lamp back?"

"No. It was Mr. Cooms's switch that was bad. I'm glad, because it's hard to find nice lamps."

"Yeah, I've noticed what a winner that one is."

"That was an expensive lamp when it was—"

Dusty's words were interrupted by a knock at the kitchen door, the door she usually used.

"Who could that be?" Tag asked, immediately alert.

"It's okay. It's Jake. I'm supposed to help him turn over his garden today."

"His garden? On a day like this?"

"Yeah. It'll be fun, and it's a great day for it. The ground isn't frozen yet, nor is it too wet the way it can be in the spring." Again there was a knock. "I'd better go."

It felt good to be outside. The weather was cool as opposed to cold, and the sun was warm. Dusty actually got a bit of sunburn across her nose and cheeks. She looked more girlish than ever, as she always did with sun-blushed skin. When she came in, Tag was at the stove warming up soup for their lunch.

"Smells good," she said, feeling exhilarated and a little out of breath.

Tag studied her, his eyes coming to rest on her dirty pant cuffs and sneakers. "You'd better change."

"I will." She was heading down the hall.

"Twinkle, twinkle, little," said Louie-Louie.

"Star, damn it, you dummy."

The exercise equipment was delivered later that afternoon, and shortly after that Brent and Roger came by.

Dusty was delighted and welcomed the boys. "I'm so glad you're here." She noticed that Roger's eye looked better. "Did you go to school today?" she asked him.

His gaze dropped. "Yes."

"I hope you haven't gotten too far behind."

The boy shrugged a thin shoulder. Although he was much smaller, Dusty knew he was ten, almost a year older than Brent. His pale coloring and worn clothes added to his sorry-looking state. Dusty wondered if he was getting enough to eat. She knew better than to move too fast, however. She needed to gain his confidence, at least partially, before he'd feel comfortable about her stepping into his life.

"I see you brought your books. Perhaps between the three of us we can figure what to do without bothering your teacher. But I'd like to know her name and room number just in case."

This sounded reasonable to the boys and they cooperated. Dusty would get in touch with the woman at any rate. The more help she could garner the better.

She was also grateful that Brent had come and was showing an interest. By serving as a good example for Roger in trusting Dusty he made things easier. He acted as a buffer, so Roger could feel more relaxed, less in the limelight. The boy's natural reticence, which not only compounded his problem because it kept him from seeking help, made times like this more difficult for him.

He couldn't face Dusty directly, except for a few seconds at a time, and either lowered his eyes or turned away altogether. By the same token, Dusty could see he admired Brent. Anything Brent said that was even remotely funny caused a chuckle in Roger. This quality about him endeared him to Dusty, and she wanted all the more to help him.

"Well, that should tell us where we are," she said. She was finishing up her compilation of page numbers and familiarizing herself with Roger's books. "I'll see if Tag will fix some hot chocolate while Roger and I have our first lesson."

Brent rolled his eyes. He obviously felt this school business after school hours had gone on long enough. Roger laughed at Brent's antic, and Dusty had to chuckle, too.

"Tag," she called out, knocking at Tag's door. "Brent and Roger are here, and I was wondering if you'd mind fixing some hot chocolate."

Tag filled the doorframe. "You want me to fix hot chocolate so you can have a few minutes alone with Roger?"

"Right."

"Okay."

Going straight to the stove, with Brent lighting up at seeing him again, Tag set about putting the chocolate together. Even Louie-Louie came to life, shifting over on his perch to call out the few words he knew.

"I can tell we won't be able to accomplish much," Dusty said to Roger. "Actually, I'll be satisfied if you read a little for me. Do you think you can do that in the living room where it's less noisy?"

"Yes, ma'am."

Roger was invariably polite and cooperative. He seemed willing if not confident as he read the paragraph Dusty pointed out. At least he had those things going for him, Dusty thought, wanting to reach out and smooth the blondish hair that fell across his forehead. He was so obviously in need of someone to love him—someone who would not only teach him but who would cook regular meals for him and sew on the two buttons that were missing from his shirt. He was a motherless child, and Dusty understood that.

"You read well," she said truthfully. Being honest from square one was the most important thing she could do to build her relationship with Roger, and she was glad she had this truth to tell him. "I know it's not easy to concentrate with all the noise in the kitchen. Hopefully it'll be better after today when it's just you and me. But for now, why don't you help Tag and Brent with the hot chocolate? That's more fun than this."

"Yes, ma'am," Roger said, his voice barely a whisper.

"And you'll be sure to give this note to your dad, won't you?"

Roger sobered, her request threatening even the little confidence she had established.

"He'll need to know where you are each day after school and what we're doing. That's all this note says."

Roger nodded and took the envelope. He was obviously still unsure.

"Is there just you and your dad at home?" Dusty ventured.

Again Roger nodded, his eyes immediately lowering as a warning to her.

She knew they had done enough, come far enough for now, and got up from her chair.

"Tag? Is the chocolate ready?" She was moving into the kitchen where Tag and Brent stood in front of the stove. She noticed that Roger was tagging along behind her and hoped that was proof of her not having pushed him too hard. All Roger needed to decide was not to come, and then where would she be? Where would he be?

"I'm glad I watched you make this or I wouldn't know what to do," Tag said, glancing up at the new arrivals. His quick, smile at Roger, showed he was sensitive to how easily the boy could be overwhelmed.

Dusty was again impressed with how good he was with the boys. He had a natural affinity for children.

She went back to the living room, then. One adult at a time was enough for Roger. But as she went, she was thinking about Tag. He was more complex than she would have thought. There were layers to Tag— layers she'd like to know.

CHAPTER TWELVE

A WEEK LATER Dusty and Tag were having breakfast together in the kitchen, laughing and enjoying themselves. Over the past days, Tag had surprised Dusty by the changes he'd made in his schedule. He'd get up, use his bike, have his shower and dress, and then actually emerge from his hole to spend time with her.

They'd eat, of course, but the conversation, the contact, was the best. Indeed, Dusty warned herself against liking it too much.

Hearing the doorbell, Tag bolted down the last of his orange juice and went to answer it. When Dusty picked out the crisp speech of Ellen Daniels, her heart sank.

"Hello, Dusty," the visitor called, hovering in the kitchen doorway.

Dusty answered cheerfully enough. "Good morning, Ellen."

"Ellen has some stuff from headquarters," Tag said.

"Okay, I'll bring in coffee in a little while."

Ellen nodded brusquely before she and Tag walked off.

As soon as she could, Dusty flew the coop. She was wary of Ellen, and had an appointment for discussing Roger's problem with his counselor at school. That was disappointing. Nothing much could be done for Roger at this point. The evidence was too sketchy.

Ending her afternoon by finishing her Christmas shopping, Dusty slipped into the apartment just before she had to get supper together. She felt a little guilty when Tag and Ellen came into the kitchen. He looked done in by their marathon listening session.

"I'll help with the salad," he announced, stepping over to the sink and picking up the lettuce. Louie-Louie was quick to note Tag's arrival, but fell silent when he got a look at Ellen.

Tag had started helping with the cooking by fixing hot chocolate a couple of times, and he'd progressed steadily ever since. Dusty was teaching him the basics, and he was always anxious to put his new skills to use as soon as he learned them. Now she automatically made room for him at the sink, then turned back to the stove to stir the pot of chili she was watching.

"Something smells good," Ellen said directly to Tag, making no move to leave.

Dusty wasn't about to answer when she'd been so obviously left out, but Tag stepped into the breach by commenting over his shoulder, "Dusty's a good cook, and she's sharing her expertise with me."

"I can't imagine you cooking," Ellen said.

And then the inevitable happened. "Can you stay?" Tag asked.

Walking over, Ellen peered around Tag's shoulder. "I'd like to. Is there something I can do? I'm afraid I'm not much better at cooking than you are."

"I can't imagine you not being good at anything." Tag said.

Since Ellen remained where she was, Dusty felt she had to say something. "You don't need to help, Ellen. Just sit down."

"I could, at least, add my place setting to the table."

Dusty had hoped to remain aloof, but knew she had to be at least polite. She wouldn't want Tag to notice her ongoing "whatever it was" with Ellen Daniels. Really, she didn't know what Ellen's problem was. The woman certainly couldn't be jealous of the position Dusty had in the apartment. That seemed too unprofessional for this very professional person.

"Our tableware is rather primitive," Dusty said, "but you can help if you want. The gate leg on the table swings out, so I'd better do that. It's a little tricky."

Dusty proceeded to set up the table for three. She handed a place setting to Ellen, showed her how to tuck a napkin in a basket and add the little oyster crackers Tag liked to eat with her fire-starter chili. Tag was finishing the salad dressing, and then everything was ready.

"Shall we eat?" he asked.

Ellen and Tag talked about tapes and police work for the first half of the meal. Dusty could tell Ellen felt uncomfortable when she herself said something, so she satisfied herself with listening. She enjoyed hearing Tag talk, and just how good he was at his job was revealed in the bits and pieces of information that were dropped.

And soon Dusty was feeling better—maybe because she'd gotten some food into her stomach or maybe because it was a relief having Ellen's attention focused somewhere else. But whatever else it was, she certainly liked looking into Tag's animated features no matter who he was conversing with.

"Well, this little place certainly isn't like that hotel where we had our stakeout," Ellen said. "This place is positively... homey."

"Dusty's worked hard to get it to look like this."

Dusty could read the displeasure Tag's praise elicited in Ellen's pretty features—even if Tag couldn't.

"Of course, you didn't offer to foot the bills for putting that place in shape," Ellen added.

Dusty's eyes shot to Tag. "I thought your budget from the Department was paying for what I do here," she said, stunned by Ellen's news.

"It pays for some of it," he hedged, switching his clear blue eyes to the last of the chili in his bowl. "I'm thinking of staying on, so it's been no problem."

"Staying on?" Ellen repeated with her first show of emotion.

"Yeah. I've never really had the time to look for a place. I lived in a hotel my first few weeks in St. Louis, and then there was the downtown stakeout and the hospital. This apartment suits me, as does the neighborhood, so I'll probably stay here. We'll see." Tag ended with a casual shrug, spooning the last of his chili into his mouth.

But Ellen seemed unable to accept Tag's explanation. "Still and all, you could do better than this."

"Yeah, I could. But why should I? I'm never at home. Even when I do get a few weeks off."

"What do you do with your time off?" Dusty asked.

"I travel."

"Where?"

"Wherever I have enough time to go. I've seen a good bit of the country and most of Europe. The year before last, when I had a month and a half together. I took the Trans-Siberian Railroad across Russia. Nothing fancy. Just cheap travel like that."

"It sounds fantastic to me," Dusty said.

Ellen sat back on her chair, obviously reluctant to be part of a conversation involving Dusty, as well.

Tag, however, didn't seem to notice. He was smiling into Dusty's animated features. "It's definitely not the luxurious way to travel, but I see everything from a perspective most people wouldn't. It gives one a sort of grungy, meat-and-bones view of the world. But I like it."

"Give me a 'for example,'" Dusty coaxed, her palm to her chin and settling in.

"I have a friend who's a deep-water sailor, and I've hitched along with him a few times. He gets me a place on the crew of his ship as a fill-in for whoever's laying off. I work my way to wherever they're going. When we get there, I look around a bit and then fly home when my time's up."

"Sounds great," Dusty murmured. "A woman could never do that. As much as I like to travel, I haven't done much. Aside from a couple of trips to New York to visit my sister, my only big trip was a horrible spring vacation in Florida my junior year in college."

Tag's eyes were the warmest Dusty had ever seen them, picking up the candlelight and shining into hers. "You'd be good at my kind of traveling. Of course, you'd have to be tucked up in my bunk every night to

keep you safe from the clutches of the other crew-
men. Those guys are rough.''

"I've seen you face tougher," Ellen interjected.

Tag leaned back in his chair and sighed. "I suppose," he said in reluctant agreement.

"Suppose?" she repeated, as if displeased. "I've
seen you."

"I don't like to think about that day, Ellen."
Switching his gaze to Dusty, he said, "Would you get
the coffee, babe?"

But Ellen didn't fall in with Tag's attempt to change
the topic. "You have every reason to be proud of that
day, Tag. And I, for one, hate to see you running
down such a special day over a mere accident."

"That accident wasn't 'mere,' Ellen. To take a life
is not a 'mere' type of incident. It's a major thing.
About as major as you can get."

"Not so major as to let it ruin your life. You've allowed that accident to change you, Tag."

"I've told you before that I don't want to talk about
that day, Ellen, and I mean it."

"All right," the woman said, obviously not wanting to back down from her position but not wanting
to argue with Tag, either.

While Tag and Ellen had been arguing, Dusty had
put together the cheesecake and coffee. She set the
dessert, first before Ellen, and then Tag. Things were
still quiet when she sat down and added sugar and
cream to her cup. Tag looked unapproachable, his old
irritation written all over his face.

"Where else have you been, Tag?" Dusty ventured. For a moment she thought he wouldn't an-

swer, but then he did, his stare losing some of its intensity when he gazed into the warmth of hers.

"Brazil was interesting, if only because it was so different."

Ellen surprised them both by suddenly standing up. "I suppose I'd better go," she said, not really addressing either of them.

It was Tag who responded. "Why don't you finish your dessert first?"

An unlikely heat entered Ellen's green eyes. "Any good cop would give his eyeteeth to bring in the people we brought in that day. And I'm proud of what we did. To have you not be proud denigrates it for me."

"You can be as proud of that day as you want, Ellen. You can discuss that day ad infinitum for all I care. But don't keep bringing it up with me. I don't want to remember it. I don't want to think about it and dream about it. Do you understand?"

Ellen was immediately patient. "Of course, I understand, Tag. None of us wants to kill children, and I know how you must feel. But you have to get over it. Try to forget it. It was an accident. Why, you didn't even see it happen."

"It didn't take seeing the child die to make me feel this way. I'm still responsible, accident or no accident. Maybe I could have done something differently. Maybe not. I don't know. And I don't want to talk about it."

Things were really awkward after that. Within twenty minutes Ellen was gone, Tag was in his bedroom, and Dusty was finishing up the dishes and heading for her own room. After going through her usual evening routine, she lay awake, trying to put the bits and pieces of what she had heard at dinner into a saner whole. While her eyes were focused on the distorted blue rectangle on the ceiling of her bedroom, she wasn't considering that.

Tag and Ellen had been in a stakeout in a seedy hotel somewhere downtown. Tag had been new on the case, as well as to the city, and when it had come down to closing in and catching their quarry, a child had been killed. It had been an accident. Even Tag admitted that. Still, a child had died and Tag was suffering from it. He still dreamed about his tragic mistake. Yes. He had commiserated with her on her bad dreams. She remembered that now.

No wonder he couldn't sleep and wanted to be alone. No wonder he dreaded the day when the operation would finally come to a head and the police would close in to make their arrests. No wonder he disliked having her on his hands as an additional burden.

Alvarez had admitted that Tag had argued with him about not wanting to be responsible for her. Now she understood why. And, finally, she understood one of the few things she could remember him saying to her on the night when she had broken down and sobbed. He'd said that he too had cried and that he had done so recently. She realized now that he had wept over the child he had killed, and her heart wrenched at the thought. She could also understand the night he had stood with her in the dark of the hall with his gun in his hand, shaking like a leaf.

Dusty looked at the lighted dial of her clock. It was nearly two in the morning. She wondered if Tag would get up at three, as he said he usually did, and go out to the kitchen. She could picture him padding about, making a pot of coffee and sharing a word and a cracker with Louie-Louie. Her heart tore for him.

She really enjoyed their shared breakfasts and especially his talk at dinner. His eyes had been warm, reaching out to her in understanding. New visions crossed her mind. Tag working his way to foreign shores, walking unknown byways, solitary and...

Dusty thought she heard a sound—an unusual sound. She was accustomed to the regular noises the old apartment made. Wood would creak, radiator pipes would clank, but this was different. This sound was almost eerily human, almost...

It was Tag. He was groaning.

Without giving it another thought, Dusty was speeding, barefoot and clad only in her flannel pajamas, over the polished floorboards. She was out of her room and into Tag's in seconds.

Enough light filtered into Tag's room for her to see clearly. Tag was lying across his cot, dressed in slacks and an open shirt. He was quietly writhing, struggling with a dream.

Dusty reached a tentative hand to his forehead. The fact that he operated on a hair trigger made her go slowly. His brow was clammy, and Dusty sat back on her heels, trying to decide how, or even if, she should wake him.

When Tag groaned again, this time even more loudly, Dusty knew she couldn't watch him suffer. She moved close to him and, as gently as she could, laid an arm across his chest, pressing her cheek to his. "Tag," she whispered softly.

He didn't awaken with a start as she feared he might. Nor did he sit bolt upright. He opened his eyes, stared at the ceiling and gathered himself together by degrees. Dusty hung on to him, and he made no move to disengage himself.

"Tag," she said again.

"I'm awake."

Dusty felt herself yearning for his embrace.

"I'm okay now," he said, reaching a hand to switch on his bedside light.

Both Dusty and he squinted their eyes against the sudden sanity of the harsh glow, and she pulled away from him so that he could sit up.

"I'm sorry I woke you," he said, running his long fingers through his dark hair.

Dusty's heart thudded. He was the most attractive, the most vulnerable she had ever seen him. When he looked at her, however, his eyes were cool, reflecting his normal self-containment.

"I guess I'll go if you're all right," she murmured.

"No, don't. I mean, I'm all right. But if you're not sleepy..."

Dusty no more wanted to leave than he wanted her to. "Should I fix some coffee or hot chocolate maybe, or perhaps some warm milk?"

Tag actually chuckled. "I'm no invalid. Coffee'll be fine."

"I'll get my robe and slippers while you put on yours," she said.

"Robes and slippers are too relaxing."

"Not to relax doesn't sound healthy."

Dusty moved off to get her slippers and robe in her room, and Tag followed to watch. "I'm purposely so rough on myself that it's unhealthy," he said. "I use things so I don't forget where I am and what I'm doing. Things like the cot and staying partially dressed when I lie down. The cushy life you represent takes a guy's edge off. And when you lose your edge, you make mistakes."

Tag accompanied Dusty into the kitchen where she set up the drip coffeepot. She was reluctant to mention what Ellen had revealed at the dinner table, but felt compelled to. Maybe she could help Tag, if only by getting him to share his problem.

"You said tonight . . . to Ellen that you may have made a mistake on your last case."

Tag stiffened, pausing just as he was reaching for the mugs. Dusty thought for a moment that she had lost him, but then he spoke.

"I'm not sure if I made a mistake exactly. God only knows I've been over and over that afternoon to see if there was something I could have done differently. There are things, of course, but I wouldn't have known at the time . . . only in hindsight. . . ."

Dusty leaned against the counter, listening, while Tag stood looking into the pot of water she had put on to boil. If a pot could be stopped by watching, certainly theirs would never bubble, she thought, staring at the hard set of Tag's features.

"In that kind of a situation—in a shoot-out—things are happening so fast that it's training, experience and instinct that carry you through. It wasn't so much that I was thinking, but more that I was reacting like I'd been trained to react and as I'd reacted a dozen times before in similar situations. I don't know." Tag paused. "I was certainly trying to consider the possibilities. You just naturally do."

"Maybe if you told someone, shared it with...me."

Tag's eyes ran over her speculatively. His expression didn't reveal anything of what he might be thinking, and Dusty had no idea how her suggestion was being received.

"There's not much to tell," he finally said. "I came on the case toward the end of it. We were after a small crime ring, much like the Desotas and their henchmen. Ellen and I had been cooped up in a single room with a hot plate and a coffeepot for two weeks. Of course, in that kind of a neighborhood, no one notices or cares about their neighbors, so a cover isn't much of a problem. Anyway, I went out to pick up some groceries, and when I came back all hell had broken loose in the lobby. Things hadn't gone according to plan, as so often happens, and we had to close in right away." Again Tag paused, but once again he went doggedly on.

"I have to hand it to Ellen. She's a really good cop. She acted fast and called in the backup. Those guys were pinned down just outside the main entrance, so I ran in another way and, after a little more fire, it was over. Evidently...one of the children belonging to a woman who lived there had hidden behind a large overstuffed chair. It was no protection, of course, and...the bullet that was removed from the body was matched up to my weapon. Internal Affairs cleared me, but..."

While Dusty held in her groan, she couldn't keep the sympathy from shining in her eyes.

Tag rejected it immediately by stiffening his stance and hardening his voice. "Don't start with the platitudes. I've heard 'em all. I've even offered them to other people and meant them. Somehow words don't help, Dusty," he said more gently. "And they certainly don't change things. It's something I'll have to learn to live with."

Tag sank onto a kitchen chair and sat, staring down at his hands, while Dusty turned to pour the now-boiling water into the top half of the prepared drip pot.

"The boy was the same age as Brent," Tag said very quietly. "Nine years old."

This was the most poignant of all, and it took all of Dusty's restraint not to run to him and take him into her arms. As if things weren't bad enough for Tag, every time he was with Roger and Brent he was reminded all over again of the boy who had died that afternoon downtown.

Both Dusty and Tag listened, in the stillness of the room, to the water trickle through the coffee grounds. She wished with all her heart that she had some words of wisdom that would comfort him or at least soothe the fresh pain.

Thankfully Tag got up and walked over to uncover the parrot. "Louie-Louie," he said, rousing the bird. He had evidently shelved his most sensitive subject yet again.

The parrot began his little speech, but Tag didn't respond. He had his back to Dusty, and she barely heard it when he spoke to her instead. "Thanks for not saying anything, Dusty."

Dusty took that as her best reward. It was enough that he had shared with her and that she had listened. That she couldn't console him, that she couldn't mend his wound, didn't count. What did matter was that Tag and she had come close tonight, and that closeness wouldn't be easily undone.

Dusty carried their mugs to the table, along with the last slice of cheesecake, which she split with Tag. He didn't say anything when he came over to sit down and take part in their three o'clock snack. The silence was comfortable, however, and Dusty could feel herself growing sleepy in spite of her emotional turmoil.

She observed Tag over the rim of her coffee mug. He didn't seem to be suffering, either, and that helped her more than anything.

"What have you been advised to do about Roger Maddox?" he asked, breaking the silence.

"Louie-Louie," said the parrot at the sound of Tag's voice.

"He thinks I've forgotten his cracker."

"I'll get it," Dusty offered, getting up from her chair. "I don't know why I do this. He doesn't like me at all."

"I've noticed that he hasn't taken to Pam, either." Tag watched while Dusty handed the reluctant parrot the cracker. The old fellow took it in a hoary claw, biting into it with a relish only when she looked away.

"Maybe I could bribe him into liking me with crackers and cookies," Dusty said, smiling and sitting down. She sighed, thinking of Tag's question about Roger. "It's a complicated business. I've got the right people alerted, and now we wait and watch. His dad hasn't been around enough lately for anything to have happened."

"It's too bad you have to wait until next time," Tag said caustically.

"I suppose you've seen cases like this before."

"Yeah. Too many. It's another pleasant chore in my pleasant business." Again he lapsed into silence, and Dusty also remained quiet until she thought of something she'd been wanting to ask him—of something that would change the subject. "Christmas is coming up. Do you think I should get a tree?"

"Yeah, it'll look good."

Tag's comment showed Dusty how continuously he evaluated everything in terms of his work and their job here. It was somehow disappointing.

Dusty got up to wash their dishes and Tag came over to help. When they were finished, she turned from hanging her dishrag on the towel rack she had installed with her handy screwdriver and bumped into the wall of his chest. Her eyes ran immediately to his, her mind just as speedily zipping back to the day he had kissed her very near to this spot.

"I . . . I guess I'd better get some sleep."

"Yeah, you better," Tag said softly. He stroked the back of his fingers against her cheek, but disappointed her by stepping away.

"Don't worry. I won't come on to you anymore." He smiled. "I want to, but I won't. You don't like it, and I've grown to respect you for all the good things you do—things like waking me so sweetly and listening to me so quietly. I guess what I'm trying to say is I want to be your friend, Dusty. It's hard to believe that a guy could have such a valiant little friend in such a cute little package, but, well, I'd like for us to be friends.''

"So would I," Dusty said breathlessly.

She couldn't believe it when Tag offered his hand for her to shake, but she took it, his large grasp enveloping hers in its warmth.

"God, this is unreal," he said with another chuckle. "I'd feel much more natural with a good-night kiss.''

"All right," Dusty said hopefully.

Again Tag chuckled, leaning forward to kiss her forehead. "Look at what you've done to me. Handshakes and brotherly kisses. I think I've been unmanned.''

"I doubt it," she replied with an answering twinkle.

"So do I. Especially with the way I'm feeling right now.''

Dusty sobered quickly. "Do you think you can sleep?'' she asked, hoping to reroute the conversation.

"Yeah. I guess. At least I won't have the dream again. It doesn't usually repeat, thank goodness.''

"How often do you have it?''

Dropping her hand, Tag walked over to cover Louie-Louie. "A few times a week.''

Dusty was appalled, but the one thing Tag couldn't accept from her was her sympathy. "Well, good night,'' she said at last.

"Good night, babe," he called after her.

THE HEIGHTS AND DEPTHS Dusty and Tag had traversed together the night before spilled over somewhat into the next day. It was obvious they felt closer and, although it went unacknowledged, it colored their interaction. They had a pleasant breakfast, Dusty getting permission to purchase a hassock at Mr. Getty's. Tag claimed he'd want a couch—if he decided to stay on—but Dusty's idea of using a hassock with the big armchair seemed like a good one for the time being.

Not ten minutes after Tag disappeared down the hallway, Dusty had to leave her dishes in the suds and answer the front door. She was amazed to find Ellen Daniels on the stoop, but especially to see, by the look on her lovely face, that she had probably slept as little as either Tag or Dusty had.

"Ellen." Dusty was even more amazed that her heart went out to the definitely subdued beauty. "Won't you come in?"

"No," Ellen said, stiffening a bit. "There were two tapes I didn't bring yesterday, and I promised Tag I'd drop them by."

"Are you sure you wouldn't like to see him?" Dusty asked, wondering why she was being so generous. Ellen had never responded to her least overtures.

When the woman actually lowered her eyes, Dusty softened completely. "Come in, Ellen. Talk to Tag."

Although she stepped over the threshold, Ellen still didn't say anything. Nor did she send Dusty the usual cool signals. She was truly unsure of herself. Dusty couldn't believe it.

Draping her coat over the back of one of the living room chairs, Ellen went to Tag's room and Dusty went back to the kitchen. She'd barely gotten to her dishes when the door to Tag's room clicked shut. Turning, she saw Ellen coming toward her.

The woman appeared ashen, even distraught. Dusty couldn't figure either what to do or how to react. "Do you think you should sit down, Ellen?"

Ellen shook her head.

"How about a cup of coffee? I just made a fresh pot."

The woman seemed reluctant but finally nodded, so Dusty poured coffee and carried it to the small table by the sunny window. "Come on, sit down."

Louie-Louie moved over on his perch, trying to get farther away from the two women and working his mouth in silent displeasure.

"Can I do something for you, Ellen? Call someone? Are you unwell?"

"No, I'm all right. It's just that I don't know... what to do about Tag."

"I'm sure Tag isn't angry with you," Dusty ventured as Ellen also sat down. "He's not the type to hold a grudge or remain upset for long."

"No. He said he isn't mad at me."

Ellen took a sip of coffee, and Dusty couldn't think of what to say. She couldn't even imagine what was wrong.

"It's just that... well, you seem so easy with Tag."

"I'm hardly easy—"

"No, no. I could see that right off. And he's always been complimentary about you as well."

Dusty felt tongue-tied in her amazement. Still, she wanted to help Ellen if she could. Once a woman like Ellen managed to open up to someone, the hearer certainly had to respond.

"Tag's always spoken highly of you, too," Dusty offered. "I know he respects you and how you handle your job. He said so just last night."

Ellen peered at Dusty as if she was also surprised. "He did?"

"He said that you handled the last case you were on together very well. Especially when you arrested those men at the hotel."

Just that quickly Ellen's face fell back into an expression of despair. "That's when I started feeling that he disliked having me as his partner. I've gone over and over that day, and I don't know what I did wrong. Tag's attitude toward me changed that day, and I don't know why."

Dusty felt a sudden relief at realizing what had probably happened. Reaching across the table, she squeezed Ellen's beautifully kept hand. "Somehow you've gotten things wrong, Ellen. I mean, I'm the last one to claim I understand Tag, but I do know some of how he feels about what occurred that day. What he's struggling with has nothing to do with you. He's wrestling with himself... with his feelings for that little boy."

"But he didn't even know about the boy until two days later. How can he feel culpable when it was so obviously an accident?"

"I don't know really. But he does. So you see, it doesn't have anything to do with your being his partner. In fact, as soon as this is over, as soon as he begins to deal with his turmoil, I'm sure you'll have the same old Tag back as your partner again."

Ellen sat up straighter, looking into Dusty's eyes. "I've been unfair to you. I've been so tied up in trying to figure out what's wrong with Tag and me that I saw you as part of the problem. I thought that I should be here, and—"

"I understand."

Ellen actually smiled a little. "You have to let me apologize, you know."

Dusty smiled more broadly. "Okay, apologize and get it over with. Then I'll get us each a fresh cup of coffee."

CHAPTER THIRTEEN

"DUSTY?"

"I'm in the kitchen."

Tag walked to where Dusty sat at the table and, reaching over her shoulder, took a long swallow of her diet cola. "Didn't you say something about going to the grocery store this morning?"

"That's why I'm making this list. I'm buying my Christmas cookie baking stuff. Why? Do you want anything in particular?"

"No. I'm coming along."

Tag sported sweatpants and a white T-shirt from his morning's exercise, and was wiping down his head with a yellow towel. He looked wonderful to Dusty. He seemed healthy, and she loved being on easy terms with him. He hardly ever scowled now, and their conversations had become natural. Of course, she didn't see much more of him than she ever had, so their occasional walks through the neighborhood were a treat.

"Do you have an excuse for going to the hardware store?" he asked.

"I can always go to the hardware store."

"Anywhere else?"

"We could go to the Laundro—"

"Oh, no," he protested. "The Laundromat is permanently out."

"Mr. Getty's, then?"

Tag chuckled with relish. "Yeah, Mr. Getty's. I haven't been there yet." After setting her empty glass beside her, he sauntered back toward the bathroom. "Just remember, no more buying from him. I don't care what the old fox offers."

"Just wait. Mr. Getty'll be a test for even your willpower."

"Fat chance."

A half hour later the pair hit the sidewalks in a mood of camaraderie. There was a brisk wintry wind, and Dusty pulled her knit cap down to cover her ears. Reaching over and taking her gloved hand in his, Tag smiled at her. "This is the best part, being able to use your lovely little person in order to look like newly-weds."

Dusty smiled and faced the wind, a tiny thrill scuddering over her nerve endings.

They reached Hauptman's Market first. It was one of the last of the mom-and-pop grocery stores in the area, and it was small, jam-packed and totally disorganized—three qualities that made it one of Dusty's favorite haunts.

While Dusty exchanged greetings with Mrs. Hauptman, who was manning the new computer at the checkout, Tag fetched a metal shopping basket. Dusty recognized Mrs. Hauptman's immediate show of interest and realized how right Tag was in coming. His appearance was sure to be recounted by the small circle that shopped at Hauptman's, especially since he was so good-looking.

He was large and vital as he walked through the cramped aisles, pausing while Dusty picked out her purchases. She was as careful a shopper here as any-where, and double-checked prices on items Tag would have just dumped into the basket.

"Well, you shouldn't have come," she said when he gave her an arch look.

"I don't mind," he answered. "But spending five minutes on a difference of two cents for a box of hot cereal is going a bit far."

"It's your two cents."

"Exactly. And I say spend it."

As if to prove his point, Tag tossed two boxes of the slightly more expensive brand of cereal into the basket with a flourish. Dusty shrugged.

The pair split up in the last aisle, Dusty to take their purchases to Mrs. Hauptman's checkout while Tag went on to get the soda that wouldn't fit in the basket. There were two people waiting to be checked out ahead of her, and she smiled into the faces that were vaguely familiar before going on to double-check her purchases against her coupons.

Coming up on her unawares, Tag put his soda on the floor and wrapped her in a bear hug from behind.

"Did you miss me, babe?" he said, close against her ear.

Dusty glanced at the group around the checkout. They were now, naturally, watching her and Tag. She actually blushed, but suppressed her automatic urge to squirm away.

Tag didn't let go of her, either. He leaned over her from behind, smoothing his cheek against hers. "Your blush is just the right touch," he whispered, only for her.

Those words were the very ones to quell her mounting warmth. *This is an act, Dusty.* Still, she had to lower her eyes to her coupons. Even when Tag's hold loosened and he stood closely behind her with an arm around her waist, she tried not to wriggle away.

When they stepped forward to put their goods on Mrs. Hauptman's conveyor belt, Dusty could see that Tag was making the impression he wanted to make. Mrs. Hauptman's eyes ran to him every chance they got, while her little glances to Dusty said, "How lucky can you get?"

Finally Dusty was able to replace her powder-blue cap and gloves and leave. Tag followed in her wake. He carried their groceries in his arms and seemed to be quite jovial. Dusty was torn between gritting her teeth against his smiles and squeezes and succumbing with an answering happiness.

"So," he asked, "where to next?"

"Mr. Getty's?"

"Ah, yes, Mr. Getty's," Tag repeated, the light of battle shining in his eyes.

Dusty led the way into the glass-plated storefront with its gilt-and-black lettering on the dirty window. The tinkling bell, which was now as familiar to her as any sound, rang when they walked in, beckoning Mr. Getty from behind the draped opening of his store-room.

"Hold your ground, Dusty," Tag whispered watching the old man shuffle in their direction.

Mr. Getty peered over the rim of his glasses, sizing up this new quantity that was John Taggert. Dusty's eyes slid to the pale blue of Tag's. She was surprised to see that he was sizing up the wizened old man, just as he was being weighed by the shopkeeper's watery gaze. Dusty could almost see the men coming to their conclusions. Then, with an almost imperceivable nod on the old man's part, the battle was joined.

"Can I help you?"

"No," said Tag lightly. "We're just browsing."

"Good, good," seconded the old man, falling in with Tag's ploy.

Mr. Getty stepped aside, letting the couple pass. The normal confusion of used goods and grit hadn't changed, and Dusty watched while Tag's eyes slid over the odd collection of discards. He walked through the narrow aisles, with his hands clasped behind his back and a definite swagger. Dusty followed.

"The old fellow seems innocuous enough," Tag murmured when they were far enough away. "Frankly, Dusty, I don't see why you can't say no to the man."

"I do say no to the man," she whispered, her eyes sneaking a reassurance that the subject of their conversation couldn't hear them.

"Then why does over half the stuff we live with come from here?" Tag was teasing, but there was a subtle goad in his words that served to raise Dusty's hackles. What was even more frustrating was her inability to answer him.

Just then Mr. Getty called to her. "I've got something you might be interested in, girl."

"I . . . I'm not interested, Mr. Getty. We've got the apartment furnished now, and Tag's only looking for something to hang on the walls."

"I haven't got much for hanging on walls," Mr. Getty actually admitted, rubbing his chin in thought.

"But I do have a box of Christmas ornaments. Just came in yesterday, and I thought about you."

"I'm afraid I'm not interested, Mr. Getty."

"Certainly you're going to have a tree, aren't you, girl?"

"Yes, we'll be buying a tree. But I plan to use natural decorations," she said, confidently, even as Mr. Getty pointed to the open cardboard box that yawned at their feet.

Dusty could see ancient strands of lights, the bulbs still in their sockets, and everything tangled around a bedraggled tinsel garland. There were shiny Christmas balls, some of them broken, and even a lopsided angel for the top of the tree.

"Sorry," she said with a sure smile and without the slightest hesitation. "I plan to string popcorn and make gingerbread boys."

"Hey, those are bubble lights!" Tag exclaimed.

Dusty looked up to see that Tag's gaze was riveted to the contents of the box. "I haven't seen bubble lights since I was a kid."

Dusty couldn't believe it. "I'm going to buy ribbon and candy canes."

"Most of the light bulbs are good," Mr. Getty commented. "I plugged them in myself."

Dusty's eyes sliced immediately to his and, seeing that familiar, knowing look there, she flashed them just as speedily to Tag's. But his were held fast to the box.

"It's a real good deal," Mr. Getty was saying. "Especially when popcorn on a tree can attract mice."

"I don't know." Tag's gaze was now locked with Mr. Getty's. "The stuff's awfully beat-up."

"Who knows," Mr. Getty coaxed. "Some of it might be collectible."

Tag snorted his disbelief at this artful try, his gaze not leaving Mr. Getty's wrinkled features.

"It's certainly usable," the shopkeeper countered.

Tag lifted a broad shoulder. "Yeah, it's usable, but just barely."

"I'm going to cut doves from white felt," Dusty said.

The men merely glanced at her; she was out of the discussion altogether.

"Mr. Getty's right, babe. Food on a tree attracts mice."

"It does not," she insisted.

"Seeing as how you two are just getting started, I'll throw in a tree stand," Mr. Getty said magnanimously.

"Let's have a look at it," Tag replied.

"Oh, no," Dusty murmured. She could see her dreams of a yummy Christmas tree fading away fast.

Mr. Getty produced the battered stand almost magically and definitely as if he'd had it ready for precisely such an occasion. Tag scoffed when the rusted thing wobbled at the touch of one of his long fingers.

"So put a book under one leg and wrap a pillowcase around the base. It'll look like the tree's standing in a snowdrift, and the stand will still hold a nice-sized tree, even with that kink in one leg."

Dusty made a last-ditch effort. "I'm going to string cranberries."

"Cranberries rot," Tag said without looking at her. His gaze was still locked onto the equally piercing gaze of the shopkeeper.

The old man murmured one more price and, with a victorious look springing into his eyes, Tag shouted, "Done!"

He, too, had been bamboozled. *Only he'll never admit it,* Dusty said to herself. *Not any more than Pam did.*

Tag and Mr. Getty shook hands while Dusty counted out her pennies. When Mr. Getty turned his back to get a pencil, Tag even sent Dusty a quick wink—very like the one Pam had given her.

"Come back," the wily fellow called out when Tag hefted the box onto his shoulder, a silly smile planted on his features.

Even when the cardboard box opened at a seam and showered Tag with a fine sprinkling of dust, he barely noticed. He continued to bear the same sweet smile of victory—the very one that Pam had worn the day she had matched wits with Mr. Getty and "won" Louie-Louie.

Dusty caught a final glimpse of the now-familiar glint in the shopkeeper's eyes when she passed him by in his window. At last he confirmed what she had always guessed. He sent her a barely perceptible wink that said it all—and that he would surely deny if she claimed he'd done such a thing. But he had shared it with her nonetheless, and she had to smile back.

"How'd I do?" Tag asked, almost gloating.

Dusty chuckled. "I don't know. How did you do? That appears to be one box of very garish junk to me."

He was a tad insulted. "But think what all this stuff would cost new."

"And that's my point. I wasn't going to buy any of it new." Dusty's quip took a bit more of the shine out of Tag's eyes. "Don't feel bad," she added. "I know the feeling. In fact, I'd be willing to bet there's not a single person in the neighborhood who doesn't know the feeling."

Since Tag continued to look down in the dumps, Dusty turned perky. "Come on, let's go to Mr. Cooms's hardware store and buy some light bulbs. We'll go home and plug in the strands, and then we'll know what kind of a bargain you've struck with Mr. Getty." As Tag looked only grimmer, Dusty continued. "If you want, I'll bake cookies. Do you like chocolate chip?"

"Who doesn't?" he muttered as Dusty helped him into the door at the hardware store.

"Dusty!" Mr. Cooms called out, coming over with a broad smile marking his grandfatherly features.

"This is my husband, Mr. Cooms."

"Mr. Taggert," replied the man.

Tag had to put his box on the floor before he could accept Mr. Cooms's hand.

"I see you've been to Mr. Getty's," the shopkeeper commented, peering down into the box of Christmas things.

"Yes," Tag admitted.

Mr. Cooms laughed softly. "Don't feel badly, son. He's been digging that box of decorations out for the past few years. He's tried to sell it to everyone who's stepped over his threshold, and I'm glad to see the pair of you came to an amicable agreement."

Dusty switched her eyes to Tag's, uncertain as to how he would react. This revelation had definitely tarnished the last of his glow, so when Tag's gaze sliced just as swiftly to Dusty's she was surprised at her sense of relief. Their locked stares filled with laughter, the resultant merry sound drawing Mr. Cooms into its embrace.

"Come on, Tag," he said. "Seeing as how your wife is such a good customer, the light bulbs for those strands are on me."

"That's not necessary, Mr. Cooms."

"No," the fellow agreed, "but it's not long until Christmas and I want to do it. You have a grand little gal there, you know."

"Yeah, I do know," Tag announced as if he meant it.

After the hardware store, all they had to do was get a tree and make their way back to the apartment with their load of purchases.

"Didn't you mention something about cookies?" Tag asked once they were back in their apartment and had dropped everything in mutual relief.

Dusty was out of her coat, her face rosy with their stint in the cold air. "Okay. I don't have an electric mixer, though, so it'll take a while."

Tag was already moving toward his room. "Let me check in with headquarters and I'll be back."

"Have you ever made cookies?"

"Me?"

"Yeah, you."

"No, but I have a feeling I'm about to."

The chocolate chip cookie dough was heavy going without a mixer, but Tag stuck to it. He even went on to make a second batch.

THE NEXT DAY Tag set up the Christmas tree and decorated it, while Dusty cleaned all the various odds and ends in the box. She finally insisted on throwing out the tinsel garland altogether. It was simply too shabby, and even Tag had to admit it. But Dusty was the one to capitulate when Tag put the refurbished angel on the uppermost spot—for the tree was charming.

"What next?" he asked with a big grin.

"I'm wrapping boxes in the kitchen. You can arrange them under the tree." Dusty moved to the table of gay Christmas wrap with Tag following.

"These boxes feel awfully light," he said hefting each one.

"That's because they're empty."

"Empty?"

"Well, except for the ones for Pam and Brent and Roger. But I thought it should appear as if we were exchanging gifts, so I got the boxes."

Tag followed Dusty into the living room, where he helped her place the false packages around the tree. Stepping back to peer at her handiwork, Dusty sighed contentedly. "It looks like a real Christmas."

"It sure does. It feels and smells like it, too. Do you miss your sister?"

"Yeah. We've never been apart at Christmas. I sent her things in the mail. Do you have a spare sock?"

"A sock?" Tag was obviously puzzled.

"To hang by the chimney with care."

Tag laughed. "In case you haven't noticed, we don't have a chimney."

"The windowsill will do," Dusty said. "I'm using a striped knee sock, but I know you don't have anything that imaginative."

"Nor do I have anything that will hold so much," he teased, playing the game. "I'll get a sweatsock."

Tag was the one to thumbtack the odd socks to the high sill on the art glass window in the living room.

"There," Dusty announced with a final look at her efforts.

"It sure looks and feels like Christmas to me," Tag reiterated, as if finding it hard to believe. "I haven't enjoyed the holidays this much since I was a kid. I almost wonder if Mr. Claus might just bring me something, after all. What do you think, pal?" he asked, turning a broad grin on Dusty.

"You never know," she replied. "Well, I guess I'll run back to the hardware store for those two extra bubble lights we need. You don't mind, do you?"

"No, no. Only stay away from Mr. Getty's."

Dusty was glad to get out by herself for a minute. She'd been feeling...oh, touchy, lately. And it wasn't just the situation. That much she did know.

She felt fortunate when she saw Brent ahead of her on the sidewalk as she neared the apartment on her way back. She wasn't up to examining her "touchy" feelings too closely and welcomed any distraction. Coming up behind him, she reached forward to put her gloved hands over his eyes. "Guess who?" she called cheerily.

"Aw, Dusty," he said.

Matching her step to his, she noticed the droop to his shoulder that accompanied his unusual lack of welcome. "What's wrong, honey?"

"Nuthin'."

"Come on. That's no answer. You can tell me. Remember, I'm a good listener."

The boy looked at her from the corner of his eye. "Yeah, you are. It's just that . . ."

"Just that . . . ?"

"You can't do anything."

"Try me."

Glancing at the passing traffic and back, Brent swallowed hard. Dusty's heart went out to him, and she put an arm around his shoulders, just as so many people had done with her in the past.

"Come on, honey."

At last the tears filled Brent's eyes. "Mom was crying last night—while she wrapped the Christmas gifts she's sending to Memphis."

"Oh," murmured Dusty. "I see."

"She cries every year, but . . . I don't know. It bothers me."

"I know it does. The whole situation seems a shame."

"Yeah," he said, almost using his sleeve for his nose before she pulled a tissue from her pocket.

"I've been wondering, in fact . . ."

"Wondering?" he asked, peering at her.

"If you might not be the one to do something."

"Me?"

"Who else *can* help?" she asked. "Your mom says everyone in the family has tried, but that your grandfather won't listen. You're a member of the family, too, you know. Maybe you're the one he'll listen to."

"But I've never talked to him."

"You don't need to use the phone if that idea scares you. There's such a thing as the U.S. Mail, you know."

Once again Brent peered at her, the possibility beginning to take hold. "Would you help me write?"

"Oh, no," she said, jostling him. "This has to be your letter... your thoughts."

The boy still looked dubious when she left him on the stoop. Even so he gave her a quick hug, and she prayed that she might have helped.

CHAPTER FOURTEEN

TAG'S EYES DRIFTED over the familiar sight before him. The crummy little room was as crummy as ever. He was trying to settle into his early-afternoon routine, but the usual restlessness was making it difficult.

The Nikon sat, ready to go, in the window. The tape deck was slowly revolving, recording Syd's naptime sounds. His police radio was alive with the ongoing events of the world of cops and robbers—a world he knew as well as this little room.

Damn dull stuff.

He prodded himself to remain alert. A stakeout like this was dull to the point of being deadly. Things could heat up before he knew it, and all hell could break loose right under his nose.

He had to stay sharp. But this surveillance was taking his edge off. He wasn't much more than a robot running on automatic, but he had to be alert.

He knew the work that had always filled his life and thoughts, the work that had taken up most of his hours, was still important. But it was no longer important to him.

This stunning truth wasn't so new anymore as to be shocking, but it remained frightening. It was imperative that he be interested in what he was doing, both to do this assignment well and for his future. Police work was all he had ever wanted to do and all he had ever done. He couldn't imagine what his life would be like or what *he* would be like if he got so he couldn't stand to do it anymore.

Oh, it had always been hard for him. He hadn't escaped the anxiety that all cops live with. He had taken that fear in stride, however, just as did most of his peers. But it was different now—had been different since his last case. He didn't know, in fact, if he could face doing it anymore, and that scared him most of all.

Resettling himself on his metal chair, he let his head drop back and stared at the ceiling. He wanted something to happen. He wanted the case to move to its natural conclusion so that he could get out of this room.

On the other hand, there was a part of him, a growing part, that wanted his days to go on as they were. He was learning things here that he had never known before. The simple things in life had entered his experience when Dusty Landry had moved in with him. She was affecting him more than even Alvarez would have thought possible. She was introducing him to parts of himself that he would never have thought existed.

He'd found that he liked to cook, for example, and had spent the morning trying to produce a pot of potato soup that was as good as Dusty's. Hell, he'd been pleased when she'd said he'd done it. And that was oddest of all.

But it was more than cooking. He had always liked his nephews and one niece, had always communicated with them as easily as he had with Brent when he had first met him. But he saw now that that aspect of himself ran deeper. Something in the way Dusty cared for little Roger Maddox had sparked a like reaction in himself. Roger needed caring and, like Dusty, he responded to that deep down inside.

And then there were the feelings he had for Dusty. Naturally those feelings hadn't always been entirely on the up-and-up. But while he still desired her physically, something gentler—again, one of those better things in life—had developed between them. Friendship. A friendship that he wouldn't have thought possible with a woman now meant a lot to him.

Oh, he had a friendship with Ellen Daniels, as well. But that wasn't the "best friends" sort. His and Dusty's was the kind where he could say anything he wanted to say, and she would, if not understand, then at least not stand in judgment. Ellen was too good at making judgments.

And thus the most amazing aspect of all. He, who had always been labeled the strong, silent type, had discovered he was something of a motor mouth. He spent hours talking with Dusty.

It had started because she'd encouraged him. She was a good listener, and her listening had brought out tales of his travels. Those had led to his retelling of the stories he had almost forgotten, but that he loved so well. The ones his dad had told him. Stories of police work and adventure. Stories that had filled his heart and mind when he'd been a child and that had inspired his own desire to be a policeman.

No one had ever listened to him the way Dusty did. Now he even felt tempted to try putting the old stories that had intrigued him as a child down on paper.

But there were other unexpected pleasures in his life. Conversations with Jake, just like conversations with Roger, interested him. They made him laugh and feel something he hadn't felt in a long time—warmth. Contact with other human beings was good. But he hadn't allowed himself that kind of real contact since the best friend he'd ever had died. His dad.

Another unexpected pleasure was the growing affection that Louie-Louie demonstrated for him. There was no doubt that the old bird brightened when he walked into the kitchen and that really pleased him.

But this tug of pleasure scared him. It was dulling his edge, and he knew he had to be razor-sharp—especially for the day when it would all go down, when they'd move in to make the bust. That day would try him, perhaps, once and for all, and he didn't know if he could handle it. What were little pleasures in comparison to a day like that? Nothing. He had to somehow get through that day before he could fully experience anything else.

So, as much as he could, he made himself stay in his room. And away from Dusty.

Unfortunately Dusty didn't always take the hint. Oh, she knew when he wanted to be alone, but she didn't let that deter her. If she wanted to say something, she'd simply walk in—closed door or no closed door. In fact, he'd given up on that ploy.

There. He could hear her. She was supposed to be at the kitchen table, getting ready for Roger's lesson, but he could hear her coming down the hallway. He swiveled his head toward the doorway, feeling both disgruntlement and...yes, damn it, the expectation of pleasure.

He watched as she stopped in the doorway, her determination plain in her pixie features. He experienced an urge both to smile and to toss her out. And also that other urge that was invariably there.

"Tag," she said "I've been thinking."

"Um."

"Don't 'um' me."

"Um."

"I've been thinking that you should write down some of the stories you've been telling me. You know, the ones your dad told you."

"Um."

"I'm serious."

"Do you realize how many times you've said that in one way or another over the past week or so?"

"I guess I've tried to say it a lot. But that's because I mean it. You tell a great story. That's a gift, you know."

Tag looked at the floor between his knees. "I suppose. But there aren't all that many people who want to sit around and listen to me weave tales, and I doubt I could make a living by passing the hat. You just happen to be a captive audience as well as an extraordinarily appreciative one."

"It's not just me. Everybody likes those kinds of stories. That's why you can see cop-and-robber capers on TV almost any night of the week."

Tag's eyes narrowed as he studied Dusty's solemn regard of him. "I know what you're thinking."

"What am I thinking?"

"You're thinking that my dad got me so enamored with police work that I was caught up in it before I was old enough to know better."

Dusty switched her gaze to the toe of her sneaker. This talk wasn't easy for either of them. "Maybe before you could make an adult's choice would be closer."

Tag shrugged. "Either way it amounts to the same thing."

"But you are considering leaving the force?"

"I've considered it in the past. Even before the last case. But, it all comes down to the same thing. I don't know what else I'd want to do—or even what I'm capable of doing."

"You said you enjoyed being with your friend, working on that tanker."

She didn't say this as if it were a good idea, and Tag had to chuckle. "There's no way I'd do that on anything but a temporary basis."

"You could cook," Dusty said, also chuckling before she sobered. "You could write."

This time Tag didn't laugh. "I don't have much education, Dusty."

"But you certainly know your subject and you tell a great tale." When he didn't answer, she went on undaunted. "Have you ever tried?"

Tag could feel the irritation building. "Of course not."

"Why don't you try?" Dusty was no longer put off by the frosty look he sent her. She knew as well as he that that was for other people, not for her.

"I wouldn't know how to even begin," he muttered.

"You're an avid reader."

Tag shrugged a shoulder. He didn't know how to say no so that Dusty would listen. Fortunately the doorbell interrupted. "Didn't you say Rog is due here for a lesson?"

Dusty hurried out to answer the door. "How are you?" she said as she let Roger into the apartment. The boy seemed all right. He showed no visible evidence of having been abused since she'd last seen him.

"Come in out of the cold. Are you hungry? Would you like a bowl of Tag's soup before we start?" She realized that neglect was a part of Roger's problem and tried to feed him as often as he would eat.

"Okay."

Dusty hung Roger's coat on the rack and followed him into the kitchen. She wasn't surprised to see that Tag had come out, too. He had obviously been thinking along the lines that she was because he'd put a pot on the stove and was getting the soup he had made out of the refrigerator.

Roger didn't hesitate as he might have in the past, and Dusty took that as a good sign.

"Hi there, Rog," Tag said with a bit of a smile. "How's it going?"

"Fine."

"How about giving me an opinion on this soup I made? I say it's better than Dusty's and she says it isn't."

"Okay."

Tag continued to chatter as Dusty slipped out of the room. She wanted the pair to have time together so that the boy wouldn't feel he was being constantly monitored by her.

Curling up in a chair by the lit Christmas tree—it always seemed to be on—Dusty looked over Roger's latest assignment. He was bright, but so far behind it discouraged him. After a little while he came in to where she sat, and Dusty heard Tag go back to his room.

"I thought we'd sit in here today and talk about this little writing assignment I asked you to do. The one on yourself."

Roger nodded.

"Come on. Sit down next to me," she coaxed him, making room for him in the big armchair.

She felt the slight reluctance in this little body, but noticed that he relaxed as soon as she put his assignment in his lap.

"You did a really good job. I've marked the few mistakes you made and thought we might discuss it as a whole."

Once again he nodded, and Dusty plunged ahead.

"You say that you moved here from Miami last summer to live with your dad. Miami's a hard word to spell, so I wrote it there on the side. Anyway, your grandma died, and her house was sold. You don't say anything else about your family. And while I liked hearing about the neat park you played in every day after school, I thought you might tell me more about your family."

"I don't have no one else. My mom died when I was a baby and my grandma raised me."

Sensing the sadness in Roger's eyes, Dusty knew to move on—at least for now. "And your dad? You don't say anything about him."

The boy shrugged, his eyes glued to his papers.

"It's just you and your dad in . . . in what? Do you have a house or an apartment like Tag and I do?"

"An apartment."

"Do you have your own room?"

Roger nodded.

"Do you want to tell me about it?"

The boy shrugged, but then shook his head. "I don't like it much," he finally said.

"Are you at home alone most of the time?"

"Yeah. My dad's gone a lot to Miami."

"And there's no one to cook for you? To be there when you get home?"

"We have a neighbor, but my dad doesn't like her much. I mostly find things in the kitchen to eat, and she shops for him and cleans up sometimes."

"I see."

Dusty felt a growing anger, but knew enough not to show it. That would confuse the boy more. A least he'd had his grandmother. That accounted for his being such a nice boy. The neglect and abuse had only begun since his dad had taken him.

The child was probably living a nightmare of confusion and grief. The sooner she and the authorities could do something the better. It was unfortunate that these things took time—that the neglectful, abusive parent had all the rights and the child none.

Poor Roger.

Dusty hoped she'd be able to spend more and more time with him, to lighten his burden until it could be done away with entirely.

SINCE BOTH PAM AND DUSTY liked the movies, they went as often as they could. One evening after watching a film that had required several hankies for each of them, Dusty came home to the apartment and was met at the door by Tag. As she walked in, he put a finger to his lips, and she immediately saw why.

Roger Maddox was curled up in the armchair by the Christmas tree fast asleep. The room was unlit except for the string of lights on the tree, which cast a warm, rosy glow.

"How was the movie?" Tag asked, ushering her into the kitchen.

"Wonderful. It was a blatant advertisement for marriage. A real example of the June-moon-spoon kind of love."

Tag expressed his opinion with a snort and headed in the direction of his room.

Dusty followed him. "What about your parents?" she asked. "From what you've told me, theirs was a prime example of wedded bliss."

"I told you that I'd grant you a few exceptions to the rule," Tag said, then turned his back on her and checked in with headquarters.

Dusty waited him out. "And your brothers and their wives?" she asked as soon as he hung up.

"I have you there. Both of them have been divorced and remarried, and my older brother's latest attempt isn't looking so hot."

Dusty didn't have a reply handy, so she just followed Tag back out to the living room.

She watched as he crouched before the still-sleeping boy in the armchair. "You keep the lid on for a while. I'll walk Roger home," he told her, shaking Roger very gently.

The light from the Christmas tree washed Tag's now-softening features with a suitable glow. Dusty was suddenly brought up short by the expression in his eyes. She'd been able to recognize his more caring side all along and certainly had known of his affinity for children, but what she saw now was somehow different. This seemed more akin to the expressions she'd seen on the faces of the proud papas on parents' night at school.

She was startled at such a comparison and stood transfixed while Tag ran a long finger down the boy's cheek.

"Hey, you," he whispered, his eyes never leaving Roger's peaceful features.

Roger moved in protest, but Tag continued to gently coax him awake. The boy's shy smile when he finally opened his eyes proved that he was unaccustomed to gentle treatment, and Dusty's heart went out to him. How could a father treat such an innocent creature so badly? She'd heard that abused children became abusive parents, but she couldn't really comprehend the process. She could, however, help the child, just as Tag was doing.

"Come on, fella," Tag whispered. "Get your bag of cookies and I'll walk you home."

"No," the boy said, his mood changing.

"What do you mean? You don't want more cookies?"

The boy looked at his hands. "No," he said softly. "I want the cookies, but I don't want you to come to my place."

"Okay. But I can walk you some of the way, can't I?"

The child looked up, staring at Tag who was still crouching in front of his chair. He was so obviously torn between wanting to be with Tag, wanting to trust

Tag, and his fear, that Dusty's heart again faltered. But Tag remained patient and persistent, waiting for Roger to arrive at his decision.

"Okay."

When Tag's eyes flickered to Dusty's, she knew that he was sharing his moment of victory with her.

"I'll get your cookies," Dusty offered, moving into the kitchen while Tag helped Roger into his coat.

Tag was soon back, and he was just taking off his sheepskin coat when there was a knock at the door. Tag motioned Dusty aside, but his caution melted into a ready smile when he saw that it was only Pam.

"What's up?" Dusty asked when Tag stepped aside.

Pam's eyes were alight. "Oh, I'm so happy and so sorry."

Dusty noticed the envelope her friend was waving in her hand and smiled, as well. "What's going on?"

"You did this! You did this!" she said, grinning and pinching Dusty's cheek.

Dusty couldn't help grinning back. "What did I do?"

"My parents sent plane tickets for Brent and me to go to Memphis for Christmas. I just got to my mail, and Brent told me that about a week ago you talked him into writing my dad."

"I didn't exactly—"

"Oh, yes, you did. And I thank you. Thank you so much. The only thing is, we're supposed to have Christmas Eve together, and—"

"Don't even say it," Dusty said. "Nothing should keep you from going to Memphis and enjoying it. But can you get away from work?"

"Honey, that's the best part. I called my supervisor, and she said, 'What the hell, it's Christmas.' Would you believe it?"

Dusty gave her friend a squeeze. "It'll be great to see your family again, Pam," she whispered. "Especially your dad. I know everything will be just fine."

"It will, it will," Pam whispered back. "Oh," she added, more her usual self. "You know that couch I ordered as a Christmas present for myself? I mean, I could hardly pass it up, what with its being damaged and my discount."

"Yeah, I remember."

"My problem is that they want to deliver it while I'm gone and—"

Dusty held up a hand. "Say no more. Just get the key down here and I'll watch for it. Or rather, Tag will watch for it."

Dusty looked at Tag. While his eyes weren't alight like hers, she could tell he wouldn't mind helping out. "What are you going to do with your old couch, Pam?" he asked.

"Why, I was going to pay extra to have it hauled off."

"As I recall, it's nubby and brownish..."

"Yeah," Pam said, focusing on Tag. "It's pretty worn, though. Brent's grown up on that couch."

"I'm sure that Dusty's told you I've been wanting—"

Now it was Pam's turn to interrupt. "Take it. Give the movers a little extra and I'm sure they'll be glad to haul it down. And don't offer to pay me for it. I was going to get rid of it, anyway."

Tag nodded and, turning to leave, smiled at Pam. "Thanks. And enjoy your trip."

"Oh, I will, I will, I will," she chanted. "Are you sure you don't mind about Christmas Eve?" she asked Dusty when Tag disappeared. "I know you aren't acquainted with many people here, and it's your first Christmas away from home."

"Don't worry about me. Just go and have fun."

With one more squeeze, Pam left, and Dusty felt oddly lonesome. It would be just Tag and her and Roger for Christmas now. She almost missed Pam and Brent already. They had come to mean a lot to her. Turning back into the apartment, she found Tag moving toward the kitchen.

"Are you upset that she's going?" he asked.

"No. No, I'm happy for her. I'll miss her, though."

She would miss her a lot. Suddenly she was feeling very emotional, with lots of feelings tugging at her heart. Most of all she realized what she was feeling was love for Tag. She admitted to herself that she'd loved him for a long time and wondered if she would regret not having made love with him once they had to separate.

It suddenly occurred to Dusty that Tag couldn't have made love in a long time. He must be feeling the need more and more as time went on, but he was obviously coming to see her less and less in the light of that need. They had become friends. That meant they would also part as friends...and that Tag and she would lose touch at some point in the future.

Oh, he would probably call her a few times, and they would more than likely meet at the trial if they ever arrested the Desota gang. They might even meet for lunch or supper once or twice. But, in the end, they would go their separate ways. Their sort of friendship needed the nurturing of constant contact and would eventually disappear without it.

Truly their little round in life was without foundation. Just as was Dusty's love. The only good thing was that it would be over soon, more than likely in a month's time. Dusty began to think about her reentry into her old life and how it would be. Would she take it up smoothly, without any of the bumps and hitches that the entry into this one had caused? And, most of all, would she be able to forget John Taggert and their days of friendship here in this little apartment?

"You're in an oddly contemplative mood," Tag said, interrupting Dusty's thoughts.

Dusty realized she had ground to a halt in the kitchen doorway. She was leaning there, absently watching Tag talk to Louie-Louie.

"What? Oh, yes. I'm fine. I guess I'm just tired."

"Why don't you take your usual long, hot soak, get into your cozy pajamas and tuck in with a book?"

"What about your time to get out?"

"I was out enough when I walked Rog home."

"Did you see where he lives?"

"No. He's a canny little guy when he wants to be. He made me stay about a block away while he went the rest of the way alone. At least I have a good idea where it is, and he'll probably let me see next time."

"He's either embarrassed about how he lives or he's afraid you'll run into his dad."

Tag sobered. "The bastard. Every time I think about him I want to...I don't know...to get even for some of what he's done to his kid. I just can't understand a situation like that. Rog is so..."

"I know. It's fortunate that Roger's been able to remain Roger after all he's been through. He isn't going sour or turning mean like most kids do in these situations."

"The question is, how long can he go without some sort of caring and normalcy?"

"At least he has us for part of the time," Dusty ventured, feeling what Tag was feeling.

"As far as I'm concerned, that's not good enough." Tag was as grim as Dusty had ever seen him, reminding her of the old Tag. "I guess I'd better get back," he added, moving toward his room.

Once again he had left her, this time feeling more alone than she had ever felt.

CHAPTER FIFTEEN

DUSTY HEARD TAG GROAN, and was out of bed and speeding down the dark hall within seconds. He had appreciated her waking him the last time he'd had his nightmare, and she had no qualms about doing so again.

Kneeling alongside of his cot, she put her arm across his chest. She also placed her cheek to his, just as she had the time before. The stubble on his face was oddly comforting against the smoothness of hers, and the smell of his cologne filled her senses.

Oh, goodness, I love him, she thought.

Deepening her embrace to a tight hold, she whispered his name into his ear.

Tag came slowly awake, just as he had before. But this time he didn't jolt them into hard reality by reaching over and switching on the light as he had the last time. Instead, his arms went around Dusty, returning her embrace twofold.

"Dusty," he whispered, and not as a question.

He obviously knew where he was and what was happening. His mouth was seeking the warmth of her neck and rested there in a tentative kiss. When Dusty didn't move away, Tag soothed his lips under the collar of her pajamas, searching out the heat of her sleep-warmed skin. Still, Dusty didn't resist, and he moaned his pleasure. His hands began a gentle rubbing at her back, a nudging at the flannel that covered the silkiness of her.

"Let me kiss you, babe."

Lifting her head from Tag's shoulder, Dusty looked down into his face. His hair was black against the white of his pillow. Enough light came into his window to delineate his features but not the special blue of his eyes. Those, too, looked black, but she knew he was staring into her face where it hung above his.

"Kiss me," he whispered, going perfectly still.

Slowly Dusty lowered her mouth to his in a sweet, if still unsure, contact. When she began to pull away, Tag's response was gentle, but definitely restraining. He wanted to return her kiss. But his was deep and consuming, reminding Dusty of the pent-up desire she'd seen in his eyes in their early days together. He still wanted her, and her heart lifted with that knowledge.

With that knowledge also came the desire to give herself to him. She loved him and longed for his touch. She tugged herself away from him, but only enough to allow his hand to slide beneath her pajama top, where he tenderly cupped her breast.

"Oh, Dusty, you're so small but so perfect. So sweet."

Here again was the gentle Tag that Dusty had glimpsed before. The sound of his voice, the plea in his praise, encouraged her. With trembling fingers, she slid the top button of her pajama shirt through its hole. Desire shot through her at the flash of his tongue across his lips. He was waiting to see her, wanting to take her into his mouth.

Slowly her fingers moved to her next button and then to the next. She could only hope her nerveless fingers could accomplish the feat, and all the while the soft darkness lent her courage.

Tag swallowed so hard that Dusty could hear it. "Don't."

Dusty went still, trying to decide if she had heard him right.

"Oh, babe, don't. Don't," he said more loudly, sitting up.

Dusty clasped her shirt across her breasts. She had never been so mortified as when he reached over and switched on the harsh light of his metal lamp. She lowered her gaze. She knew her face was already as red as it got and her hands were trembling.

"Oh, God, babe," Tag said, getting up. "Don't look like that."

Striding the short space to the door, he turned back and faced her squarely. He was just as unraveled as she. But instead of being flush with embarrassment, he seemed incredibly nervous—unsure of himself. Raking his fingers through his hair, he met her gaze, his eyes dark and troubled. "I can't do this," he said, coming back to stand over her. "I'm sorry. I . . . I just can't."

Reaching down, Tag helped Dusty to her feet and began to button her pajama top. "I want to, babe. I've never wanted to more, but . . ."

All Dusty knew was that she was mortified. She was around him and out of his door before he could react to her unexpected move.

He followed her into her bedroom, though, and as she dived under her covers, he snapped on her light.

Luckily her lamp cast a much softer glow. But she no more wanted her red face to be seen by its light than she had by the illumination in his room. She wished, in fact, that he would leave so that she could collect herself and told him so.

"No. I'm not leaving."

Dusty turned her back to him, hoping her heart would stop pounding the blood into her cheeks where he could see it.

"Don't think that I don't want you or that I wasn't turned on by what you were doing."

Dusty couldn't hold in the groan of embarrassment. She pulled her knees to her chest, curling into a ball.

"Oh, God, Dusty, I want you. I have since the beginning. And you know it."

"Just go!"

"I want you now. Especially now. I want to climb into that bed with you and comfort you and make love to you."

"Stop it!" she rasped, putting her hands to her ears.

But Tag was relentless. "Don't you think I know what it took for you to unbutton your top? Don't you think I could feel you trembling in my arms? Don't you think I wanted to make love, too?"

Grabbing one of her pillows, Dusty put it over her head, but she could still hear his voice.

"Don't you see I can't? When we first came here I could have in a minute. But I've grown to know you and to like you. Hell, I more than like you. I respect you and admire you. How many women could have moved in here and, in a couple months, made a place for herself? Every bone in your body is caring. So how can I casually bed you? How can I take someone like you without a thought for the future? You need love and commitment, and I can't give that. I told you that from the beginning. If there was ever anyone I wanted it with, it's you. But it's not in me. I'm not meant for this setup, and it's tearing—Oh, hell!''

Dusty heard Tag leave just as surely as she had heard every word he'd uttered. She wasn't embarrassed anymore. Instead, she felt miserable. But she didn't cry. All she could think was that she was in love with Tag and that he was in pain.

Getting up and putting on her robe, she went looking for him. She knew he'd no more be attempting to sleep than she was and discovered him seated in an armchair, glowering at the Christmas tree.

Tag didn't look up when she sat down in the chair next to his, and she remained quiet for a moment, her eyes absorbing his dark, good looks in the rosy glow of the tree. Still, he didn't say a word or move a muscle.

"Tag, can't we talk about this? I know you're too honest, too good, not to have your reasons, but—''

"Don't make me out to be a saint,'' he growled.

She could see the immediate regret in his eyes, together with his pain. She didn't flinch, and that seemed to help more than anything.

"Look,'' he said more reasonably. "It's very simple. I'm not capable of the kind of love you need and want. Some white knight will come along someday and the two of you will deserve each other. In the meantime, I'm not going to take advantage of this situation. It'll only get us both all tied up in knots when we're done here.''

Dusty didn't reply, but Tag could read her effort at understanding. "This sort of thing happens all the time," he told her. "A stakeout is a natural setup for a hot affair simply because it's so unnatural. With someone like you, I was bound to... Look, the Desotas are getting together a good, solid deal. It's just what we've been waiting for. They'll be bringing the stuff back here to sell, and then we'll have them. We're talking about a month. At the most. Then it'll be over. And we'll be over, too," he said, softening. "You're not the kind of a girl who wants a fling. You're—"

"I'm not a girl. I'm a woman," Dusty said, finally losing patience.

"Oh, yeah? You can't fool me on that score. Who's made you a woman?"

"Me! I'm twenty-four years old. I've been on my own for most of my life. I've educated myself and made a useful place for myself in the world. I can also make my own decisions."

"This decision would be based on what you think you're feeling."

"What I *know* I'm feeling."

"What you *think* you're feeling. And that's no way to make a decision."

"Just let me account for my own feelings and decisions."

"But you want me to feel good about our love-making, too, don't you, Dusty?"

Dusty looked Tag levelly in the eye. "Maybe I can read you as well as you can read me."

"I admit you might be seeing something in my eyes. But I can also assure you that it won't last. And that's the sticky point. You need it to last for it to be good.

And knowing that, I'd be a heel to go to bed with you." He said this with so much assurance that Dusty could tell he'd given it a lot of thought.

"What happened to you, Tag?" she asked softly, changing her tack. "Why can't you love?"

For a while Tag stared at the tree in silence. "I was raised much like you were," he said at last, "on the same kind of street, right next door to a girl two years younger than me. My parents and her parents were close and made no secret of their wishes with regard to Viv and me. I didn't object, either. Viv is beautiful and always has been."

Oh, go on, go on.

"One day I finally told Viv I loved her and, glory of glories, she said she loved me, too. Well, that day marked the beginning of a long wait. But all I needed to do was look at Viv to know I'd wait forever. Even when I joined the force while she was finishing up high school I waited.

"God, I would have been embarrassed if anyone had known that. In fact, I've never told anyone but . . . you." He sent her a flickering look, and Dusty nodded, accepting his confidence and urging him to go on.

"Anyway, it only got worse, because when Viv came to me and said she wanted to go to college, I told her I'd still wait. I wasn't particularly happy about her going out east to school. But she had earned a scholarship and it would have been selfish of me to insist she skip college to marry me.

"She graduated the year after my dad died. I remember, because going to her commencement was the first thing to interest my mom since he'd gone. We packed up the car and drove to Massachusetts. Viv looked gorgeous but seemed nervous, too. I figured it was just the hustle and bustle surrounding the event and couldn't wait to get her alone. I'd waited. I had a diamond ring and I was...proud, I guess.''

Dusty's eyes wavered when Tag looked at her again, but even so he continued.

"After it was over, I took my mom's arm and we went to look for Viv. God, there was a crowd, and any blonde in a black gown caught my eye. Finally we found her, standing with her parents and a guy who was also in a cap and gown. Viv's eyes ran nervously to mine, and I thought the guy was some kid who was bothering her. When she introduced him as her fiancé, I was floored.

"She had wanted to tell me, she said. Tried to call, but I'd already left for commencement. They would have waited, only they wanted to share their news with the people they knew at college. And on and on...

"I managed to congratulate her on her diploma and on her ring, too. She was sorry. I could see that in her eyes. But it was still this other guy who took her home.

"Mom had made arrangements with Viv's parents for the drive back to Cincinnati. The Neals liked the guy well enough, but had the grace to commiserate with my mother.

"I drove into Boston and picked up the first girl I met," Tag said, his voice hardening. "She was willing..." he shrugged. "I gave her the ring the next morning."

Finally he looked at Dusty, a grim smile curving his wonderfully shaped mouth. "So you see, Dusty, being a virgin at twenty-four isn't so unusual. In fact, this should be your lucky year."

Dusty didn't smile. "That . . . that was only one—"

"Let me finish, Dusty. You're usually more polite when you sit listening to me tell a tale. Last year, around Christmas as a matter of fact, I went to visit my mom. This was before I left Cincinnati, and there sits Viv Neal. She and her two kids were staying with her parents until she could decide what she'd do next. It seemed 'the bum,' her ex, had run off with a younger blonde."

Dusty could imagine the ready sympathy she knew Tag was so capable of.

"Viv was still blond and beautiful, and I even liked her kids. Our parents were delighted when we said we were going out. Good ol' Viv didn't even make me wait beyond dinner. We checked into a motel right after dessert. I could barely manage. We were both disappointed. Somehow my heart just wasn't in it," Tag finished. "The fact is, I had no capacity for love, and I still don't."

"But, Tag, you're talking about one woman. Only one. Sure, you were hurt by her. But that's not the sum total of love, nor even part of it. You were a kid—"

"Not this last time," he cut in. "I loved her, loved her in the way you mean it. I thought that all I wanted was her, even up until last year. And when we finally had our chance, I found I didn't love her, after all."

Dusty had no answer for this and they both knew it.

"I didn't even like her much," Tag said. "I sympathized with her. I spent time with her children. What if I'd married her in the beginning the way I'd planned? I'd have hurt her as badly as her ex did. And

I'd have hurt those kids just as surely as they're hurting now. Oh, no, what you want doesn't exist in me—if it exists at all. I'll stick to my approach. And that, of course, means steering the hell clear of you.''

Again Dusty had no reply. She sympathized with him simply because he had been so young when he'd first fallen in love and had been so enthralled for so long. But she couldn't see how Tag had gotten older without being able to shake off his experience with Viv Neal.

But though he obviously wasn't right in his assessment of his capacity to love, he was implacable in both his belief and his pain. And he was also correct about her. She didn't want a brief affair. But if that was all she could have . . .

Dusty sighed and leaned back in her chair, her eyes following Tag's to the lighted tree.

One more month, she told herself, *and then you can begin to recover. He'll be gone and you'll be forced to get over him.*

''Are you still angry with me?'' Tag asked softly.

''No, I'm not angry,'' she said, equally softly.

''I would hate to lose your friendship, Dusty.''

She turned her head to gaze into Tag's eyes and found he had a very serious look on his face. She had to smile. ''I'd hate to lose your friendship, too.''

His grin was lopsided. ''I've never had a girl . . . er, a woman, for a friend before.''

''Well, I've had lots of male friends,'' she replied.

''Wouldn't let anyone get any closer, huh?''

''Not on purpose. It was more that I was too busy to meet anyone I wanted to have more with.''

"I feel...honored," he said seriously, and even with a twinge of sadness.

"I'm sure it will pass."

Much to her delight, Tag laughed. "You've probably broken a dozen hearts without even knowing it. I know you've broken mine."

"I thought yours was already broken."

Tag's eyes reverted to the lighted tree. "I'd thought so, too. But now I'm beginning to wonder."

CHAPTER SIXTEEN

"PAM AND BRENT LEFT this morning?"

"I just kissed them goodbye."

"So it looks like it'll be just you and me for Christmas Eve," Tag said, taking a big swallow of orange juice. "Poor Rog. I'd hoped he could come for a while."

"Still, it's nice of his neighbor to include him in her Christmas Eve plans. Even if he doesn't like her much, I think it's good that he'll be with her and her family. It might help him get to know them better." Dusty turned from her dishwashing to peer at Tag. "Do you mind?"

He looked puzzled.

"Do you mind that it'll be just you and me?"

"No," he said with a wicked grin. "We can get sentimental and pour out our guts to each other."

Dusty didn't deign to answer that, so Tag went on.

"I don't have time for Christmas, in any case."

"You mean crooks don't spend the holidays with their families?"

"Sure crooks have families and observe Christmas," he said, coming over and pushing in beside her at the sink. She knew he preferred washing to drying and, because it didn't matter to her, she picked a towel off the rack and let him get his hands wet. "The Desotas are celebrating in Florida, except for the one wife they're having trouble with."

"Do they divorce like other people, or will the Desota brothers simply knock her off if it comes to it?"

Pausing in his dish scrubbing, Tag looked down into Dusty's twinkling eyes. "I swear, sometimes you have the weirdest sense of humor."

"I do not."

"It's rather like getting punched in the stomach and tickled at the same time. There are things about you, Dusty, that are so special."

"Yeah, like my sense of hearing. Isn't that headquarters calling?"

Tag grabbed her dish towel. He was drying his hands and walking off before Dusty could offer to answer the call for him. He didn't, in fact, return until Dusty was finishing up.

"Twinkle, twinkle, little..."

"Star. That was Alvarez. He says you deserve time off for good behavior."

Dusty lifted an eyebrow. She couldn't imagine what Tag was suggesting.

"Your sister and brother-in-law are in town. They want to see you."

"Leslie?" Dusty couldn't help lighting up at this unexpected news.

"They're at the Grand Hotel."

"And the boys?"

"No mention of boys."

"When do I go?"

"Not until this evening. They'll send a car after supper. Alvarez says you can have three days if you take the beeper in your purse. That way we can reach you if we need to.''

When Dusty's face broke into a broad grin, Tag looked away.

''Three days!''

Stuffing his fists into his pockets, Tag nodded. He didn't appear nearly as pleased for her as she would have thought he'd be.

''I've so much to do! I have a load of washing, packing . . . Oh, my gosh, I didn't bring a single dress. I'll have to—''

''No, you can't go to your house,'' Tag said categorically. ''We can't take a chance on anyone seeing you.''

''But I can't stay at that kind of hotel over the holidays without a dress.''

''You'll have to run out and buy some new things. I'll loan you the cash and call a car.''

''Oh, Tag,'' she said with a beaming smile. ''Thanks.'' Dusty gave him a brotherly kiss.

''Yeah,'' he said. ''You're welcome.''

Ignoring his growl, Dusty organized her thoughts, planning what had to be done. She was too busy to react to Tag's behavior, and she threw herself into her day.

''Well? What do you think?'' Dusty asked that evening after supper as she appeared in the kitchen doorway in a delicate little apricot dress.

Tag, who was seated at the table with a game of solitaire spread out in front of him, looked up and let his eyes pass quickly over her. "You've got great legs," he muttered.

Dusty chuckled. "I should have expected something like that from you. I'm talking about the dress. Do you know what a feat it was to find the things I needed in the last-minute Christmas rush? Maybe that's why I did so well. I didn't have time to vacillate."

"You never vacillate."

Dusty ignored his grouchy reply. Looking at the clock, she saw she had just enough time to give Tag his gift.

When she set the large, gaily wrapped package on the table, he peered at her with questioning eyes.

"For you," she announced, smiling. "Merry Christmas."

"I thought our gifts were fake."

"They were until I ran across this at Mr. Getty's." Not even her mention of the wily shopkeeper brought Tag around. He was as sour as he had been all day. "Aren't you going to open it?"

At last, he nodded and pulled the gift toward him. "It's heavy."

"Open it."

Tag's fine fingers made quick work of Dusty's wrapping, the box yielding up a used—very used—typewriter.

"A typewriter?"

Dusty produced another package, this one unwrapped. "Here's a box of paper, a new ribbon and a big fat eraser. Now you can be a writer."

"Dusty..." Tag murmured. "I don't have a gift for you."

"That's okay. Write me a first chapter by the time I get back." She was still cheerful, moving toward the door. "I'd prefer a story about your dad and the organ grinder. I mean, it would be really interesting to make a villain out of an organ grinder."

"Dusty."

"Merry Christmas, Tag," she called back before closing the front door.

"Merry Christmas," Tag muttered under his breath.

Louie-Louie was left to catch Tag's blue stare. The bird ruffled and shifted his weight on his hoary feet. "Twinkle, twinkle, little star, damn it."

Tag got up from the table. He left Louie-Louie, the lights on the Christmas tree and the coziness of the kitchen for the sanity of his dingy room. He should have known better all along than to go into the other rooms.

No one heard the parrot begin a cheerful chorus of "Meet me in St. Louie, Louie..."

DUSTY PAUSED ON THE STOOP outside their apartment and breathed deeply of the cold air. The car Captain Alvarez had sent was just pulling up, giving her little time to wipe the sudden tear from her eye. That tear was caused by the unexpected cold, she told herself. She certainly wanted to see her sister and brother-in-law, and she needed the familiarity they represented. But somehow the apartment, with Tag in it, had grown to be home to her. Drat.

The place she felt was "home" wasn't even going to exist in a month's time. She climbed into the police car. Why couldn't her head rule her heart? She kept trying to force herself to face reality, but somehow kept getting suckered into living a dream.

Dusty watched the passing scene. It was definitely Christmas. She could glimpse other Christmas trees in other cozy rooms, but couldn't seem to force the picture of Tag's tree from her mind. There were wreaths on doors and decorations on lampposts. Dusty even saw a group of carolers singing for charity.

But Dusty arrived at the Grand Hotel with a picture of Tag, grumpy and alone, still in her mind. She was ushered through a side door and into a service elevator, then followed her plainclothes escort down the hushed corridors of the elegant old hotel. Dusty endeavored to get herself under control. Leslie was sure to notice anything wrong, and Dusty didn't want to spoil her sister's holiday any more than it was being spoiled already.

At last they stopped in front of a door. "I'll stay out here," the officer told her as he rapped on the door. It was immediately opened by Dusty's brother-in-law, but Dusty only had eyes for the slender young woman behind him.

"Dusty," Leslie cried.

The pair were in each other's arms before Dusty could speak. She hadn't realized how much she'd needed her sister until now, and she forced down an unexpected flood of emotion. Stepping back enough to look into each other's face, they broke into unsure grins at the same time.

"Are you all right?" Leslie asked.

Dusty felt the old urge to protect her sister. As anyone could tell, just by looking into her refined features, Leslie was less strong than she. Dusty had known that even as a child.

Smiling broadly, she said, "Of course I'm all right. Juan wouldn't let me be anything but all right, would he?"

She was gratified, not only by her sister's relaxing stance, but by the more knowing look she exchanged with her brother-in-law. Eric, too, would do what he could to make things easier for Leslie, and he gave Dusty an understanding smile.

"Well, you two," Dusty said, moving to the cushy sitting area in the luxurious suite "let's have the best news. How are the boys? And how did you ever get away for Christmas?"

"The boys are fine," Eric said, still smiling. "They send their love."

"I can't imagine spending a Christmas without them," Dusty said.

"We couldn't imagine spending a Christmas with them in a hotel." Leslie replied. "In any case, we only convinced Juan just yesterday morning that we needed to be here with you for Christmas."

"For Christmas?" Eric repeated. "If it had been Groundhog Day, Leslie would have used that as an excuse for managing this."

At that moment Dusty was more than grateful for Eric's presence. His easygoing nature and smile were what both she and her sister needed most of all.

As always, Dusty was glad she'd chosen Eric for her sister. She had introduced them and had encouraged the match every step of the way. She patted herself on the back, just as she always did when she was with them.

"Alvarez didn't have time to tell us much about the progress of the case," Eric was saying. "He told us that you could let us in on the latest."

Dusty snorted in an unexpected imitation of one of Tag's worst mannerisms. "I'm afraid there isn't any 'latest.' The 'latest' is what's been going on all along—nothing."

Leslie sat forward on the couch they were sharing, gazing intently into Dusty's face. "But when we were talking just before you went into this surveillance situation, you said that there's a gang member living right next door to you."

Dusty chuckled, glancing to where Eric had gone to relax in a comfortable chair and light up his pipe. "Really, Les, if you saw the circumstances for yourself, you'd realize you're being . . ."

Reaching over, Leslie took Dusty's hand. "Please, Dusty, don't make light of this. You can't imagine what it's been like for me, living all the way in New York and not seeing you after Dad's death. We've only had a few phone calls."

Dusty peered into the soft brown of her sister's eyes. Leslie had always been called the pretty Landry sister, while she had been called cute and gamin. Indeed, Leslie, with her chestnut-colored hair and willowy figure, had never been lovelier. Still, Dusty could see the wear and tear that the trying circumstances of the past months had taken.

"I've never lied to you, Les. I understand now what it's been like for you, and I see why it was so important for you to come to St. Louis. I know that if our positions were reversed, I'd feel the same way. But you have to believe me when I say that Juan has done the best for me that he can. Usually, after the six months of a protection program run out, a person is simply left to fend for himself. What with Dad's killer not having been caught, well, Juan's done a good thing for me."

"Oh, Dusty, if only you could come home with us. I've wanted you there all along."

"Now, Les," Eric interjected, "you know Alvarez said that Dusty'd be no more safe with us than she would be in your dad's house. This kind of mob has worldwide connections, and the papers mentioned we live in New York."

"Besides," said Dusty, "I might just identify the murderer if I'm in on the stakeout. I've been told there's not much chance of it, but I might."

"And what about this mobster who lives next door?" Leslie asked. "The very idea scares me to death."

Dusty patted her sister's hand. "Now there's where even you would laugh. This 'mobster,' as you call him, is a shriveled little old man who doesn't do much more than sleep and watch TV."

"Have you seen him?" Leslie's brown eyes were wide with wonder.

This time Dusty's laugh was genuine. "Oh, Les, of course I've seen him, and I'm telling you he looks no more threatening than any other old man you'd see hanging on to a bench at a bus stop. In fact, he's never been much of a mobster. He's only tolerated because he's an uncle to the gang members we're trying to arrest."

At last Leslie seemed somewhat satisfied, and she sat back on the couch.

"Have you had dinner, Dusty?" Eric asked in an obvious ploy to change the subject. "We thought we'd attend Christmas Eve services at the new cathedral and then have a light supper. Alvarez says it'll be all right."

"That sounds great to me," Dusty said. "You haven't seen the new cathedral, have you, Eric? It's beautiful, and I've never been there for Christmas."

"Now wait a minute," Leslie objected. "I'm not through talking about what I want to talk about."

Dusty smiled. "Talk away. We've got a lot of time for talking."

"No. I want to clear my mind now. As much as it can be cleared."

"Okay."

"Are you still having nightmares? You said you were doing better with your emotional adjustment, but I would think your present circumstances would be awfully hard on you."

"I'll admit that I have my ups and downs. I cried one night, but the dreams are pretty much under control."

"And this officer you live with? Juan says he's an excellent man and that he takes good care of you."

"Juan's right," Dusty said. "Detective Taggert is a very dedicated policeman, and I feel safe with him. It's strange, but his first day on the force here in St. Louis was also the day Dad was murdered. I think I told you about him at the time. He was the one who drove me to the safe house, the one who was so nice to me."

Leslie sighed. "I don't think I remember you mentioning him."

"That's understandable, sweetheart," Eric said. "Those days were difficult. I'd be surprised if you had remembered Dusty mentioning Detective Taggert."

"I suppose."

"Well," Dusty said. "How are the boys doing? I've had some news about them through Juan and Aunt Marge, but I've missed hearing about their everyday antics."

She could see that her sister wasn't quite ready to move the conversation on, but luckily Eric was on Dusty's side and all three were soon beginning to really enjoy themselves.

Christmas Day dawned bright but cool and went more easily than the night before. The trio ate in the hotel restaurant and talked and talked and talked. Leslie had brought her gifts for Dusty, while Dusty had already sent hers to New York. The boys, who were staying with Eric's parents, sounded cheery when Leslie and Dusty telephoned them later in the day.

But while Dusty was glad for this time with her sister—and she experienced the real meaning of Christmas in her company—she couldn't help thinking of the little apartment that wasn't too far away.

Oh, she knew that Tag was doing all right without her. He'd done without her before and would do so again. She wasn't so sure about herself, however, and her occasional lapses into thinking of him had to be explained to her sister. Always in evasive and general terms, of course.

The morning following Christmas, on what was to be their last day together, the two sisters walked across the street from the hotel and into Forest Park. It seemed funny that at the park's other end—which was some distance—the object of her straying thoughts sat in his dingy room. She could picture him easily, could see the hard set of his handsome features as he worked over his card table.

Suddenly Dusty realized that her sister had said something.

"What?" Dusty asked.

"I was saying that the fresh air smells good after living in pipe smoke for two days."

Dusty chuckled. "I know you don't really mind. I mean, Eric has so many wonderful qualities that they far outnumber a little pipe tobacco."

Leslie sent Dusty an arch look, then let her gaze return to their surroundings, just as Dusty did.

The park was special in many ways, a tribute to the men who had had the vision to establish it when parks in cities weren't considered necessary. Dusty allowed herself to simply enjoy strolling arm in arm with her sister. She even managed to stop thinking of Tag and of her imminent parting from Leslie.

"What?" she asked, again brought up short.

"I said, out with it."

Pausing on the sidewalk, suddenly aware of the quiet rustling of winter-bare tree branches above them, Dusty looked into the soft brown of her sister's eyes. "Out with what?"

"Come on, Dusty. We don't have much time, and if you don't tell me, I'm going to worry."

Slipping her arm back into place, Dusty coaxed her sister into resuming their walk. She had wanted to tell her all along, but had been afraid it would add to

Leslie's worry. Now that her sister had sensed something, however, she knew she had to tell.

"Don't be shocked, but I've fallen in love with my guardian angel."

Leslie stopped dead in her tracks. "What?"

"You heard me. I'm in love with John Taggert."

"The detective who—?"

"The very one."

"Are you sure? I mean, Dusty, well, these are unusual circumstances, and one hears all the time about how people who wouldn't normally be drawn to each other can easily be in this kind of strange situation."

"You sound like you've been watching too much Phil Donahue."

"I'm serious, Dusty. Are you sure? You've always been so levelheaded, so practical, that I can't imagine you doing...doing..."

Once again Dusty simply had to laugh. "Doing anything dumb? It's not like I volunteered, you know. It's something that just happened to me. Just like Eric happened to you."

Leslie lapsed into silent contemplation. "I've heard nothing but good things of him," she finally admitted. "Really, if you've fallen for him, he must be quite a guy."

"Oh, he is that. Quite a guy."

"Actually," Leslie continued, "the fact that you love each other makes me feel better about your going back."

"Oh, don't get this wrong, sister dear. I said that I was in love with John Taggert. He, however, isn't in love with me."

"What?" Leslie asked in disbelief.

When Dusty had once tried to explain that her short stature, freckles and youthful appearance, were problems, Leslie had reacted the same way. Leslie simply couldn't imagine anyone finding anything wrong in the sister she loved.

"Are you *sure* he doesn't love you?" Leslie asked at last.

"Positive."

"I can't imagine it."

"I didn't think you could."

"Maybe he just doesn't know yet."

"Get the stars out of your eyes, Les. He's told me that he's not capable of love."

Once again Leslie came to a standstill. "I've never heard of such a thing."

Dusty sobered. "What about Dad, Les? Oh, I know, I know," she added, lifting a hand to stop her sister's reply. "Just before he died he told me that he'd loved us all. But his work certainly kept him from really feeling and living his love and, I'm afraid, that the same is true of Tag. I mean, maybe he can feel love, but he's so...so *absorbed* with his work and with himself that he can't really live his love—can't act out his love... Does any of this make sense to you, Les?"

"Tag hasn't sworn off women altogether, has he?"

"He says he has."

"I can't imagine," Leslie insisted. "Surely you're misunderstanding the situation. He'll come around."

Dusty sighed in exasperation. She could see that her sister had decided that Tag was in love with her—whether he knew it or not, or admitted it or not. And nothing was ever going to change her sister's mind—nothing ever did, once she'd made her mind up.

When they got back to their hotel room, where Eric sat in a cloud of pipe smoke reading the paper, Leslie argued her case before him. Eric simply relaxed into his chair, smiling affably at the sisters.

"Leslie," Dusty finally protested, "the man I love is not in love with me."

"Nonsense."

"He doesn't believe in love at all—not in the June-moon-spoon kind."

"The what?"

"The June-moon-spoon kind of love. That's Tag's sarcastic name for what other people call true love."

"Why, I've never heard of such a thing as not believing in love."

"I'm telling you that he's like Dad, Leslie. He might *care* for some people, but love . . . ? No way."

"But you also say that Tag has *demonstrated* a certain amount of caring, which Dad never did. Look at that little boy. What's his name? Roger? It's obvious from what you've said that Tag cares very deeply for the boy."

At that, Dusty jumped out of her chair and headed for the door of her bedroom.

"Where are you going?" Leslie asked.

"What you're saying is actually starting to make sense to me. I've got something I have to take care of, so, if you don't mind, which I'm sure you don't . . . I mean, seeing as how you're convinced you're getting a brother-in-law out of this . . . I'm leaving a little early."

CHAPTER SEVENTEEN

WHEN DUSTY ENTERED THE APARTMENT she was amazed to hear the old typewriter clacking away in Tag's room. Obviously Tag had taken her advice and had started to write. After setting her bag on the floor, Dusty walked to his room. She was pulling off her coat when Tag looked up and saw her in the doorway. He paused, momentarily frozen, his index fingers poised over the typewriter keys as he stared at her.

"You're home early," he said, something flashing briefly in his eyes. "I wasn't expecting you."

Dusty smiled. She hadn't missed his inadvertent reference to the apartment as home. His little slip demonstrated that this arrangement meant something to him, as well. She didn't dwell on that small hope, however.

"My sister was anxious to get back to her children," she fibbed. "So how's the typewriter?"

Tag had the grace to smile. "A typical product from the classy showroom of Mr. Getty."

"What do you mean?"

"I mean, among other things, that the letter *n* doesn't strike."

Dusty shrugged. "Do you use *n* all that much?"

"Only all the time. But I thank you, anyway."

"You do?"

Tag nodded. "I'm of the hunt-and-peck type-writing school, so it doesn't throw me off too much. Actually, I've gotten into the habit of leaving a space and then penciling in the *n*'s along with my other corrections."

"How far have you gotten?" Dusty asked, moving into the room.

Tag grinned again. "Two chapters."

"Two whole chapters?"

"Almost. I had a story pretty much in mind, but I had to put together a sketchy outline."

"And you've written two chapters besides? Of course, I don't know anything about writing, but that sounds great to me!" Dusty's eyes meandered over Tag's card table. She had hopes of catching a glimpse of his story amid his orderly piles of paper.

Tag chuckled, sensing her intense curiosity. He even seemed a bit interested in her being interested. "This is my outline, this is my clean paper and this is my finished product," he said, indicating three separate piles.

Dusty looked down at the wastebasket and saw only two balled pieces of paper. Catching the meaning in that glance, Tag chuckled again.

"That's all there's been. Just two pages that I threw out and rewrote, and those were at the beginning when I was getting my main character set. But as soon as I had my first sentence, my thoughts and fingers began to fly."

Dusty smiled. "So you enjoy it?"

"Actually I can't believe how much. Nor how easily it comes. The hours speed by. I've never experienced anything like it. I stay up almost all night, then

I fall asleep plotting, I even woke up yesterday morning with an answer to a plot twist already set in my mind . . ." Tag seemed almost embarrassed by his unabashed relish. "I do need a dictionary, though. I can't seem to spell a damn thing."

"Sounds great." Dusty was still eyeing his finished chapters. But she found she couldn't read upside down, especially with Tag's penciled-in corrections running this way and that.

"Would you like to read some of it?" he asked, his tentative smile touching Dusty like nothing ever had before. Was Tag feeling vulnerable? The thought floored her.

"Would I ever!" Scooping up his neat little stack, she plunked herself down on Tag's cot.

He turned even more unsure. "Oh, no, not in here. Take it . . . take it somewhere else."

"Okay. I'll just unpack and . . . Do I smell something burning?"

"Oh, my . . . damn it!" Tag jumped up from his chair. "I've got cookies in the oven."

"I'll get them." Dusty left Tag's room without putting down his manuscript. Considering the mood he was in, she was afraid he might change his mind about her reading it. Rushing into the kitchen, she stopped dead in her tracks. The place was a mess. Dishes were piled in the sink, and leftovers littered the table.

Tag came sheepishly in while she was whisking his chocolate chip cookies out of the oven. They were as much a disaster as the kitchen.

"I, uh . . . haven't gotten around to cleaning up yet. I thought I'd do it all at once before you got home."

Dusty scraped the burned cookies into the waste-basket. "And what have you been living on?"

Tag didn't answer. He stood shifting from one foot to the other. Dusty felt an odd and heady sense of power. What was happening here? Had she caught him so off balance by her early return that he didn't know what to say? But why? Why would he feel that way in front of her? He had always been so self-assured.

Suddenly, as Dusty's eyes met Tag's blue gaze, she realized he had missed her. He'd been busy writing, even enthralled with his new discovery, but he had missed her. Perhaps all the more so because he'd wanted to share his phenomenal discovery with her.

The smile in her eyes triggered something in Tag, and he stepped abruptly forward, scooping her into his arms. His embrace was hard. "God, but I missed you, babe. The apartment was so quiet. I...I took up writing more out of desperation than anything else."

"Oh, Tag, I missed you, too. I lied when I said I came back early because Les wanted to see the boys. I returned early because I wanted to be with you."

Dusty stared up into Tag's face. He was so much taller than she, but he looked sweet and approachable. Her eyes passed over his unshaven face, his rumpled shirt, his ruffled hair.

"I've been living off cookies and coffee," he admitted, his own gaze moving over her. Evidently he was pleased with what he saw. "I was a fool the other night. I've wanted to make love to you for so long, and now, if you..."

Dusty leaned into Tag's hard body signaling her surrender. But Tag didn't react as she would have expected. He didn't ravish her with pent-up kisses or sweep her off her feet. He simply smoothed a curl behind her ear, his eyes devouring her.

"I'll have to run up to the drugstore first . . ."

"No, you won't. I went by a clinic."

Tag nodded, a soft smile spreading across his face. "What were you planning to do, seduce me?"

Dusty repeated his nod.

"So, seduce me," he whispered, finally lowering his mouth to hers. His kiss was gentle, and when Dusty lifted herself on tiptoe to take a better grasp on his neck, he didn't allow her a tight hold.

"Easy, babe, slow and easy this time. It's been a long while for me, so don't push me. It'll be hard enough as it is. I want you more than I've ever wanted anybody." Tag kissed her again, lightly, easing himself from her tighter grip. "Are you sure about this? I'm afraid there'll be no going back once I get started, and I . . ."

"I'm sure," Dusty said, putting her fingertip to his lips.

Tag kissed her finger. Looking intently into her gaze, he dragged her finger into his mouth, his tongue curling around it, stroking its underside. Tag's gaze suddenly became filled with passion. He groaned as he released her finger and began kissing her palm.

Desire shot through Dusty, leaden and hot—unlike anything she had ever experienced before. "Tag," she pleaded.

"I know, babe. Believe me, I know."

When Tag finally lifted his eyes to hers, they were those of a stranger. She hadn't witnessed desire, not like the desire in Tag's eyes, not in the light of day. But for all her inexperience with his sort of fire, she could tell he was restraining himself, putting her first and, that made him all the dearer to her.

"Come on," he said huskily.

Tag led her through the apartment to her bedroom. It was broad daylight, and the yellow curtains were diffusing the winter sunlight into a golden glow. A single, solid yellow shaft of light fell across Dusty's bed like a spotlight. She felt as if she were about to be put on display.

"Come here," Tag coaxed, his smile softening. Sitting on the edge of the bed, he eased her between his knees. "I want to undress you." His familiar voice was thick with an unfamiliar rasp.

Dusty's heart responded to that sound, her eyes seeking a steady contact with his while he began unbuttoning her apricot dress. Tag treated each revealed patch of her skin to his expert ministrations, kissing her breasts where they swelled above her bra, trailing the soft pad of his thumb between her cleavage, then along the edge of her lacy undergarment.

"I've fantasized about where you'd be freckled and where not, and I'm glad to finally see the reality." Bending, he kissed the round of her newly exposed belly. "I couldn't have applied the sprinkling more perfectly myself."

Tag had stripped Dusty down to her underwear and now slowed to a luxurious pace. Her white panties and bra were her best. They were also her most fragile, mere wisps, which Tag seemed intent on peering through. Finally he reached around and undid the bra hooks, allowing the sheer strip to slip down her arms to the floor.

Tag slid his hands upward along Dusty's waist as if measuring her, until each palm covered a small rosy-tipped breast. His thumbs stroked slowly across the soft peaks, bringing them to hard red beads.

"Tag," she murmured, her knees weakening.

Tag responded by lifting his eyes to hers. "Hang on, babe. I can't seem to get enough of looking at you. Your skin is like the finest...the most translucent porcelain. It...it's..." Tag gave up trying to express how beautiful, how infinitely desirable she was and instead took a nipple hungrily into his mouth.

Dusty looked down, and the sight of his full lips sucking the tip of her breast into his mouth sent a sensual jolt through her system. Suddenly her legs became unsteady, and she clung to Tag's broad shoulders for support. He pulled her close, his tongue and lips now playing over her skin. Leaning back, Dusty arched her body toward him, offering herself to him.

"Tag," she whispered.

"Yes, babe?" His voice was more ragged than before, and when he looked up at her, Dusty felt another spasm of desire shake her body.

"Would you remove your shirt, please? I want to..."

She knew what she wanted. She wanted to feel his warm skin under her fingers. But would her naive explorations please him? Why hadn't he removed any of his clothes?

Tag smiled a slow, sensual smile. "You want what, babe? Say it," he coaxed.

At her continued hesitation, he tucked her more closely within the circle of his arms and legs. "I want you to say it, Dusty. What do you want?"

"I want to touch you, too."

"And I want you to. But I wouldn't do anything to make you uncomfortable, and I know you're new at this."

Dusty lowered her lashes. "I'm sorry about that now."

Tag suddenly went still, his gaze seeking to pierce hers. "Sorry about what?"

Dusty shrugged a bare shoulder. The golden light running along the soft roundness of it also fashioned a glorious nimbus in her lush red hair. "About not knowing how to please you. I never really planned . . . It just worked out that way. I was always so busy, and . . ."

Tag was smiling another of his new, soft smiles. "If you're trying to explain your virginity to me, babe, you're talking nonsense. That's something no one should have to defend. Besides, you can surely see how much you're pleasing me. You're also forgetting that I waited until I was the same age as you are."

Dusty smiled. "You also told me this was my lucky year."

"Yeah, I did. And now I don't know which one of us is luckier." Tag reached to touch the fiery light that was Dusty's hair. "You're so beautiful in your own special way."

Releasing Dusty for the first time, Tag stood up. Quickly he undid his shirt buttons, then the hook and zipper of his pants. His pace was so quick that he was out of his clothes before Dusty could request a chance to enjoy the same slow pleasure he'd had, looking at her while removing her clothes.

But Tag even seemed to have forgotten his promise to let her explore him as he had her. He caught Dusty up in an embrace that was bone-crushing. His mouth enveloped hers. His hands smoothed down the curve of her back and under her panties, his long fingers stroking the soft entrance to her femininity. Stripping her panties away, he grasped her by the swell of her bottom, pulling her into contact with his arousal, then fell with her onto the bed.

He held her close, his hands stroking her heatedly and his kisses moving over her skin. But somehow his pace seemed to be slowly, becoming . . . uncertain.

She gave him a questioning look, which he answered with a slight smile. "I'm not so sure now," he whispered. "Oh, I know you think you are, but this . . . is different."

"Why is this different?" she whispered back.

"Because I don't know what I'm doing."

Dusty found his qualms both sweet and silly. "Just because I haven't . . . doesn't mean I've been raised on the moon, Tag. Or that I haven't gotten close to . . ."

Tag lifted his head so that he could stare down at her. "Who'd you get close with?" he demanded, sounding a tad offended.

Dusty smiled a wise smile. "No one I can even remember."

Tag groaned and, kissing her possessively, lost his qualms.

While there was tenderness in his kisses, in his coaxings, there was no longer any hesitation. He only waited until he was sure she was ready. Then, pressing the length of his body rhythmically against hers, he moved into her, accomplishing the union she was aching for.

Dusty's gasping sigh was inarticulate, but she couldn't have spoken more clearly to Tag. His response was just as clear. *What's happening in you is happening in me,* he said with his bold blue gaze.

Tag's rhythmical thrusts were building toward a goal—for them both. Right away Dusty discovered what that goal was. She could feel it gathering gloriously inside of her until, at last, it expanded into the brightest, most ringing realm she had ever experienced.

Her soft gasp and little cry of pleasure brought a pleased, almost relieved, look from Tag. Then he, too, was overtaken by a shuddering spasm that left him suddenly drained of tension.

"I knew you'd be sweet," he said in a lesser language than the one his eyes spoke. "I've thought about you...dreamed about you."

Kissing her once more, Tag rolled to the space just beside her. Dusty turned her head to gaze at him. He looked beautiful in the golden patch of light, and she smiled a satisfied, female smile.

Tag's kisses became languorous. There was no sense of urgency now. He stroked her slowly, smoothing his hand gently over her skin, which obviously fascinated him. Until this day, Dusty had never been grateful for her dustings of freckles. Beauty was, indeed, in the eye of the beholder, and Tag found her beautiful.

At last Dusty curled herself comfortably into Tag's arms, while he tucked her in close against his larger body. She heard him sigh, then listened as his breathing slowed and deepened. She studied him in the fading beam of light shining through her window, and skimmed a fingertip along his arm. Tag grunted, snuggling more closely into her. Dusty didn't think she'd ever been so happy. She was in love with John Taggert, and he was hers—at least for the time being.

CHAPTER EIGHTEEN

GENTLY REMOVING HERSELF from Tag's embrace, Dusty got out of bed, being careful not to wake him, and headed for the kitchen. She retrieved the first two chapters of his manuscript. To discover he was writing a book—and at her coaxing—was nothing short of thrilling. She wondered if this wasn't the best day she would ever have.

After the warmth of being in bed with Tag, the apartment air felt cool against her bare skin, and she went quickly back to their haven. The golden light that had suffused their lovemaking had disappeared, leaving the room in twilight.

Fetching a couple of blankets from Tag's room, she covered his sprawling naked form. She loved looking at him and regretted the need to cover him up. Then, taking his flashlight and his manuscript, she crept carefully under the covers. When she sat back against the rattan headboard, Tag insinuated himself around her and as much into her lap as he could manage.

Since she knew he didn't normally allow himself this kind of deep sleep, Dusty waited until he was again breathing slowly and steadily before switching on his flashlight and beginning to read.

It was as good as she'd known it would be. The tale was a male adventure story—the sort you might purchase on any paperback stand. Tag obviously made no claims to being an author of fine literary works, but his words swept you up in the very first paragraph into a world that was real and gritty.

Tag's hero was a rumpled, savvy detective who was hard as nails yet entirely principled. His name was Louie Starr. That name, however, was the single thing she could connect with their life in the apartment. His use of Louie was funny, but only because it was personal. The rest of the wit salted through the pages was strictly dry, growing out of his main character's view of life—the sort of wit that might prompt the reader to smile and say, "Yes. Yes, that's what the world's like. Tell me more."

Dusty wanted to shout with joy. Here was something her love could do. Here was his best talent—his means of freeing himself from a life that was tearing him apart. She wanted to wake him and tell him so. But she didn't. Instead, she began to read it all again from the beginning.

"Dusty, what are you doing?" Tag asked, peering up at her from her lap. The light from her flashlight was obviously shining through the paper and into his face.

"I'm reading the first pages ever written by a fabulous new writer."

"So. You like it?" He didn't seem nearly as anxious for her opinion as he had been earlier in the afternoon. He was, in fact, insinuating his face more deeply into her lap. "Um, Dusty," he whispered, his grip on her tightening.

"Tag," she said, beginning to feel more than a little distracted, "don't you want to discuss your book?"

"I can think of something I'd rather do."

"But…" Dusty hemmed, liking what Tag was doing with his mouth, but not quite comfortable with it.

She was relieved when he chuckled and pulled himself up and her down in order to be level with her.

"Seeing as how you aren't ready for that move and I'm not quite up to snuff as far as finishing what I'm starting, I guess I have no choice but to discuss my book."

"What would you like to hear?"

"That I'm a fabulous lover and have a perfect body."

Tag got the laugh he wanted. "You almost deserve those phrases. But I'm talking about your literary abilities."

"What do you mean, 'almost deserve'?" he asked with a frown.

"Well, I'm hardly the one to say you're a fabulous lover since I have no point of comparison. You are, however, definitely a lover."

"And what about my perfect body?"

"For my tastes, I must admit it is rather perfect."

"Aha!"

"But … others might find these little scars and this big one on your thigh, which are obviously tokens of your trade, a bit less than perfect," she added, taking the luster out of his pale blue eyes.

"I guess we'd better move on to discussing my literary abilities if that's where you'll give me the praise I deserve."

"Yes, let's, because you, John Taggert, are going to be a star."

Tag sobered a bit. "You really like it that much?"

"I love it." Dusty looked him straight in the eye. "And I think you've picked the perfect type of book to write. What with your store of tales, your underbelly view of the world, your firsthand experience, your talent for weaving a story, your cynical nature, you can't miss."

"I guess that's praise enough," he said with a soft smile.

"I'm your first fan as well as your number one fan."

Tag kissed her. "And I'm a real fan of yours, babe. I'm so glad you're in bed with me. I'm so glad you're my lover, and that I was your first."

"Do you provide sustenance for your lovers?" she asked pertly, wanting to lighten the tone. What he said thrilled her, but she was afraid he would see her need for even more from him in her eyes.

"What would you like? Cookies?"

"I saw your cookies, thank you—and I saw the way you keep a kitchen, too. Which reminds me, who cleans up?"

"I've got this sweet little redhead who cleans up," Tag said, kissing her cheek.

"That's what I was afraid you'd say."

"Tell you what, I'll send out for pizza and help with the kitchen. That way we can turn in early."

Dusty looked into Tag's face, a slow smile spreading across her features. "Okay."

"That's what I like to see—an enthusiastic beginner. Promise me that you'll always say yes."

Dusty looked him straight in the eyes. "I'll always say yes."

With another quick kiss, Tag was on his feet. "I'll call for the pizza."

"Do I dress in a towel to answer the door?"

Tag stopped dead in his tracks. "Like hell you will."

"I was quite a success with the delivery boy the last time I did."

"Yeah, well, I'll get the door this time."

Dusty sighed. "Tag, you're being silly."

"I don't care. I'll answer the door, and I'll do it fully clothed."

"I don't get this." Dusty was chuckling. "I mean, we'd only be living up to the reputation we've established."

Tag pierced Dusty with another stuffy stare. When she laughed even harder, he went off to his room. She heard him checking in at headquarters, and then calling the pizza place.

Over the next few hours she learned how terrific things could be. Kisses in the kitchen, caresses over the pizza, sweet urgings that drifted into lazy cajoleries under the Christmas tree, all made her feel as if she'd entered some unknown and even unimaginable world. It was a far softer and more sensual one than the world she was used to, and she decided she'd like to live in it forever.

That night Tag moved into her bedroom. They had been friends first, and being lovers came easily. Dusty could sense that he was as happy with their new arrangement as she was. She could see it in his face and hear it in his ready chuckle. For if Tag was anything, he was a natural tease.

The following morning Tag forced himself back to work in his little room, but by late morning he was diverted again. The movers had come with Pam's couch and he paid them to carry her old one downstairs.

"Let's try it out," he said as soon as the door closed behind the retreating workmen.

"Okay." Dusty plopped down on their new piece of furniture. "Switch on the TV."

Tag immediately sat down beside her, his mouth seeking the warmth of her neck. "That's not the kind of trial run I'm interested in," he said, his hand stroking the outside of her thigh.

"I thought you said that when you had some time this morning you needed to get into your first confrontation scene."

"I thought you said you'd always say yes," he replied, his palm caressing the top of her thigh.

"I didn't say no." Dusty was already slightly breathless with anticipation.

"I wouldn't be able to concentrate now," Tag whispered, stroking the inside of her leg. "Especially since it's a confrontation scene. I'd much rather write a love scene." Tag's fingers fumbled at the snap on Dusty's waistband.

Dusty blinked. "Are you actually going to write love scenes?"

He paused to chuckle. "Sure. But they won't be sweet and tender."

"They won't?"

"No. My main character is—"

"Louie Starr."

"Yeah, Louie Starr. He's strictly out to use and cruise."

"I'm beginning to dislike Louie."

"Don't go viewing good old Louie in a bad light. He's a heartbroken guy. A guy you ladies should sympathize with."

Even though she wasn't sure Tag was being serious, Dusty was curious. "What happened to good old Louie?"

"The love of his life was killed by the Mafia. Now he wanders the world lonely and alone. Where women are concerned, he takes what's offered. I mean, why shouldn't he? But everyone of them is willing and goes into it knowing he has no heart to give."

"Just when did you decide on this?"

"When I decided that this is only the first in a whole line of books with the same character. It's called The Starr Series."

"Talk about delusions of grandeur." But while Dusty scoffed, deep down she believed that what he said would happen. "So, tell me what happened to Louie's lady love. And, please, spare the gory details."

"I can't tell you just yet, but it'll all be exposed in a tender and touching flashback. All I can say is that her name is Rusty. Rusty Starr. And that she had red hair and a freckled posterior that will someday be world-famous. You see, that's to become his measure for all the women he meets."

"He sounds more than a little chauvinistic."

"But somehow adorable just the same."

Dusty had to chuckle. "Rusty Starr," she said softly, caught by the world Tag was building on paper in his dingy little room.

"Yeah, Rusty Starr," he said, smiling at her contemplative look. "Now, can we get back to trying out the couch?'' His hand was again smoothing its way along the inside of her thigh.

''I suppose Rusty, with her freckled posterior, would never have refused Louie.''

''Never. She, too, swore she would always say yes.''

''And naturally Louie always says yes to the ladies he meets.''

''Naturally.'' Tag grinned wickedly. ''It's sort of a personal memorial, a way he pays tribute to Rusty.''

She wished she could manage a disapproving look, but Dusty just laughed. ''Nothing like killing off your one true love and then paying such a high tribute to her through fifty books.''

''I thought it was sort of a nice touch.''

''And you? What about you, Tag? Do you always say yes?''

''Only to you,'' he said, still smiling, but no longer laughing.

''You'd better be careful. 'Only' sounds awfully close to June-moon-spoon.''

Tag sobered a bit more, looking steadily into Dusty's eyes. ''Yeah, it does.''

Dusty felt oddly disconcerted. It was as if something was dawning in Tag. Reaching over the short distance between them, she touched his knee. ''Then I can be sure you won't say no to me now?''

Covering Dusty's hand with his own, he pulled her to him. His kiss was surprisingly steamy.

Smoothing her hand over his leg, he traced ever-expanding circles. Dusty could see his eyes cloud over with desire, and experienced her own need to respond.

''Dusty,'' he rasped. ''Touch me.''

Dusty did as Tag asked, her intimate grasp setting off a storm in both of them. Soon the couch seemed too confining for their desire, and Tag carried Dusty to the bedroom. Later, after the passion was spent, she fell into a light sleep, wondering how she would ever live without him.

"WHAT'S THE MATTER, BABE?"

Dusty peered groggily up from where she lay in the rumpled covers of their bed. "Nothing's the matter."

Tag was sitting across from her, a tray of sandwiches and apples in his lap for their lunch. "Are you sure you're all right? I thought maybe you were having a bad dream."

"No. I'm fine."

She found that the food helped. By the end of their lunch she had established a fresh resolve. She still wanted Tag and whatever he would share with her. Just looking at him—even doing such a mundane thing as munching on his sandwich—confirmed that. She simply had to accept the temporary nature of their time together and, with that acceptance, would also come an ability to enjoy the bittersweet hours they would have.

Dusty's resolve was only shaken once more, and that was during the following night. Tag and she were sound asleep, wrapped in the comfort of each other's arms and the warmth of their bedding. Disturbed by something, she woke up to find that he was caught in the throes of one of his nightmares. From the way he was moaning and twitching, this one seemed especially tormenting, and when she reached out to gently wake him, he sat upright as he hadn't before.

Again Dusty reached out. This time she was accepted into his embrace. He was so clammy with sweat that she dragged their covers tightly around them and held him fast. His recovery was slow. Dusty even felt the accelerated race of his heartbeat, the slight tremor in his hands.

"Tag?" she said, coming close to declaring her love for him.

"I'm all right, babe."

When Dusty reached for the lamp on the beside table, he told her not to switch it on. "Just cuddle with me under the covers and I'll be fine," he told her.

Dusty lay back down with him, curling around his upper body, holding his head against her breast as one would with a child. He responded to her quiet presence and gentle strokings, and she felt him gradually relax.

"Do you want to tell me?" she asked.

"I haven't been able to tell anyone."

Dusty stared up at the familiar blue patch where the streetlight cast its glow on her ceiling, quietly waiting for Tag to speak.

Finally, drawing in a deep breath and holding her even more tightly, he told her. He spoke of dreadful visions of faceless people, some dead, some bleeding. He felt again the impact of the bullet he had taken in his own body, and said it was all confused with a faceless child feeling the same thing. His scream was the child's scream.

Dusty didn't answer with any more than a continuation of her gentle stroking and the offer of the warmth and softness of her body.

"I'm torn, Dusty." Tag confessed, sounding more like his usual self. "I want to get out of this business and yet . . . yet I feel I have to prove myself one more time or I'll never be able to walk away from it and be free." He paused, obviously dredging up his darkest worry. "I have to show myself that I can...that I won't fall apart. And then I'll walk. I'll put it all behind me. And between you and me, I won't look back."

"Tag," Dusty murmured, and in that one word offered a world of understanding and comfort—all she could give. And once and for all, she gave up the wish to add "I love you" to her sweet utterance of his name. She knew if she'd been able to hold it back at this most intimate moment, she would be able to keep it from him for good. She was both relieved and sad, and a tear slipped down her cheek before Tag began to suckle her tenderly, leading her in the now-familiar direction of making love.

CHAPTER NINETEEN

DUSTY SPENT a couple of long afternoons with Roger Maddox. She wanted to take full advantage of the Christmas holidays to spend as much time with him as she could. She'd been exchanging notes with his teacher, and they felt pretty good about his progress. He seemed to be doing better, mainly because his father was absent for so much of the time.

For some weeks now the boy had been spending more and more of his time with Tag and herself, dropping by shyly and being welcomed into whatever they were doing. He was even looking better, and Dusty was certain the new glow in his eyes was the result of good food and more attention.

But Dusty's best times were spent with Tag, their days and nights running the gamut from exquisite passion to peaceful companionship. Now she sat on his cot, her legs tucked underneath her in her usual position for what had become their regular editing sessions. She fixed the *n*'s, checked Tag's spelling and made occasional suggestions.

"Did you say Pam called while I was talking to headquarters this morning?" Tag asked.

Dusty looked up from the typed page she was reading. "Yeah. Pam telephoned all the way from Memphis to wish us a happy New Year."

"Did everything go well for her and Brent? I mean, with her father?"

"It went so well that I've never heard her happier. She also says she's pretty much decided to move back."

"Move back? To Memphis?"

"Well, it's not like it's a bolt out of the blue. She's been thinking about going home for some time. She doesn't have anyone here, and she calls the store where she works, 'the coal mines,' and the nicest thing she calls her boss is 'slave driver.' So why not move?"

Dusty shifted uncomfortably on the cot, letting her eyes drift to the crack in the drapes. "I'm going to miss her, though. It's surprising what good friends I've made here. My only regret is all the lies I've had to tell Pam. She's constantly catching me up in them. When it's time to tell her the truth, I hope she'll understand."

"Dusty," Tag said, his tone of voice suggesting she was being silly, "once you've explained the circumstances, Pam will definitely understand. Fibbing to protect your life is understandable."

"Yeah, I guess so."

"And," Tag said, "speaking of New Year's Eve. How will we celebrate? It's tomorrow night, you know."

"Actually I hadn't thought about it. What are our choices? You can't get away, can you?"

"Not for any length of time. But do you have a dressy dress?"

"The only dressy dress I have here is the one I bought for dining out while I was with Eric and Leslie." *The one you removed a few days ago,* she thought.

"Oh, that one."

"Yes, that one."

"Er...I thought I might rent a tux."

"And...?"

"And we'd spend the evening here."

"Here?" Dusty felt as if she were pulling teeth.

"Yeah. We can order in some Chinese, do a little dancing..."

Dusty brightened. "Do you like to dance?"

"No," he replied with a sexy grin.

Dusty sent Tag a knowing look. "In short, you want to get all dressed up just to get undressed."

"This is getting scary."

"What is?"

"You're starting to know me too well. We think alike, we get along without really making an effort—"

Unfortunately the doorbell rang, and Dusty got up to answer it. "That's probably Rog. He's a little early, though, and I wanted to take some soup up to Jake and Bessie."

"Just send him back to me," Tag said.

"But what about your equipment?"

"He saw it the other day. I told him it's a special tape playing system."

Dusty nodded. "I'll send him back then and run up to Jake's. I won't be long."

"Aren't you forgetting something?" Tag called after her.

"What?" Dusty asked, puzzled.

"Come here and kiss me. Heaven only knows how long Rog will linger. Poor kid. And I want a taste of tonight." When Dusty only sent Tag a smile over her shoulder, he cocked an eyebrow and said, "You promised you'd always say yes, remember?"

Dusty walked back to him, a minor shiver of anticipation running down her spine. Even Tag's little kisses had their effect. This one was no exception.

"Can you find your way to the door?" he asked when the doorbell rang again.

"If I can't, I'll call you."

"Then we'll never get there."

Precisely what happened after that took some piecing together later on. Dusty had planned on a tutoring session with Rog. After that she wanted to keep him for dinner, and then Tag would walk him home. But after delivering the soup to Jake and Bessie upstairs, she returned to find that all hell had broken loose in the apartment.

On the doorstep, Roger careened into her, and Dusty was unable to stop him. Giving her a terrified look, the boy dashed off down the street. She called after him to stop and come back. When he didn't, she raced to Tag's room.

"What happened?" she asked.

"The Desotas are back," he said, flinging the words over his shoulder as he worked with his tapes. "They got out of Miami without our knowing. They're here in St. Louis, and it looks like the deal's going down now. They've got the merchandise on them, so it's time to put them away." Tag spoke in a terse language that was barely recognizable to her. He had reverted to being a cop.

"But isn't it too soon?"

"It's never too soon. It happens when it happens. And that's precisely why sitting on a case is necessary—no matter how innocuous it looks."

Tag took a moment to use his police radio. Dusty understood only half of what he was saying. She was trying to calm herself. She couldn't imagine what would occur next.

Finally Tag turned to her. She had the sudden feeling she was staring into the gaze of a stranger. His eyes hadn't looked so icy in weeks, and she tried to come to grips with what he was saying.

"Rog and I were talking when the machine clicked on. Naturally I was caught up right away, and when I looked back, he was as white as a sheet. I tried to explain, but he ran off. I'll simply have to deal with him later. The voice that was piped in was a new one, and I have no idea whose it was."

"No names were mentioned?"

"They seldom are when it's critical."

Dusty nodded, licking her lips. "The merchandise," as the drugs were called, was here and ready to be disposed of. This was it. A chill ran down her spine. The day she had always known would come had finally arrived—and all too soon.

Swallowing hard, Dusty fought for control. She hadn't expected to react this way, to feel so anxious. She especially wanted to remain collected in the face of Tag's cool demeanor. God, he seemed a stranger. And, oh, it hurt.

"Are you all right?" he asked brusquely.

"Yes," she managed, stiffening her shoulders.

Tag looked at her for only a moment more, examining her with his impersonal blue stare. Evidently she measured up, because he began stashing his tapes and papers in a slim black attaché case.

When he reached for the holster and gun, that always hung in his closet, Dusty felt her first jolt of real gut-twisting fear. Of course, somewhere in the back of her mind, she'd known all along that Tag kept his gun in this room. Hadn't she seen it that night in the hallway? But somehow she'd forgotten it.

Hadn't Tag warned her against forgetting the reality of their situation? But that was exactly what she'd done.

Another jab of fear struck her as she watched him strapping on his holster. God, she thought, don't let him be hurt.

His eyes scanned the room, a last check before finally focusing on her.

She felt like a butterfly pinned to the wall, and knew that to struggle, to flap her wings in protest, would be both useless and, in the end, shameful. So she stood before him, mute, watching with her rust-colored gaze.

"I've got to go."

"Next door?"

"No. Across town. A nearby patrol car is coming to pick me up, but we'll have to fight rush hour."

"And what about Syd Desota?"

"He's too old to go. He merely relayed the message to several of the minor fish. We've got a good chance at getting them all."

"Even the one who killed my dad?"

Tag was shrugging into his coat. "Since we haven't identified him, I can't say. But this is our best chance yet."

Dusty nodded her understanding.

"I want you to lock up. You're not to open the door for anyone. Do you understand?"

Dusty nodded again.

"I'll come back as soon as I can," he added, and just for a second there was something besides ice in his eyes.

Still, all Dusty could do was nod once more.

"Don't do this, Dusty." Tag said with sudden anger in his voice. "Don't make demands on me. I've got enough in my craw."

"I know." She did know, and she would no more drag him down than she would do anything else to harm even so much as a hair on his head. "I'll lock up and won't answer the door until you're back."

Dropping his case on the table, Tag grabbed her roughly into his arms and stared down into her face. He looked as if he wanted desperately to tell her something, but was just as desperately afraid of doing so. In the end he said nothing, but seared her lips with a kiss. When Dusty attempted to respond, tried to cling to him, he pulled away.

"I've got to go." He left her with a glance that revealed something raw and hot burning in the ice-blue depths of his tortured eyes.

Dusty didn't cry. She didn't react at all. She walked to the door and locked it, just as he had commanded, then went back to his card table to keep her vigil. Maybe she would hear something over the police radio.

TAG STEPPED INTO THE COLD, the chill in his heart easily matching that of the waning day. Even his searing kiss for Dusty hadn't been able to reach the ice in his blood. God, he was in love with her. She had enough warmth to heat even his frozen soul, but he couldn't let her. Not yet, and maybe never.

He had things to prove, possibly tonight. But it was going down across town, so it was possible he wouldn't make it. He didn't know which he dreaded more—getting there in time to have his piece of the action, or missing his opportunity to purge himself. If he missed it this time, his hellish wait would be prolonged. He'd have to hold on to his sanity until his next chance to prove himself, and he dreaded that wait most of all. If he had to wait, he'd have to give up Dusty.

He couldn't ask her to live with the bitterness of not knowing. That would only sour them both. No. He would go to her only when he knew he was whole. She deserved better than half a man.

Just then the patrol car swung into the block, its lights and siren already screaming a warning. Tag glanced at his watch. Eight minutes. Not bad, he told himself. Only eight minutes since he'd heard that call piped into his room from Syd's apartment. Eight minutes since he'd phoned headquarters to tell them where the deal was going down.

It was too bad he was so far away. It would take almost half an hour, forty-five minutes maybe, to get there through rush-hour traffic.

Swerving in to the curb, the patrol car screeched to a halt. Climbing in, Tag nodded to the youthful policeman who was driving. "You know where to go?"

The kid snapped a "Yes, sir," and Tag told him to do his best.

Looking out the window at the city blocks flying by, Tag tried to concentrate, to think of what lay ahead of him as a cop.

He'd had his guts wrenched out that afternoon at the hotel stakeout. What guts he'd had to begin with. Dusty might have been right about his having chosen this work too early in his life. But then he shoved that thought to the back of his mind. He would give himself no excuses.

How he had gotten to this crazed point in his life didn't count now, anyway. All that was important was that he resolve his inner turmoil so that he could sleep nights and get rid of the ache in his gut. And he knew the single way to accomplish that feat was to face the same hell and to emerge either whole or not at all.

At last their mad plummet through dodging traffic came to an abrupt halt. The youthful patrolman sent Tag a glance as he pulled the car to a jolting stop.

"Good job," Tag told him.

"Thank you, sir."

Getting out of the car, Tag could already see what had happened. Even before he walked the last half block from where the patrol car left him, he knew it was over. It was like a scene from a grade B movie— the bombed-out look of the half-abandoned city neighborhood exposed in the harsh, whirling light of police cars.

Tag was torn between relief and his dread of the next time that was already building inside of him. His trial by fire that he'd hoped would come tonight would still come, but now it was postponed.

He would have to give up Dusty.

Feeling his insides wrench, Tag swore that no one would see his pain. Not even Dusty. Not even the object of his enormous and newly discovered love.

Captain Alvarez was picking his way over the debris in the alley, coming to meet him.

"It's over," the older cop said, stating the obvious.

"How'd we do?" Tag watched the captain's dark features, which were garishly exposed by the revolving bar of lights on his police car.

"The second Desota wasn't here when we arrived, but someone just picked him up."

"And the others?"

"We got all but one."

"Which one?"

Alvarez looked steadily into Tag's scowl. "Ox Landry's killer. One of the Desotas decided to make it easier on himself and started pointing the finger. He not only named the name, but told us it was an execution, just like we thought."

"Oh, hell."

"At least we know his name now."

"And?" Tag was trying to come to grips with this bad news. Dusty's stint with him might never bear fruit.

"It's Maddox...a Roger Maddox."

Tag didn't react. He stood staring into Alvarez's face. "Oh, God. He must have been the one...the new voice that called Syd. He... Oh, my God," he whispered.

"There's no way he can know about Dusty," Alvarez said, seeing but not understanding Tag's sudden, black fear.

"Oh, no?" Tag was already heading for the driver's side of the police car. "Dusty's been tutoring his kid, and his kid heard his voice over the bug."

After that it was Alvarez's turn to scramble into the passenger side.

DUSTY WAS AMAZED by her composure. She would have expected her excess energy to make her restless. But here she sat, glued to the now-familiar bank of equipment in front of her.

From what she could gather on the police radio, Tag's case was an important one but was resolved fairly easily. She listened as, step by step, the police surrounded their quarry and closed in. In fact, it was almost that simple. By her reckoning, Tag had barely gotten to the scene before it was over. She was relieved, and realized that her knowledge that Tag was almost certainly safe accounted for her steadiness.

In fact, she was so relaxed now after being so anxious that she barely heard the first knock at the front door. She listened to be sure, then heard it again. Getting up from her chair, she walked toward the door. Halfway there, Tag's warning popped into her mind.

"Who is it?" she called out, her hand at the lock.

"Roger."

The boyish voice was definitely Roger's, but the strain in it caught her ear. Her concern for the child was quickly aroused. He was probably still upset about what had happened earlier.

Dusty fumbled with the lock, sorry that she hadn't turned on a light in the living room and cursing the stingy landlord who'd made the stoop lights inoperable in order to save a penny. When she finally opened the door, she bent to gather the boy in her embrace, but even as she reached for him, she was shoved back into the room by an enormous man.

"What are you doing?" she sputtered indignantly.

She couldn't see him at first, but when he stepped into the light, panic erupted inside her. The picture in her mind had at last come to life.

"You're Dusty?"

"Y-yes."

"Dusty Landry?" he asked with a sneer.

Dusty didn't answer, couldn't answer.

"That's what I thought."

Dusty recoiled in revulsion. This man had killed her father and had somehow found her out. Her eyes switched to the small figure of Roger Maddox. He was held fast by the man's hand on his thin shoulder.

Dusty was torn between her fear and her worry for the child. "Don't hurt the boy," she heard herself say. "This is between you and me and doesn't concern him."

"I'll do what I want with him. He's my kid."

That statement explained everything, even without the man going on.

"When I got your note that you were going to teach him, I looked a long time at that unusual first name of yours. But, no, I told myself, her name is Dusty Taggert. And the Dusty that Ox Landry called to that night was Dusty Landry. Of course, I never would've recognized you. I didn't get a good look. Who'd have thought I'd get this lucky? I should have had this luck at the track."

Maddox moved farther into Dusty's apartment, and she backed up a step. "But when this kid comes home this afternoon," Maddox continued, "and says he's heard my voice on a tape player, it all clicks. It was too late to warn anyone. The damn cops stepped in too fast. Anyhow, Roger here wouldn't tell me where you lived without a little persuasion."

The brute of a man shoved his son forward, and the boy stumbled into Dusty's arms. Reaching out, she pulled him against her. He was trembling, the feel of his thin little body adding sympathy to her already overwhelming mix of emotions.

Stepping toward her, Maddox motioned with a thick hand. "I wanna see this tape deck the kid told me about. I wanna see if there's anything with my voice on it."

"There isn't." Dusty was glad to have the truth to tell. "The detective took it all with him."

"Let's just have a look to be sure."

Not letting go of Roger, Dusty led the way back to Tag's room. As the man came in behind her, she noticed the bulge in his pocket, something heavy that dragged down that side of his cheap overcoat. He, too, had a gun, and the menace of it sucked away Dusty's ability to think.

Tightening her grip on the boy, who now had a grasp on her that was desperate, Dusty watched while the man tore through the room and smashed everything in it. As she watched this brutal display, she realized the daily terror the boy had lived in for all these weeks. Something primal and protective was struck in her, and she looked, with as much reassurance as she could, into Roger's terror-filled eyes.

"Rog," she said, just as his father was winding down because there was nothing more to smash, "why don't you go into the bedroom and let your dad and me work this out."

Even as the boy pressed his head against her shoulder to protest leaving her, Maddox turned on them with a roar. "He doesn't go anywhere, lady! He stays right here where I can keep an eye on him. I can't trust the little bastard."

Maddox's eyes drilled even more deeply into Dusty's, and she could almost read his mind as he made his decision.

"I'm gonna have to take you out."

Removing the gun from his pocket, this murderer who she had seen kill before reached into another pocket to retrieve a silencer. A kind of disbelieving daze gripped Dusty's brain. She couldn't think of how to escape. Even as she recoiled, Roger jerked from her clutches, launching his little body at the hulk that was his father. It was a ludicrous sight, the bravery of it tearing at Dusty's insides.

"No!" the boy shouted.

The brute who had brought him into being backhanded the child as if he meant less than nothing. The blow was so untempered that it threw Roger against a wall. The boy crumpled like a rag doll, slumping unconscious. Dusty moved to grab him.

"Stay where you are, lady." Maddox said quietly. "He knows too much, so he'll have to be snuffed, too."

The brute's stare kept Dusty frozen as he twisted his silencer onto the muzzle of his gun.

Dusty's gaze flew to the boy who lay in the smashed debris. He was out cold, but he was breathing. And then it hit her. She was about to die. With Roger soon to follow.

Turning again toward Maddox, she saw Tag crouching in the doorway behind the killer. Tag's arms were extended, the revolver in his hands aimed point-blank at the unsuspecting Maddox.

"Hold it right there," he growled.

Maddox looked over his shoulder, his gaping expression almost ludicrously comical.

Safe. They were almost safe.

But Maddox didn't cave in. He raised his own gun. Dusty's eyes sliced automatically to Tag's, and then she felt as if she'd stepped into the final nightmare. *Oh, God, Maddox is going to shoot. And Tag . . . and Tag's shaking.*

A grotesque grin spread across Maddox's large features. He appeared even uglier. "What's the matter, cop? Gone over the edge?" he taunted. "You're not gonna blow me away. In fact," the man said, turning so Dusty couldn't see his face. "It's me who's gonna off you. You're already shot. I'm just doin' you a favor."

Tag's eyes and stance held. He didn't so much as flinch when Maddox shifted his weapon. But it wasn't Tag's gun that sounded in the nightmarish silence, nor was it the brute's. Maddox fell forward onto his face as Captain Alvarez stepped into the room. His revolver emitted a wisp of smoke. Tag's gun dropped onto the floor, and the clatter sounded faint against the echoing din of Alvarez's shot.

Dusty looked at Tag. Everything else was forgotten. She was vaguely aware of Captain Alvarez seeing to the boy, doing the things she should be doing. She was caught up in Tag's agony—even as she could see that he was already backing away from her.

"Tag," she whispered, her heart breaking for him, her hand reaching for him. She knew he was seeing this night as his failure.

"No," he said, the word a stony warning. "Can't you see? Maddox was right. I'm burned out. I'm shot. I'm no more good for you than I am for myself."

When Dusty protested, stepping toward him again, Tag walked out.

CHAPTER TWENTY

THE SWEET WINTER DAYS of seclusion had come to an end. Spring was in the air. Maybe it was still officially winter, but the day definitely had taken on a touch of balminess.

The children in Dusty's afternoon kindergarten class seemed to be most attuned to the changing seasons. Besides herself, that is. They ran over the newly green lawn in brightly colored boots, glad to be free in the out-of-doors.

"Ith that a robin, Mth. Landry?" Tracy asked. The little girl's lisp was so cute that it seemed a shame that a speech therapist was working to rid her of it.

"It sure is a robin. If we stand really still, we might be able to see him pull a worm from the ground." Taking the hand the girl was offering, Dusty squeezed it. Tracy was the sweetest child. With her pale blond hair and shyly affectionate ways, she reminded Dusty of Roger Maddox.

Roger... As always, all it took was a single stray thought and Dusty's mind would begin to go over it all again....

Juan Alvarez had taken her in his arms after Tag had left the apartment the night Maddox had been shot down. Alvarez's wife—"Aunt Marge" to Dusty—had come and helped her pack and move out of the apartment. Alvarez and Aunt Marge had listened to her go over and over what had happened.

Shock, they'd said. She'd been suffering from the shock of watching one man killed and another man, a really good man, lose his sense of self-worth. All of that had to be talked out.

Aunt Marge's loving hands had turned her over to Leslie's, and even more loving and listening had been provided. It was because of all of that understanding that Dusty had recovered so quickly. She'd bounced back in a matter of days.

Then she'd come home and gone to work. That, too, had been good for her. But none of it had reached the core of her problem and, although both Aunt Marge and Leslie knew what that problem was, they'd been helpless to heal it. Healing would come with time, they'd promised, with time...

But time hadn't worked its miracle. It hadn't even begun its task. She wasn't any better. She was merely carrying on.

And Tag? What was he doing? She didn't know.

She'd thought that surely he would come to her. They had been so close. Surely he had loved her...

No more, she ordered herself. Switching her eyes back to the children and the robin, she repeated that ragged inner caution. *No more.*

Out of the corner of her eye, Dusty saw that a few cars were beginning to pull up by the schoolyard. "Oops," she said with a smile. "Here's your mommy, Tracy, and that robin still hasn't caught his worm."

"Maybe he'll catch him tomorrow, Mth. Landry," Tracy said with the hope of a child.

"Maybe tomorrow."

More parents were coming now, arriving in a quick rush, and all of the children were leaving just as suddenly. Quitting time. Dusty always dreaded quitting time. It meant going home and taking up the endless struggle with her own thoughts and questions.

"Mrs. Taggert!"

Mrs. Taggert? She must be hearing things. But turning around, she saw a small boy standing just on the other side of the chain-link fence separating Brockham Elementary from the busy street the school was on.

"Roger," she whispered in utter surprise.

Dusty had tried to find Roger after she'd left her sister's house in New York and gone back to St. Louis. Captain Alvarez had told her the boy had recovered from his head wound and said the child had been placed with foster parents until he could be put up for adoption. Very gently Alvarez had suggested it might not be a good idea for Dusty to see the child. "Might bring up bad memories," he'd said. Two weeks later Alvarez had told her the child had been adopted, and Dusty had given up her gentle insistence on seeing the boy.

But she'd often wondered who had pushed so hard to have him. As far as she knew, the boy didn't have a living soul to whom he could turn.

"You look great!" she exclaimed, peering into Roger's smiling face. "Meet me down at the end of the fence," she said.

"Okay. Race ya!" he called out, seeming more boisterous than she'd ever seen him before.

Dusty laughed, taking up his challenge and running along her side of the fence. She kept watching him through the quickly flying screen of interlocking gray diamonds, amazed at the change in him.

"Beat you!" he crowed reaching the end of the fence just before Dusty.

"Yeah, but you had a sidewalk to run on and I had squishy, lumpy ground."

"Yeah," Roger said, generously giving her her point. "I guess we'll have to call it even."

Dusty simply had to reach down and give him a hug. He returned her embrace wholeheartedly. "Can you visit with me for a while?" Dusty asked.

"Sure. I came just to see you."

"Well, that's nice. How did you know where I work?"

"Tag told me. He tells me everything."

Dusty's heart scuddered. "You're living with Tag?"

"Yeah. He adopted me," the boy announced proudly.

"I'm happy for you and Tag," she said truthfully. Placing her arm around the boy's shoulders, she gave him a gentle jostle. "How is Tag?"

"Fine."

"Good."

"Sorta."

"Oh?"

"He's up at night an awful lot."

"Oh." Dusty was sorry to hear this. Tag was probably still wrestling with himself, still having bad dreams.

"He's a writer now, you know."

"No, I didn't know."

"Yeah. He's finished his first book and is trying to write a dedi . . . ded . . ."

"A dedication?"

"Yeah. That's it. He says it's been an awful lot of trouble and that he's gotta mail it in. So I thought maybe you could help, since you're the one he says he wants to deditate the book to."

Dusty didn't know whether to laugh or cry. Between the bitter and the sweet, she felt torn in two. "Rog, I really don't think Tag ought to dedicate his book to me."

"Oh."

The boy was obviously disappointed.

They had reached the doors to the school building and there they paused. Both were reluctant to part.

"Does Tag know you've come to see me?" Dusty asked.

"Nope."

"How did you find me?"

"We were in the car yesterday, and he said this is where you work."

"You're still living in Tag's apartment, then?"

"Yeah."

"Well, that wasn't too far to come."

"It only took one bus."

"Did you see Brent before he moved away?"

"We had a day together."

"Yeah," said Dusty. "Pam and I only had an afternoon. They moved so quickly that it made my head spin."

Dusty still missed her friend, though they talked to each other twice a week on the telephone. Dusty was also keeping in touch with Charlotte Ross, the officer who had sat with her through the six months at the safe house.

Truly Dusty realized how lucky she was. Her dad's house had been waiting for her and so had her job and her friends.

Both Dusty and Roger continued to hang around the school door, Roger dragging the toe of a heavy-duty sneaker through a patch of dirt.

"Would you like to come in for a minute?" Dusty finally asked. "I could fix us a snack."

"Sure."

Dusty couldn't help noticing Roger's new coat and nearly new clothes underneath. Tag was obviously taking good care of him.

Once they were inside, Dusty fixed a light snack—milk from the cooler and leftover cookies from a birthday party. With Roger following, she went to her own classroom where she sat down at the child-sized table by the sunny window.

This room was more of a home to her now than the empty house she'd grown up in. The neatly stowed toys on the shelves, the gay area rug where she and the children sat to read, sing and talk, the bright bulletin boards full of fanciful drawings made her as comfortable as she could get. Somehow she disliked her childhood home. It reflected the emptiness she felt, and not just because her dad was gone. Heck, he'd hardly ever been there, anyway.

Dusty watched while Roger looked around the cheerful room. He'd come from something that was far different from this, and yet it was obvious he was putting that behind him. *What a good little guy.*

"What's that paper you've got there?" Dusty asked, pointing at a roll of crumpled and twisted pages that stuck so far out of Roger's coat pocket that it looked as if he might lose them.

"That's the deditation."

"Dedi-*ca*-tion."

"You wanna see it?"

Even as she said, "Yes," Dusty knew she should refuse.

The boy happily tugged out the wad of pages, which Dusty suspected had been retrieved from the wastebasket.

There were, of course, no *n*'s, but Dusty gave that only passing notice. What really struck her as she looked through the small stack was that all the pages held variations of the same sentence:

To Dusty, from whom I learned the meaning of June-moon-spoon love....

To Dusty, for whom I have the June-moon-spoon sort of love....

To Dusty, who taught me there is such a thing as the June-moon-spoon kind of love....

When tears started to roll down Dusty's cheeks, Roger's features sobered. But his expressive child's face turned just as quickly to sunshine when Dusty laughed through her tears.

"Where is Tag?" she asked.

"That's just it. He got so mad at the dedita...at the dedi*ca*tion, I mean, that he had to go out for a walk. I passed him by on the bus, but he didn't see me. He had his 'mad as hell' look on his face. That's what he calls it."

"When I'm mad as hell because I miss Dusty so much," Tag said from the classroom doorway.

"Tag!" the boy called out in delight.

"May I join you, or is this a private tea party?"

Roger shot a questioning look at Dusty. It was, after all, her party.

She nodded, numb with surprise. "We could move into the office where there's a full-size table and chairs," she finally managed to say.

"Where will it be more private—in the office with the adult furniture or in here?" Tag asked.

"In here."

"Then here it'll be."

Dusty watched as Tag came toward her, where she and Roger sat at the pint-size table. He was thinner again, but as gorgeous as ever, and her heart and body responded as they always did. She knew she was feeling the thrum of that old Taggertitis.

Shrugging out of his sheepskin coat, Tag insinuated his large frame onto one very small chair and stretched out his long legs. Fortunately the chairs were sturdy and could support his weight, if not make him comfortable. Dusty still didn't know what to say, especially when he displayed a slow, sweet smile.

"I see you two are working on finishing my dedication." He reached over and retrieved the pages from Dusty's numb fingers. "It's strange, but I was on my way here just like you, Rog. Too bad you didn't give me this idea sooner."

"I just thought of it today," the boy offered. He had taken a long swig of milk, and a white mustache lined his upper lip in a perfect arc.

Dusty still couldn't think of a thing to say as Tag's pale blue gaze switched to engage hers. "I've had some other ideas for that dedication," he said softly. "I don't want to rush my fences, but the one I'd like would be 'To my family: my wife, Dusty, and my son, Roger.'"

"Yeah!" exclaimed the boy with a pleased grin. "We could be a real family, then."

Again Tag's eyes switched to Dusty's, but hers were torn between that persistent blue regard and Roger's delight.

"Maybe you'd better let us have a minute, Rog," Tag said.

The boy automatically slid his chair back and got up cheerfully. "It would be really great if you'd marry me and Tag, Mrs. Taggert," he said, putting in his plug.

"I know, honey," Dusty managed, lowering her eyes.

"Go on, Rog," Tag coaxed. "Dusty and I need to talk."

As soon as the door closed behind the boy, Tag stood up. Dusty thought he looked wonderful in his worn jeans and heavy cream-colored fisherman's sweater. He appeared large and vital in her half-pint world, and she watched while he moved around the end of the short table and came to loom over her.

"You were right, Dusty," he said, staring down at her. "I kept plugging away at the job I'd chosen, simply to prove I could handle it. I had to keep making myself face one case after another because I was never quite convinced, even case after case, that I wasn't afraid to handle the dangers involved in the next one. When I couldn't shoot Maddox, even to save you and

Roger, who I love, I thought I was in even worse shape than I'd imagined. I thought I wasn't much of a man, too much of a coward, to mean anything to you, because you're so courageous, so on top of it, despite all the bad things that have happened to you.''

''Tag—''

''No, let me finish, babe. I want to explain. After that night, I began to think about . . . well, about the things we'd discussed at the apartment. And how I'd probably been too immature to make a career choice at the age I'd made it. About how it was really my love for my dad that made me a policeman, not a love for the work. I thought, too, about the grief your dad's single-mindedness had caused your family, and I saw that I didn't want my life to go the same way. In the end, I realized I hadn't been cut out for doing police work at all. I've been beating my head against a wall for years, and I didn't even know it until I stopped.'' Tag paused for a moment, still looking down at Dusty.

She knew this was not only what Tag needed to tell her, but what she needed to hear, and evidently Tag must have sensed that, too, because he went on. ''Not everyone is capable of doing that kind of work. There's nothing shameful in not being able to do it. I've come to see that not everybody can be a doctor or a nurse, but just because you're not cut out for one of those professions doesn't mean you're weak. It doesn't mean you don't have a lot of guts.'' Getting down on his haunches in front of Dusty's small chair, Tag looked her straight in the eye.

''You taught me that, Dusty. You got me off my merry-go-round before I got knocked off. You saved me.''

When Dusty opened her mouth to deny this, Tag put a big finger to her lips. "I'm just sorry it took me so long to see it. I regret what I've put us both through in figuring it out. I want to apologize and to ask you to forgive me."

"It's not that easy. Oh, I mean, I forgive you your struggle. I've known about that all along and, naturally, I forgive you and, of course, it took you some time to sort through it. But, Tag," she added with a pleading look, "why didn't you let me share these past few months with you? Were you too proud? Was it only pride that stood between us?"

For the first time Tag lowered his eyes. "No, it wasn't pride. Or male ego. I...I was ashamed. As I've told you before, you've proven yourself to be so brave, and I...well, after I'd failed to shoot Maddox, for your sake, I didn't think I was worthy of—"

"Oh, Tag," Dusty cut in. "Surely you realize now that courage isn't as important as love. We can all have moments where we lack courage, if that's what you think you lacked that night. I don't happen to think you did. But if we're loved, really loved, those who love us understand our weaker moments and help us through them."

Tag gathered Dusty to him, nuzzling his face into her neck and shoulder. "I'm sorry I wasn't there to hold you through all those bad nights you've had. I've shared them with you in spirit and thought about you so much. I'm sorry I haven't kissed you for almost three months. But I promise you, Dusty, I'll start making it up to you right now. Stop staring at me with those big brown eyes and kiss me, Dusty. Kiss me."

Dusty smiled and kissed Tag on the mouth. Tag returned her sweet kiss with a bold one. "Will you marry Roger and me?"

"I've sworn to always say yes," she replied, grinning.

"This is the most damn, uncomfortable place," he stated, standing and pulling her up after him. His eyes ran quickly over the cheery space. "It suits you, though. You look just right here—and not only because you're little."

"I love this kind of work," Dusty admitted.

"Well, I'll be at home. What with my becoming a writer. A soon-to-be-published one," he added with his own broad grin. "I'll keep the home fires burning, juggle the baby schedules—whatever," he finished with a shrug of his broad shoulders.

"Soon to be published?" Dusty asked.

"Yeah. *The Case of the Strangled Green Parrot* is ready to go," he said proudly. "And they're already looking for more. It's a good thing I'm prolific as well as quick. I'll easily do four a year."

"I'm impressed."

"I'm glad you're impressed, 'cause that'll get me my way with you. We writers are sexy as well as being available because we're at home all the time."

"Come on," Dusty said, ignoring that familiar look in his eyes.

"Where are we going?" he complained as she stepped away from him.

"I work with the dearest people, and I want you to meet them."

Tag resisted her tug at his hand. "And I want to meet them. But couldn't we meet them later?"

"Later?"

"Yeah, like much later. Like in a day or so."

Dusty continued to look quizzical.

"I'd kind of like to go home now. We've only got a couple of hours until Rog will need his supper."

"So? That's plenty of time."

"Since you're not getting my point, I'll be blunt. I want to go home and make love to you. Seeing as how you're not only marrying me, but Rog, as well, you'll have to get the hang of his schedule and learn to catch on real quick to my subtle hints. In this case, he'll be going over to the park until it's dark."

"I suppose this means there will be three on our honeymoon."

"Actually," Tag said sheepishly, "I've got a book to start."

"Oh, I see." Dusty wasn't disappointed. Nothing could burst her balloon.

"But after that's done—and remember, I'm real quick—we'll take two weeks. I'll talk Juan into keeping Rog. He'll be feeling secure enough by then... What are you laughing at?"

"You sound like you're going to make a great house husband."

Tag grinned. "At last I've found my true vocation."

Harlequin Superromance

COMING NEXT MONTH

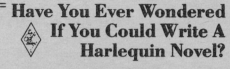

Have You Ever Wondered If You Could Write A Harlequin Novel?

Here's great news—Harlequin is offering a series of cassette tapes to help you do just that. Written by Harlequin editors, these tapes give practical advice on how to make your characters—and your story—come alive. There's a tape for each contemporary romance series Harlequin publishes.

Mail order only

All sales final

TO: **Harlequin Reader Service**
Audiocassette Tape Offer
P.O. Box 1396
Buffalo, NY 14269-1396

I enclose a check/money order payable to HARLEQUIN READER SERVICE® for $9.70 ($8.95 plus 75¢ postage and handling) for EACH tape ordered for the total sum of $_____ *
Please send:

☐ Romance and Presents   ☐ Intrigue
☐ American Romance   ☐ Temptation
☐ Superromance   ☐ All five tapes ($38.80 total)

Signature_____
Name:_____ (please print clearly)
Address:_____
State:_____ Zip:_____

* Iowa and New York residents add appropriate sales tax

AUDIO-H

This April, don't miss Harlequin's new Award of
Excellence title from

elusive as the unicorn

*When Eve Eden discovered that Adam
Gardener, successful art entrepreneur, was
searching for the legendary English artist, The
Unicorn, she nervously shied away. The Unicorn's
true identity hit too close to home....*

*Besides, Eve was rattled by Adam's
mesmerizing presence, especially in the light
of the ridiculous coincidence of their names—
and his determination to take advantage of it!
But Eve was already engaged to marry her
longtime friend, Paul.*

*Yet Eve found herself troubled by the different
choices Adam and Paul presented. If only the
answer to her dilemma didn't keep eluding her....*

HP1258-1

In April, Harlequin brings you the
world's most popular romance author

JANET DAILEY

No Quarter Asked

Out of print since 1974!

After the tragic death of her father, Stacy's world is shattered. She
needs to get away by herself to sort things out. She leaves behind
her boyfriend, Carter Price, who wants to marry her. However, as
soon as she arrives at her rented cabin in Texas, Cord Harris, owner
of a large ranch, seems determined to get her to leave. When Stacy
has a fall and is injured, Cord reluctantly takes her to his own ranch.
Unknown to Stacy, Carter's father has written to Cord and asked
him to keep an eye on Stacy and try to convince her to return home.
After a few weeks there, in spite of Cord's hateful treatment that
involves her working as a ranch hand and the return of Lydia, his ex-
fiancée, by the time Carter comes to escort her back, Stacy knows
that she is in love with Cord and doesn't want to go.

Watch for *Fiesta San Antonio* in July and
For Bitter or Worse in September.

JDA-1